THE

LOVE
FOOL

A *ROME*-ANTIC COMEDY

LORENZO PETRUZZIELLO

Published by Inkshares, Inc., Oakland, California
www.inkshares.com

Edited by Pamela McElroy
Cover design by Coverkitchen | Interior design by Kevin G. Summers

ISBN: 9781947848191
e-ISBN: 9781947848207
Library of Congress Control Number: 2017956968

First edition

Printed in the United States of America

To the ones that never were;
And the ones that should have been;
To the ones that may have once;
And the ones that could have then.
I thank you for my past, and my present,
And the future that is to come.
But, most importantly
For sparking my imagination.

-Lorenzo Petruzziello, September 2016

CHAPTER 1

Rome

Present

THE FLASH OF the cameras lit up the white backdrop of logos that stood on the red carpet outside of the venue. Alex weaved his way through the crowd. He could hear the photographers ahead of him pleading with the celebrity to "Look this way!" among the cheering fans and clicking cameras. Alex couldn't see who was walking in through the mass of people, but as the cheers grew louder, he knew that she'd arrived.

He continued to push his way toward the front, catching glimpses of her wavy chestnut hair, but he couldn't get a clear shot of her. Peering in between the crouching photographers, Alex saw sleek black boots stepping and pausing on the red carpet as she posed for a camera, then another. He needed to get just a bit closer to take a snapshot with his mobile phone, but the crowd refused to budge.

He felt a forearm on his back, an elbow on his chest, another on his shoulder. The pressure from the crowd continued to grow as he pushed farther ahead to see her. People screamed "Look here! Look here!" all around him, vying for her attention. It was a mildly crisp evening but the heat from the crowd was triggering Alex's slight claustrophobia. His breathing grew heavy and he began to sweat. He shook his head as if to brush off the tension around him and prevent himself from fainting. Although he'd never blacked out before, he didn't want that moment to be his first. He leaned his head back and tilted his mouth toward the sky, trying to calm his breathing to a slow, deep rhythm. The flashing lights continued to brighten the scene ahead.

He just needed one quick glimpse. He needed to get back to his post at the front barrier, where he had been before all the commotion had begun. But his boss, Eleonora, had called him from inside the venue, instructing him to meet her at the entrance with her briefcase. He hadn't thought it would be such an issue to get through the horde.

He was too experienced for this job. He rolled his eyes, wondering how he had managed to convince himself that a professional downgrade was worth the opportunity to work in Italy. The shouting all around him grew louder, and he was getting more annoyed. He wanted to scream, but instead he pushed forward until suddenly the crowd weakened and the camera flashes dwindled.

He'd missed it. He'd missed her grand entrance—the whole reason he was at the event, and he'd missed it. All that work, fighting through the thick crowd, and it suddenly seemed like a waste of time. All he needed was one shot of her on the red carpet giving that award-winning, movie-star smile with the meticulously designed backdrop behind her. His task was to simply post it on social media—instantly. Sure, it was a last-minute request, and a simple one at that, and he had failed.

There he stood, behind the front barricade, staring at the empty red carpet and the beautiful, clean backdrop. The crowd around him slowly dissipated. He was frustrated, upset, and angry with himself. He did not want to disappoint Eleonora, and he was worried that missing this opportunity was going to reflect on his capabilities as an employee. He was still new to the job, and he needed to prove to her that she could rely on him. The only saving grace would be if she forgot about her request altogether.

He remembered the first day he had met Eleonora. It was at her office near the Vatican. He'd been thirty minutes early, but fine with it—he hated to be late for anything. He'd been nervous as shit and self-conscious about his sweating. He'd watched the ground below as the caged, phone-booth-sized elevator climbed to the third floor. He used his blazer sleeve to wipe the sweat from his forehead and lightly slapped his cheeks with both hands, telling himself to relax.

He exited the elevator into a dimly lit hallway with five white doors, all of them closed. The sign on the third door to the right read ZERO OTTO MARKETING. Alex had walked to the door and knocked three times to no response. Finally, he tried the handle, and he slowly opened the door to a small room lit by a bright white light. He paused in the doorway, waiting for his eyes to adjust, and then he heard a voice.

"Hello? May I help you?" asked a cheerful girl behind a large white desk. She wore such an abundance of makeup that her face looked as though it was made of plastic.

"Hello . . . yes," Alex replied as his eyes fixed on the doll-like receptionist who smiled and fiddled with a blue pen between her fingers. "I'm Alex Corso. I'm here to see Eleonora Persini."

"Hello, Alex!" exclaimed the girl. She stood up and motioned for him to take a seat. Alex's eyes finally acclimated to the room's brightness. He noticed that everything around him was clean and a shiny and dazzling shade of white, save the couch he sat on with its pearlescent gray hue that matched the sleek marble tiles on the floor.

"Eleonora is on the telephone," continued the receptionist. "She should be done any minute. Would you like some coffee?"

"No, thank you. I'm okay," he replied with a smile. "I know I'm a bit early. I apologize."

"Oh, not a problem at all." She sat back down and looked at her computer. "Make yourself comfortable. I will let you know when she is available."

Alex rummaged through his bag to make sure he hadn't forgotten his pen with his notebook. The coffee table in front of him held an array of magazines: celebrity gossip, cinema, TV, and music interest. And just peeking out from behind the latest *Vanity Fair*, Alex spotted a food magazine featuring Amanda Jones—one of the world's most famous actresses—smiling wide while gripping the legs of a raw chicken. He liked the way the photographer had captured Amanda's genuine smile—she'd even been described as America's Sweetheart. The teal blue wallpaper behind her accentuated her yellow blouse. And the way Amanda held that chicken exuded strength and a sense of knowledge. His eyes focused on Amanda's. He was hoping to someday meet her.

Alex first fell in love with the onscreen siren when he was in high school. He'd gone to see a period film—a Jane Austen adaptation. The exact moment was when Amanda peered over a book during a scene in the movie. Her reddish-brown locks were tamed by clips and two ample buns. Her dark eyes coyly eyeing the object of her affection—he couldn't remember who the actor was anymore. Her graceful way of placing the book down on the settee and getting up to walk about the room, reciting the polished lines of English literature. She had enchanted Alex. Done. He was in love.

Friends teased him profusely about his love for Jones. And many a girlfriend had walked away, tired of being held to the impossible ideal of America's Sweetheart.

"Alex Corso." The voice came from a woman walking down the hall toward him. It was pleasant: excitement with a hint of that sensual Italian accent. Alex saw her black shoes through the coffee table glass. His gaze followed her slender legs hidden under loose fitting white pants that hugged her hips just perfectly. Her green satin sleeveless blouse was cut low enough to reveal the tops of her—

He caught himself staring openly at the woman's breasts, and so he abruptly looked back down to shuffle the magazine back underneath the pile. He stood quickly, his cheeks flushed with embarrassment.

"Eleonora," he shook her hand. "Such a pleasure to meet you." Her curly brown hair fell just below her tanned shoulders, which held up the thin straps of her flowing blouse. He tried to avoid taking peeks and worried he was only making matters worse. He hoped Eleonora hadn't noticed.

"Thank you for joining us." She smiled. Or was she smirking? "Come into my office. We can talk about what you'll be doing."

She led him down the bright hallway. He was nervous. He hoped she hadn't noticed him checking her out. This woman was to be his boss for Christ's sake.

The walls of her office were made of glass and had privacy panels about a third of the way up from the floor. Alex supposed they prevented the other perverts in her office from looking up if she wore a skirt. He took a seat in the black leather chair across from her desk and watched her glide around to the other side. As she sat to face him, he quickly shifted his focus out the window to avoid looking down her blouse.

They discussed the company's current projects while Alex struggled to maintain eye contact. She informed him that he would be joining her at a big launch party right in Rome. Although most of the preparations had been completed, she made Alex responsible for working with the London partners in overseeing that the plans were executed successfully.

"This is her first cookbook," explained Eleonora. "Just translated for the Italian market. She's been making her movie comeback and decided to dive into the food world. We are fortunate to be responsible for promoting her book project here in Italy." She handed Alex the cookbook and continued to explain, "I'll be running around the party, Alex, so I'll need you there as my right and left hands. Can you handle that?"

"Of course," he smiled. "It's what I do best." He ran his hand over the book cover, unable to believe he was working on a project for the award-winning movie star Amanda Jones.

In that moment, in Eleonora's office, he felt their fates were colliding; Amanda Jones and Alex Corso would finally cross paths. Now he had to consider what he would do that he was sure to encounter his dream girl.

CHAPTER 2

HIS MOBILE PHONE vibrated in his hand, a mocking reminder of his failure to get the photograph. He composed himself and read the text.

Where are you? Find me inside. By stage.

He rolled his eyes and continued through the barricade, down the red carpet toward the two women standing at the door with clipboards in hand.

"Hi. Alex," he introduced himself to one of them. "From Zero Otto Marketing."

"Hello, Alex," the woman replied as she checked her list and found his name. "So, she just walked in and should be backstage with your boss, Eleonora." She waved him in. "Take the central stairs down to the main stage."

"Thank you."

"You're welcome. And don't forget to grab yourself a drink. You'll need it."

"Thanks again." He walked up the steps and through the heavy glass doors into the venue.

The restaurant tables had been removed to open the space for the crowds of people milling about. The area was walled with etched wood panels between thick dark beams. The crowd stood in small clusters, laughing, gossiping, and posing as they sipped their cocktails. A waiter appeared in front of Alex with a tray of sparkling red Campari drinks. Alex grabbed the glass that seemed the fullest.

As he sipped the bitter concoction, he watched three blonde women giggling with a short, plump man who had apparently just delivered a joke. To his left, Alex could hear a reporter interviewing an older woman about her recent photography project. And then at that moment, Alex felt pressure from a large group pushing through the doors behind, forcing him into the adjacent room on the right.

The new room was less crowded and people were scattered on plush antique sofas. Small plates and multi-colored gilded goblets rested on ornate marble coffee tables. Each sofa was placed along a wood railing that circled a wide, carpeted staircase leading to a lower level. He placed his empty glass on the closest table and proceeded down the stairway to the large, dimly lit event space.

As he descended the stairs, hip-hop beats mixed with modern jazz melodies surrounded him. The stage was set at the opposite end of the room, directly across from the staircase. Alex looked above the sea of people and watched the performance of the four-piece band, which consisted of an upright bass, a trumpet, and percussion led by a lanky man in a silver blazer incorporating Italian rap over the bouncy beat.

Alex remained on the final step and examined the room, looking for Eleonora. To his right was a long oak bar with three bartenders attentively mixing cocktails for the awaiting guests. His eyes followed the bar toward the back and spotted Eleonora in the shadows, curly brown hair and serious expression awash in a blue light as she typed furiously on her phone.

He stepped down and slowly pushed his way through the swaying crowd and up to Eleonora.

"Alex," she smiled. "Great. You're here." Eleonora took him by the hand and led him behind the velvet curtain, down a dark corridor lined with private dining alcoves. "I need to go to the back kitchen quickly." She stopped at the third doorway. "*She's* in the private alcove here with her party. Gianni here," she grabbed the skinny young waiter, "is the only one covering *her* room." She let go of Gianni with a smile and turned back to Alex, gripping her hand on his shoulder. "He's the only one allowed in there, you got it?"

"Of course," Alex nodded.

"Thank you so much." She let go of his shoulder, grabbed her oversized green purse, and added, "If she asks for me, just let her know I will be back in ten minutes." With that, Eleonora zipped away.

The vivacious trumpeter ended the set with a solo that revved the crowd up to a roar. The bandleader removed his gold bowler hat and bowed, thanking his spectators. As the music faded, the singer threw his silver blazer on his right shoulder and fashionably stepped off the left side of the stage. The crowd cheered and quickly dispersed toward the bar. The musicians immediately tore down their instruments, while a few younger men set two chairs and microphones in their place.

Alex stared at Amanda Jones, who had now shifted to a spot behind the stage, waiting with a group of people, probably her management. Eleonora reappeared and led Amanda to a spot toward the left of the platform, and then returned to Alex, by the bar, as if to check on him.

"Thank goodness this is almost over. My legs are killing me in these shoes." She leaned on the bar and rubbed her well-sculpted calves. "Alex. Feel free to stand out in the crowd and signal to me if you can't hear."

Alex followed the instruction, grabbing another glass of the bubbling Campari and soda. He claimed a spot at the center of the bar and watched Eleonora walk to center stage with the microphone. She thanked the band for serenading the crowd and mentioned that the band members were close friends of the guest of honor. She segued into her introduction of the star and welcomed her onto the platform.

Amanda stepped through the curtain with a sparkling smile and regal wave. The camera flashes picked up momentum, filling the room with a bright frenzy accompanied by generous applause.

Eleonora calmed the crowd and passed the microphone to Amanda Jones. As the celebrity talked about her cookbook and latest film project, flashes occasionally lit her face, forcing her to blink profusely. The crowd cheered her closing speech as she thanked them all for attending. Once she walked off the stage, the crowd's chatter began once again, while the background music was raised to a party level hum.

Alex moved back down the bar toward the stage to wait for Eleonora, but he was really hoping to get an opportunity to talk with Amanda Jones, who was now engaged in a conversation with a well-dressed man in a bowtie.

Alex turned his attention back to Eleonora, who was sauntering toward him. Her face was once again lit up by the soft glow of her mobile phone. She was somehow texting while adjusting her tweed pleated skirt at the same time—she was clearly a woman who had perfected multitasking.

"Alex, I must go meet our latest client at the door. Will you hold my binder here until I return?"

"Sure. You want me to come with you?"

"No, no," she replied as she walked away. She then turned and gestured toward the stage. "Just keep an eye on her. I'll be right back."

THE LOVE FOOL 11

He took another sip of his cocktail and focused his attention back on Amanda. The area was so crowded that Alex didn't notice Amanda had somehow shifted closer to him. She was now standing with her back inches from his, chatting with her old friend. She was so close to Alex that he felt her hair on the back of his neck when she laughed. So close, in fact, that all he'd have to do was turn around to lock eyes and introduce himself to the unbelievably attractive and completely unattainable movie star.

He took a final sip of his drink, put the glass down on the oak bar, and turned around. As he spun, he found himself face to face with the one and only Amanda Jones. And she was smiling at him. She looked exactly as she did on screen—better. Millions of thoughts ran through his head like flashes of lightening. He had to make his move and say something. This was the moment. Amanda glanced past him over his left shoulder.

"Ms. Jones?" he blurted.

"Yes." She looked at him and smiled again. She was dressed in a tight black leather skirt that stopped mid-thigh and revealed her perfect calves. The neckline of her black top was silk and cut to highlight Alex's greatest weakness: freckles. She had freckles! Those devilish spots were seductively sprinkled on her golden skin.

"My name is Alex Corso," he offered his hand. "I'm with the PR firm promoting your cookbook here in Italy."

"You're American!" she exclaimed. "Nice to meet you, Alex." She grasped his hand with a firm but friendly shake. "This is a lovely party—did you plan this?" she continued. She was still holding his hand.

"Well, I helped organize somewhat. Yes," he replied. "Thank you."

Suddenly, someone tapped Amanda's shoulder from behind and grabbed her attention. Still holding on to Alex's hand, she turned to speak to the tapper. Alex stood there, hand held, waiting for Amanda to turn back, but she seemed rapt in conversation.

That was it, he thought. *I lost her.* Now he was just an idiot holding a movie star's hand. A movie star who was clearly more interested in the new man talking to her. This was probably her way out of the conversation with him. Were people staring? Was his hand sweating? Should he let go of her hand?

Reluctantly, he loosened his grip, but to his surprise she squeezed his hand! She clearly didn't want to let Alex go. Was she sending him a signal? Did she need to be rescued from the strange man? After a quick flurry of goodbyes, Amanda turned back to face Alex.

"I'm so sorry about that, Alex." She looked apologetic and ended their interminable handshake. He readied himself for their light goodbyes, but instead she continued, "You were saying?"

He was shocked.

"Oh, I . . . I . . . just wanted to let you know that I liked your cookbook."

"Thank you."

"Yes," he continued. "I was surprised—pleasantly, of course—that you pursued a cooking project. But when I read the intro, I realized how much food means to you. You showed us—the public, your fans—another side of you, and it was down to earth and real."

"Oh," she blushed. "Thank you for that compliment. It means a lot. The project meant a lot to me." She added, "Food takes up a lot of my personal life. I'm always in the kitchen feeding the family."

Right. Family. Alex had naturally wanted to forget that. She was, in fact, married to Liam Dorset—one of the world's most popular rock stars. Of course. Alex decided to ignore all that and live in the moment. What does a man say when he meets his dream girl? He had never had an experience like this. He'd never thought he would react as he was at present—star-struck and awkward.

"Ooh," she reached past him. "I've been trying to get a glass of this all night." She grabbed an opened bottle of wine off the bar. "My glass is somewhere on the other end of the room, so we'll need some new ones. Do you want some?" She reached over to a table of clean glasses just beyond her and grabbed two. As she poured, she added, "This is one of my favorite wines. With all the talking, I haven't been able to take a sip."

She handed him a glass and put the bottle back on the bar. She raised her glass and said, "To food."

"Yes, and to your book," he added. "Congratulations!"

"Ooh!" she waved over to someone. "I'm over here. Come here!" Alex followed her glance to find Liam making his way through the dense crowd that seemed to ignore his celebrity status. The man seemed unimpressed by them all. Who could possibly be too high and mighty to acknowledge *the* Liam Dorset?

"There you are." He planted a kiss on Amanda's pink, glossy lips. "I was held up at the entrance. What a crowd," he complained with his heavy British accent.

"Liam, this is Alex. Alex, Liam."

"Nice to meet you."

"Alex works for the party planners here."

"Oh, great."

"A fellow American," she added.

"Yes," Alex finally stepped in. "But I now live in Rome working for the PR firm—as Amanda was explaining." He could see Liam had no interest so he continued. "So . . . I . . . just bought your album."

"Oh really? Do you like it?"

"Well. . . " He hadn't bought the album. He lied. "To be honest, I haven't really listened to it yet—I just bought it yesterday."

"Right."

"But I hear it's amazing," he tried to recover but could tell Liam knew he was lying.

"Great." Liam looked around the room. "Where did you guys get the drink?" Amanda pointed at the wine bottle. He turned it down. "I'd prefer a pint, rather—if we can make our way out of here. Are we heading out soon?"

"Yes," she replied. "I just need to talk to a few more press folks or something and we can go. In fact, I probably should make my way . . . somewhere I suppose." She scanned the room. "I'll meet you at the door, okay?"

"You got it," he replied with a wink. "Nice to meet you, Alex. And listen to my album, will ya?"

"Of course," he responded with embarrassment.

Amanda suddenly put her arm up. "There she is. Does she see me?" She was waving to the girl who had checked Alex in at the door, who was making her way to them. "Alex, that's my cue to go. I suppose I should talk to the press." She rolled her eyes as the girl continued to signal for her to follow.

"No problem," he replied. "That's what we're here for, after all." He raised his glass.

"Listen," she added before stepping away. "It was really nice talking with you. And thanks for saving me from the weirdo earlier." She winked as she was whisked away, swallowed up by the noisy crowd.

Alex stood back in wonder. He had just met two of the most famous people in the world. He knew that this opportunity would not present itself again. After all, as Eleonora had reminded him, it was a rarity for Zero Otto Marketing to have such a high-profile project with someone like Amanda.

"Alex. Alex!" It was Eleonora waving to him from the stair-well above. "Come up here. I want you to meet someone."

Alex put down his wine glass, took one look back at the swarm of people surrounding Amanda Jones, and ascended the stairs. Eleonora was in a corner talking with a tall, very blonde, and incredibly beautiful woman. He smiled and walked up to them.

"Alex," Eleonora put her hand on his shoulder and turned to the beautiful woman. "This is Alex. He is my new staff member. He will be working on your project." She turned back to Alex. "Alex, this is Pernille Bjørn—Scandinavia's popular TV chef and cookbook author."

"Hello, Alex," Pernille smiled and shook his hand. Maybe it was the lighting, but he thought he saw an ethereal glow ema-nating from her. Pernille Bjørn's super blonde hair was ironed flat and hung down the left side of her face. As she shook his hand, the golden cascade swung like satin ribbons reflecting the rays of artificial light across her perfect skin. The same rays bounced off her striking blue eyes, causing them to appear as if they were sparkling. As she spoke those two words to Alex, her eyelids fluttered, exposing a touch of faint green eye shadow that accentuated her irises. Her Danish accent only enhanced her goddess-like appearance.

"Nice to meet you, Ms. Bjørn." Alex woke from his love-struck gaze and replied, almost stuttering. His words seemed to have come out slowly, as if he were in a dream. Pernille returned a coy smile and slowly let go of his hand.

"Pernille will be appearing as a guest on the TV show *Chiacchiere del Cuoco* next month," Eleonora interrupted. "We are representing her while she is here in Italy. Our job is to grow her brand as she launches the Italian translation of her cook-book. She will be staying in Rome for a while, and I promised her producers that we would take good care of her—that *you*, Alex, will take good care of her until then."

"Wonderful," he replied. "I look forward to it."

"I look forward to working with you, Alex," she said. "I really love Rome and need to make sure I can handle myself on Italian TV."

"Yes," explained Eleonora. "Alex will make sure you know what to say, how to say it, and what they will say to you. You don't need to worry about that. Right, Alex?"

The sound of a crowd grew behind Alex. He swung around and spotted a group of people accompanying Amanda Jones as she walked out the front door. Her security guard opened the door of a sleek, black car and guided her inside. His moment with destiny was over.

"Alex?" Eleonora addressed him with a little chuckle. Alex turned back to the two ladies and noticed Eleonora looking at him like he had three heads.

"Oh, right," he said. He was confused. This was the first time Eleonora had mentioned anything about this Pernille Bjørn project to him. Nevertheless, he had to pretend he knew all about it. "It won't be a problem, Pernille," he assured. "You're in good hands."

"Fantastic!" Pernille Bjørn practically jumped with excitement. "I am looking forward to taking over Italia."

"Great!" Eleonora grabbed her oversized bag. "I will walk you to your car." She directed Pernille to coat check, then turned to Alex and said in a low voice, "Thank you for your help tonight, Alex. We're all done here for tonight. I'll see you tomorrow afternoon, then?"

"Yes, of course," he replied. He leaned over and called out to Pernille, "It was very nice meeting you, Pernille. I will see you soon, I hope."

"You will see me tomorrow, of course," she replied as she turned the corner to grab her belongings.

Eleonora left with Pernille Bjørn. Around him, the crowd had dwindled along with the music, which played at a lower volume as the lights grew brighter. The staff rushed around, gathering plates and glasses. The event had come to an end.

Alex shrugged as he walked out the door and hopped on a bus back toward his apartment building.

CHAPTER 3

Rome

Two Weeks Earlier

ALEX HAD MOVED to Rome for a contract position—with the potential to become a full-time job—with Zero Otto Marketing. He knew he was fortunate to come by a job so easily in Italy's confusing employment market. He was aware that Italy was one of those places where it was all about who you knew. And, if you didn't know anyone, it was even more difficult to get anywhere. He also knew that he'd gotten the position through all-too-familiar networking methods. With a referral from a family friend, he had been able to get a temporary position with the marketing firm.

He was annoyed that he had to go for a lower-level position, but he needed to take what he could get. If he could prove his worth to his boss, though, there was a good chance for a full-time position or a long-term contract, at least.

Alex did genuinely have a lot to offer the firm. He was well-educated and multilingual, thanks to his Italian-born mother. And he had several years of publicity experience in the United States, where, at one time, he had felt his life was complete: he'd had an amazing job with a large global PR firm. Unfortunately, a victim of the weakening U.S. economy, Alex had been laid off.

After a few days of panicking over losing his employment, Alex decided to take a break from his American life and move to Europe. Why not? He contacted everyone he knew in Europe—especially in Italy, where most of his relatives and family friends lived. It was then that he connected with Zero Otto Marketing in Rome. Upon landing the part-time gig, Alex officially moved to the enchanted city without looking back. After thorough research and plenty of time visiting trashy apartments, he finally settled on a slightly overpriced place in the picturesque neighborhood of Trastevere.

The building had an antiquated façade with muted gray stucco and dark green shutters on every window of all five floors. It was nestled in a quiet piazza away from the frenzy of the tourist-filled areas. It was more than he'd hoped to pay monthly, but the location and view had convinced Alex to sign immediately upon first viewing.

The apartment was on the very top floor of the five-story palazzo. The wide and decorative marble staircase, located just through the ornate wrought-iron gates in the lobby, was beautiful enough to distract Alex from realizing there was no elevator in the building. After climbing up to the fifth landing, Alex would be out of breath. But the bright red door greeting him at the top of the stairs reminded him he was home, and he soon forgot his exhaustion.

Inside lay a modern apartment, fully furnished. The master bedroom housed an antique armoire and a chest of drawers filled with bed linens and bath towels. The cozy kitchen contained a tiny oven and matching refrigerator. Off the kitchen was a smaller bedroom with two twin beds and a bureau. Just around one of the small beds, through double doors, sat a tiny terrace overlooking the four adjacent buildings that shared a brightly tiled courtyard.

When Alex first moved in, he walked directly into the master bedroom and placed his suitcase by the chest of drawers. He pushed open the window and admired the view of the Tiber River. A sense of peace had come over him as he watched the river flowing around the bend. Through the trees to the right, he could make out a hint of the river's tiny island, Tiberna. And over the clay rooftops to the left, he could just about see the top of Saint Peter's dome indicating the Vatican far off in the distance.

Prior to moving there, Alex had not been familiar with the layout of Rome. Now, sitting in his living room, he pulled out a map and tried to get his bearings. On the map, he found his neighborhood, then across the map he found where the offices of Zero Otto Marketing were located—not far from the Vatican. Alex realized he would have to sort out transportation to and from the office, but settling into his new home was the first order of business.

He went into the kitchen and browsed the cabinets. He found the typical essentials: frying pan, stock pot, mixing spoons, and espresso maker. He continued his inventory and made a mental list of what he needed to start his new life in Rome.

With the long, heavy keys in hand, he dragged his apartment door shut and skipped down the five flights of marble stairs. On the main landing, he noticed that although it was mid-morning, the foyer was quite dark, lit only by the sunlight creeping through a tiny crack of the building's large and ornate front doors. He pulled the door handle, but the door wouldn't open. It seemed to be locked. On the wall to his right, he could make out a white rectangular button and recognized it for what it was. He buzzed himself out and slowly pushed one of the heavy doors open to the sunlit cobblestone streets of Trastevere.

CHAPTER 4

THAT FIRST DAY out, Alex had walked just around the corner when he heard the swish and hum of an espresso machine accompanied by lively '60s music.

It was coming from an open double doorway on the corner of a small piazza. Above the entrance were six red letters that hung crookedly: CIN CIN. He peered inside and discovered a whimsically over-decorated café.

The mismatched tables and chairs were grouped together like a colorfully curated collection from old schoolhouses and theatres. In the center of the room was a large white marble statue of two lovers sharing a kiss. The alabaster couple, in full embrace, seemed intentionally positioned so that their image was reflected in practically every vintage mirror that hung lopsided on the silvery blue walls.

Alex stepped inside.

Rich velvet tapestry and gold beads were carefully placed to appear thrown together, framing the doorway, front window, and crooked mirrors in the L-shaped room. The tin-tiled ceiling was incomplete, and partially exposed, thick wood beams supported chandeliers adorned with colorful plastic jewels.

Apart from the lovers, the main spectacle of the place was the coffee bar, which was trimmed with a decorative metal resembling silver lace. Behind it sat the source of the swishing and humming: an extravagant maroon and silver coffee machine, framed by asymmetric dark wooden shelves of mismatched teacups, vintage coffee pots, and assorted statuettes.

"Welcome!" An old bohemian bartender turned around with a smile, exposing his handlebar mustache.

"Hello," Alex replied with slight bewilderment. He felt like he was in another world. "May I have a coffee?"

"Of course you may," boasted the burly man. He extended his arms like a boisterous circus performer—the strong man, maybe—and turned back to the machine. He grabbed a flowery teacup from the slanted shelves above. He looked back at Alex and asked in Italian, "*Normale?*"

"May I have it *macchiato?*" replied Alex in Italian. He always liked that little dollop of foam on top of his espresso.

"*Certo signore,*" said the circus barman as he turned back to the machine and foamed up the milk.

Alex took a seat on a leather-topped barstool, which looked more like something out of a barbershop, as the bohemian-inspired barman set a blue saucer in front of him. After adding the dollop of foam, he placed the delicate teacup onto the saucer. The musical clink that the small gold spoon made on the saucer was the final touch. Alex sipped his coffee and examined the spoon's intricate etchings.

He looked around the café, admiring his surroundings with a smile. *Espresso in a teacup*, he thought. *How interesting.* The café owner was definitely playing up a circus-wonderland theme. As he took the second and final sip, the coffee's aroma hugged him like a deep, warm welcome. He was pleased by the amazing coffee and the establishment itself. It was then, Alex decided, that he'd found his local morning coffee bar.

On the left wall, a wooden door—resembling one on an old train car—slid open to reveal the back kitchen. The door appeared to be almost falling off its hinges, but it was tentatively secured by the wobbling metal track above. Out came another circus-like barman wearing a striped apron and carrying a stack of white dishes. He had messy brown hair and a short, curly beard. A slender woman came out behind him. Her sleek, black hair was styled up high in a way that reminded Alex of the space-age Judy Jetson. They carefully placed the dishes in neat piles behind the counter and then tidied up the tables while greeting the other patrons. The woman eventually made her way to Alex. She propped her arm on the bar and spoke with a whisper-like rasp.

"Welcome to our bar," she said to him in Italian with a genuine smile.

"*Grazie*," he replied. "This is a very nice place."

"Yes. We are happy that we finally were able to open our doors." She looked around proudly. "This is our first day."

"What a coincidence," he smiled. "I'm new to the neighborhood myself." His rudimentary Italian was improving quickly as he spoke.

"Oh, you live here? You are local?"

"Yes, I just moved in right around the corner."

"Well then, you are in luck," she walked back behind the bar and continued. "Today, we are treating our locals with special pricing. Your first coffee is on the house."

"You don't have to—" Alex began, but she placed her hand on top of his and smiled.

"I insist," she said and took back her hand, grabbed a crisp white rag, and dried the dishes she had brought out earlier. "Where are you from? Originally?"

Is she winking at me? He set down his empty cup. "You have to guess."

Her brown eyes scanned his appearance. She cocked her head, squinted, and deduced in the style of Sherlock Holmes, "You look Italian, but when you speak I hear a hint of an accent. I can't quite place it." She continued, "European, but not necessarily Italian. Your eyes have a gold hue—like the scales of a fish."

Alex tried to hide his confusion by stretching his smile; he wanted to laugh. He could tell she realized what she'd said was odd, but she continued anyway.

"You are dressed very nicely—classy, but casual." She tapped her fingers on the bar as she continued looking him over. "I sense an interesting aura about you . . . something classic. Classic is definitely a word for you."

Alex felt like she was trying to read his mind. She slapped the countertop. "You must be from Spain," she suddenly pronounced with conviction. "Yes," she continued. "You are a very handsome man, your eyes are intriguing, and—maybe because I don't know you—you are mysterious. And you have that extra handsome quality of a Spanish man."

Is she flirting with me? Alex felt his face getting warm and worried he was blushing. He tried to get a glimpse of himself in the faded mirror behind her, but her tall hair was blocking the view.

"Am I right?" she insisted.

"No," replied Alex with a smile, still hoping he wasn't red in the face. "But I'll take it as a compliment. Thank you."

"You are not French, are you?" She turned her head to the side as though avoiding an impeding blow.

"Ha, no, not French. I am American."

"No!" she exclaimed as she slammed the rag on the countertop. "You are not American!"

"Yes," Alex switched to English. "I was born and raised in the United States."

"I don't believe you," she replied in English. Her Italian accent was as seductive as the look her sparkling brown eyes gave.

Alex was intrigued by this quirky woman. She continued to dry the plates in the complete silence that hung between them until a coworker called for her.

He stood up to leave and chuckled. "Well, like I said, I'll take it as a compliment."

"Wait," she said before he left. "What is your name, American Boy?"

"I'm Alex."

"I'm Patrizia," she replied. "It was very nice meeting you, Alex."

She walked out from behind the counter. "I look forward to seeing you here every day, American Boy," she said it in a way that seemed like an order.

Alex looked at her standing there, waiting for his response. He imagined what he must look like, half-sitting, half standing, grinning like an idiot while he processed her meaning.

He snapped out of his head, about to reply, when she said, "Alex is a nice name, but I think I'll call you American Boy." She walked away leaving Alex wanting more.

PERNILLE BJØRN'S NORDIC FEASTS
SEASON 01, EPISODE 06
"Frikadeller (Danish Meatballs)"
SCENE 04

FADE IN:

INT. PERNILLE'S KITCHEN — DAY

Wide shot of the kitchen. Behind the kitchen island, PERNILLE wears a red-and-white checkered blouse. Her summery blonde hair—with flat bangs, cut just above her blue eyes—is tied in a high ponytail.

> **PERNILLE**
> Today, we visited that lovely pig farm and all those adorable piglets. We took fresh eggs and milk. And now we can honor them all with this delicious and traditional Danish frikadeller.

PERNILLE opens the refrigerator behind her and returns to the counter with a large glass bowl. She pokes at the bowl's contents with a wooden spoon.

> **PERNILLE**
> This frikadeller mixture has been cooled for about thirty minutes. The ground pork and veal are now mixed well with the onion, milk, egg, and breadcrumbs. The mixture, you can see, is still moist, but not drippy.

PERNILLE ignites the burner under a yellow enamel skillet. She drops a large knob of gold butter into the warmed pan.

> **PERNILLE**
> We Danes love our pork, and fri-kadellers are probably the most preferred choice for pork at lunchtime.

PERNILLE scoops out a large dollop of the meat mixture with a spoon. With the help of a second spoon, she forms an oval and plac-es it into the skillet, creating a sizzle.

> **PERNILLE**
> They don't have to be perfectly round balls. In fact, the fri-kadeller should be a little flat, like so.

PERNILLE flattens the oval with the back of her spoon.

> **PERNILLE**
> That is the typical shape of the Danish frikadeller. But, to be honest, I never do this with a spoon. Just like my *mormor*—my grandmother—taught me.

PERNILLE sets the spoons into the sink be-hind her and lifts her hands. She continues the frikadeller making process using her bare hands to form the flat ovals.

> **PERNILLE**
> These will cook for about fifteen
> minutes on each side. Until they
> are brown and no longer pink at
> the center.

PERNILLE flips the frikadellers.

> **PERNILLE**
> Once these are complete, I will
> show you how to make a delicious
> and flavorful brown cream sauce
> for them. Yum!

PERNILLE smiles, winks, and gives her signature flirtatious look to the camera.

CHAPTER 5

Rome

Present

THE MORNING AFTER the big event, Alex woke up early for his first full day at the office. He prepared his Friday morning espresso and watched a few episodes of Pernille Bjørn's cooking series. He wanted to be prepared for the afternoon meeting with Pernille, making notes about her style as well as ideas he could use to push her brand in Italy.

But his concentration was thwarted with memories of his encounter with Amanda Jones. He couldn't wait to write to his good friend back in the States. He supposed she probably wouldn't believe him, and he didn't even get a photograph to prove the one-on-one conversation, but deep down he knew she would be excited for him.

Penny had once been one of Alex's closest friends. They used to confide in each other about every situation. But through the years, they'd drifted apart. It was only natural once Penny got married and started a family. Just one of those things that happen as people get older. The friendship is still present. They keep in touch now and then for big moments mostly. And this was definitely a big moment to share.

Alex typed out his email and included the news about his new job and first project: Pernille. Of course, he had to tell her about the amazing Amanda Jones experience. Typing it all out made it real. Even the part when he admitted he most likely would never see her again. And even if he did, Amanda probably wouldn't remember him.

After firing off his email to Penny, he got back to work, viewing more video snippets of Pernille's series, and then researching her history and accomplishments. He discovered she was a well-known Scandinavian food personality, award-winning TV chef, columnist, and cookbook author, and had her own line of table wear—all by the age of thirty-five.

His search didn't reveal any scandals or inappropriate photos, but it did offer up several mentions of a relationship with Theodore "Teddy" Hume—a member of one of Britain's wealthier families. One such article was accompanied by a photograph of Teddy and Pernille standing alongside the Duchess of Cambridge at what appeared to be a charity benefit.

The vibration of his mobile phone interrupted his research. It was a text from Eleonora.

Buon Giorno, Alex. I'll see you this morning before the meeting. By the way, did you not post anything from last night's event? I don't see any photos on our social media.

Shit! He'd forgotten about that task. His first actual assignment and he'd botched it. How was he going to get around it? He'd hoped she had forgotten. *It's not a big deal*, he thought to himself, and repeated it in his mind reassuringly. *I'm sure it's not a big deal.*

Hi, Ms. Persini. I had some trouble last night. I meant to talk to you about that today at the office. I'm on my way. See you soon.

What he was going to say to her, he had no idea. He just hoped it was not a big deal. But he had to come up with a logical explanation for failing her. After all, the fact that he couldn't fulfill a simple task didn't look good on his part. Why would she hire him full time if he couldn't even snap a quick photo for social media? He needed to come up with some way to butter her up.

Yes. I'm just walking in. Meet me in my office at ten.

Alex immediately closed his laptop and jumped in the shower. She'd seemed upset. He had to come up with something good. Still, nothing came to mind. He dried off and dressed—still nothing. He gathered his computer, his notebook, his bag—still no idea what he was going to say to Eleonora.

He didn't stop at the quirky bar for coffee. He didn't even bother to peek in for the mysterious Patrizia. Besides, it had been a while since he had seen her working. *I need to figure out her schedule. Wait, no. That is pathetic. Back to reality.* He had a mission and needed to focus on a story to save his ass.

He purchased bus tickets from the newspaperman and waited at the bus stop, nervously fidgeting for a story. *Maybe I'll just play it cool,* he thought. As if missing a post was not a big deal. He could redirect the conversation to Pernille. That was what he settled on. He would focus the meeting on what was to come.

Bus number 23 to Clodio finally arrived. Alex climbed the steps, stamped his ticket, and sat by the window watching Rome go by as the bus traversed the city.

Alex watched scooters swerve through the morning traffic. He spotted an assortment of men and women walking dogs of all sizes. And, of course, there were the suits—*probably politicians*, he thought—rushing out of coffee bars toward a day of who-knows-what.

Amid the bustle, he noticed a small group of people with backpacks, maps, and cameras, gathering for what obviously was a day of organized sightseeing. Were they American? Maybe Canadian? Maybe British. He couldn't really tell. But trying to decipher it was enough for him to momentarily forget his upcoming meeting with Eleonora.

The bus circled the Vatican walls and made its stop at a busy intersection around the corner. Alex rushed off and treaded to via Santamaura, where his dreaded meeting was about to take place.

He set his computer and bag down on his desk and proceeded to find Eleonora in her office on the telephone. Her hair was in a bun, exposing gold hoop earrings that dangled as she laughed with whomever was on the other line. She looked up and waved him in as she put the receiver down.

"Good morning, Eleonora." Alex sat across from her and waited for her reaction. Was she angry? He couldn't tell. She scribbled something on a notepad and looked up with a smile.

"Alex," she said, exhaling a sigh of relief. Was she relieved he was there? Alex wondered. Or maybe she had just accomplished something on the phone call. He couldn't tell.

Eleonora continued, "I wanted to thank you for your assistance last night, but I was confused when I didn't see anything on Twitter, Instagram, anywhere. What happened?"

This was it. The moment. He had to be cool, calm, and collected. What was his plan again? He couldn't remember.

"Oh, right," he still had no idea what he wanted to say. "I had an issue connecting with the accounts." Where that came from, he had no idea. "That's what I was trying to tell you when I came back in. That was why it took me so long out there."

Eleonora's face was undecipherable. If she was angry, Alex could not tell.

"Of course," she said finally. "I shouldn't have entrusted that with you. Not yet."

"Oh, it wasn't a difficult task."

"I didn't say it was difficult. In fact, it was simple. I just realized that I didn't give you access to the accounts. Or did I?"

Inside, Alex was ecstatic. She had forgotten she gave him all the passwords to their social media accounts. This was his way out, and she was handing it to him. He wanted to smile, but he controlled himself.

"But I could have at least gotten the information from you last night," he blurted. What was he doing? He needed to take the way out, not bury himself further. "So much was happening . . ."

"No, you're right, Alex. Let's just call it our first mistake, eh?" She smiled, but Alex couldn't tell if she was sincere or condescending. "Did you at least happen to get a photograph? Maybe we can post it now."

Shit! Of course Eleonora would press the situation. Alex had to get himself out of this. Now. He couldn't follow up one disappointment with another. What was he going to do?

"Well, I looked through my photos this morning and they wouldn't have worked anyway. I had someone's elbow in one shot. A faded blur in another. It was chaotic out there. Should I call up one of the photographers and have one sent to us?"

Alex could see she was disappointed. She let out a long, slow breath and smirked.

"No," she finally said. "I don't think it is necessary at this point. Let's just let it go."

"I'm really sorry, Eleonora," Alex replied. He had to save himself. "I promise it won't happen again."

"No, it won't," she replied shortly.

"I am a diligent worker; I can promise you that. You will see with this Pernille project—which, by the way, I thank you for allowing me to work on."

"Yes," she replied a bit frustrated, but she also seemed glad for the change of topic. "Pernille will be coming in later in the day—I believe around four—so we may have a late evening here," she warned him. "We'll go over the publicity schedule. Of course, we are just pushing her brand right now as we wait for the Italian translation of her cookbook. It's not the norm for cookbook marketing, but we think that her look and personality will be liked on the cooking shows and talk shows . . . like a TV personality. You know? Build on her beauty."

"And her talent?" he added.

"That will follow. I want to focus on her beauty. I think that's what will resonate with the people here. Let's be honest: Italians don't need Danish recipes."

Eleonora's last comment confused him. Why did she bother to take on the project? She immediately followed up.

"I'll be honest with you, Alex. I'm doing this project for a friend of mine in Denmark. He called me and asked me to take it on. He wants to increase the series ratings—which, mind you, only just began airing here in Italy. But someone mentioned her on some talk show, I have no idea who—please do some research on that when you can," she instructed. "So, my friend thinks we can do something for her here. Let's see." She ended almost disinterested.

"Okay, I'll work on some research and will see you at four."

"Actually, let's meet again before Pernille arrives so we can review the project specifics," she said. "Oh, and take the passwords for the social media accounts. We can't have that happen again. See you later."

Alex smiled in return, a little embarrassed, and walked out.

MIDSUMMER'S DREAM
PERNILLE BJØRN'S NEW TABLEWARE

Danish TV cook Pernille Bjørn's new tableware collection is influenced by her Swedish half.

Melanie Cartwright—*Delicious Magazine UK*

[AUGUST 2004—Malmo, Sweden]—I'm sitting at a picnic table set in a field of lavender, waiting for a traditional "midsomer" dish made by the gracious Pernille Bjørn—Denmark's treasured TV cook.

She walks graciously down from the deep red barn with a platter of smoked fish. Her platinum blonde hair is tied up in a bun and her pink apron is cinched tightly around her waist. I am reminded that Pernille Bjørn started as a model before delving into the world of cookery.

Pernille Bjørn—whose name is really Pernille Vestergaard—uses her Swedish grandfather's first name as her public surname. "I want to honor both of my Scandinavian sides," she explains. "My mother's family was originally from this region of Sweden. But my mother moved to Denmark when she married my Danish father. I was raised in Denmark, but spent my summers with my grandparents here in Malmo. This collection is an honor to my Swedish grandmother."

Pernille places the fish on the beautiful navy blue plate in front of me. I examine the white flowers around the trim and imagine the flatware coming from a loving grandmother's home. This plate was designed in traditional Swedish colors, but with modern influence: two geometric lines cross at the center. The design holds true to the accompanying salad plate—both of assorted colors that go hand-in-hand with thoughts of Sweden: bold reds, yellows, greens, and blues.

CHAPTER 6

ALEX SAT AT his desk all afternoon preparing for his meeting with Pernille and Eleonora. Her list of accomplishments included culinary awards, best-selling cookbooks, and high quality tableware. He even discovered modeling photos for perfume ads and elite fashion.

He looked through her portfolio of publicity photos. Many of the shots—taken in a studio back in Denmark—were of Pernille standing behind a table, mixing, chopping, or just holding up one random vegetable or another.

He glanced at his watch. He couldn't believe it was time to meet with Eleonora already. He gathered the material he'd collected and headed toward the conference room.

Eleonora had run through Alex's responsibilities at the long glass conference table prior to Pernille joining them. She had explained how the Pernille Bjørn name, through a mutually exclusive, lucrative collaboration, was associated with a popular Scandinavian housewares brand that made everything from flatware to kitchen linens. The line was one of Pernille's strongest sources of income, and she'd invested much of those proceeds into a burgeoning fashion line for young women.

In Italy, Pernille Bjørn was not yet a household name. She was just a face on a perfume ad. Alex's job was to showcase Pernille's expertise, beauty, and sparkling personality, pitching her modeling services to Italian brands and growing her name recognition in Italy in the process. Her TV producers' goal, of course, was to eventually enter the U.S. television market—global domination.

Eleonora had explained that Alex would be Pernille's contact and her go-to guy throughout her stay in Rome. And while his first official assignment was to prepare her for her upcoming televised cooking segment, Eleonora had made it clear that Alex was to be, more importantly, Pernille's Roman concierge. He was required to be available to Pernille at any time for any reason, until he put her on the plane back to Denmark.

He was now seated at the conference table across from both Eleonora and Pernille. They ran through the specifics of the first TV segment. At first, it seemed like an overwhelming project, but he liked Pernille—her energy, her intelligence. He felt a bit at ease because he knew Italians would love her too.

"I've rented a flat near Piazza Navona," Pernille changed the topic at the end of the meeting. "Teddy should be here in a couple of days, which is when we will transfer to the hotel."

Alex raised his eyebrows, which Pernille took to mean that he hadn't heard of the wealthy Teddy Hume.

"My fiancé," Pernille explained. "You are going to like Teddy. Everyone loves Teddy." She hooked her arm into the handles of her oversized black leather purse and stood up. "Well, I'm sorry to have kept you all so late. I should be off."

The doors closed behind Pernille, but her bubbly energy continued to buzz the room.

"Isn't she great?" Eleonora's tone seemed a bit too reassuring. "This is not going to be a problem project; she seems so lovely." She waited for his reaction.

"Absolutely." He wanted to appear confident, up to the task, but he couldn't help confessing his shock that such a big responsibility was going to a relatively new, part-time hire. "I'm surprised you're allowing me to handle this one. She seems like a big deal."

"Oh, she is," Eleonora began to gather her papers. "She really is. But, still, I don't know how she will do in this market. To be honest, I think she'll do this one appearance, and then we probably won't see her in Italy again. I mean, not to sound discouraging, but as I've mentioned before, I find it hard to believe that Italians are going to buy a cookbook full of Danish recipes."

Alex followed her out of the conference room.

"Not that I don't want her to succeed," Eleonora continued.

Is she back-peddling?

"Let's see how the TV appearance goes and we'll take it from there. If they like her, it will be good. Oh!" She flipped through her pile of papers and handed one to Alex as they descended the stairs. "This is the recipe we spoke about, the one that she wants to cook on set. Share this with the talk show producers immediately. Make sure they get her whatever she needs."

"Okay, sure. First order of business," he added with a smile.

"Yes, and Alex?" She held the door for him. "This is a good thing for you. If this works out, we could consider taking you on full time. Good luck!"

"Thank you." That was what he wanted to hear. "She will be a huge success here. I promise."

"Let's hope!" She winked as they parted ways. "And don't stay too late."

Stepping off the bus, Alex strolled along the river looking for a quick bite to eat. He discovered a late-night, fast-food type pizzeria around the bend. It was a tiny eatery with no tables. The rectangular slices of Roman-style pizzas were all displayed in a glass case. Alex selected one slice with broccoli rabe and one with artichoke. He ordered a bottle of beer and sat at the high counter by the window.

Rome by night was absolutely charming. Alex slowly ate his pizza while staring at the streetlights reflecting off the Tiber across the way. Occasionally, people walked by—a group laughing, a couple holding hands, a loner out for a night on the town.

After he'd finished his pizza, Alex decided to stroll through the streets. He ended up crossing the bridge over to Trastevere and headed straight for Patrizia's bar. The faint sounds of jazz music filled the small cobblestoned street. As he approached the piazza, the music grew louder and was accompanied by the conversations of Cin Cin's patrons. He hoped that Patrizia would be working. He hadn't seen her since that first morning two weeks prior. He supposed it was a rarity to see her on the morning shift and that maybe she worked in the evenings.

The jazz bounced as Alex crossed the threshold and felt, as always, that he had entered another world. He welcomed the escape and knew that was what drew him to the place.

The well-dressed guests were all mingling, laughing, or dancing to the music. Alex scanned the room for Patrizia, but still no sight of her. He made his way around the room for a better look.

A live band was performing off in the corner, the lead songstress bouncing in her silver studded dress as she happily crooned in English about a lover who didn't love her back. A teal flower was nestled in the wavy brown hair that danced on her shoulders as she shook around the small stage between her bassist and trumpet player.

There was no sign of Patrizia. But there was still hope that she'd walk in from behind that crooked door to the back.

Alex found an empty table made from an old schoolhouse desk and theatre seats. The circus barman with the handlebar mustache approached and stood so close that it made Alex lean back as he placed his order for something with Campari in it. His preference for the bitter Campari taste was all he knew he wanted. He left it up to the bartender to come up with something. The man exposed his crooked teeth with a grin and slid back behind the counter to execute a dramatic drink-making performance.

Alex took a file folder from his bag to review his upcoming work: recipe, Q&A, photo shoot, the TV appearance, and—if the TV appearance went well—another TV appearance to follow.

Suddenly, the Dalí-esque waiter from that first morning appeared next to him dressed in what resembled a mime costume with black-and-white stripes. He wore white makeup with pink circles on his cheeks. He balanced a silver tray in his left hand. With his right, he theatrically placed a laced doily and ruby red drink onto the school desk. The mime offered a bow and disappeared into the crowd.

From behind the bar, the circus barman explained, "That cocktail is called Americano. Made for the Americano. Enjoy your Campari drink."

Alex raised his glass and gave him a grateful nod.

The room was lit up in hues of red, blue, and yellow—the simple change of lighting gave the place an even more enchanting feel. Alex sat back in the velvet theatre seat and enjoyed his surroundings. The playful music soothed him as he watched the songstress perform to the well-dressed crowd.

Again, he scanned the crowd for Patrizia and examined the patrons. Most of the women wore black beaded dresses and feathery hats, despite the early hour. The men sported blazers with pocket squares and expensive jeans. Alex hoped that he blended into the crowd with the more conservative blazer he had worn to the office.

"You're welcome to take some food, signore," the barman called out again.

"Oh, no thank you." Alex hoped he didn't look startled. "I just want the drink."

"But it is free with your drink, signore." As the barkeep said this, the creepy mime appeared from nowhere and waved his arm like a game show host to a tempting spread of bites displayed on a marble counter.

"Thank you . . . "

"Aurelio." The bartender answered for the mime.

"Nice to meet you, Aurelio." Alex stood up, shook his hand, and headed toward the food. "My name is Alex."

Again, the mime bowed his head and disappeared.

As Alex turned back toward the food, he heard someone call out his name. It was Pernille, jumping up and down, clapping her hands with excitement.

"I'm so glad to bump into you!" She put her black leather bag and bright purple jacket on the empty theatre seat next to his. "You know this singer? She's from Denmark. I am so happy to find you here. I'm glad that I have someone to enjoy this wonderful place with," she stopped and took his hand. "I hope you don't mind me sitting with you. Are you with someone?"

"Not at all." He was glad for such beautiful company. "I'll grab some food for us. Stay here and order yourself a drink. Look for that wandering mime—clown?—whatever."

"The clown?" she looked perplexed, then jumped and laughed when the mysterious waiter suddenly appeared at her elbow.

Alex and Pernille enjoyed pizza and vegetable bites while he sipped his Americano and she her Prosecco. The songstress had since taken a break, leaving the sound of the upright bass and percussion to fill the room. Behind the counter, the mime joined the circus barman for what seemed to be a magic trick. Pernille laughed as the two clowns bumbled in comedic showmanship.

"This place is absolutely wonderful!" she exclaimed. "I'm so happy I found it. And I'm so glad you're here to enjoy it with me." She held her slender glass of Prosecco aloft. They clinked glasses and took another sip.

Alex was less surprised when the mime returned, this time with the addition of a red cape and a black mask over his eyes. He placed a bowl of nuts with another round of drinks on the school desk and, instead of dissolving into the crowd like before, he smiled and reached for Pernille's hand. He led her to stand and silently danced her around the room as she laughed along. He winked at Alex as he deposited Pernille back into her chair and then dramatically turned around, allowing his red cape to flow around him as he floated away.

"What a strange place," she said to Alex. "I love it."

"Yes, I have my morning coffee here."

"Oh, really?"

"I live just around the corner."

"How lovely! We must hang out here often. This will be our place. What do you think?"

"If you don't mind trekking over the river, I will be here."

"Perfect." She slapped his knee. "Then it is done." She finished off her Prosecco. "Teddy will love it, too. Do you have a girlfriend?"

"Um . . . " Alex was surprised at the turn the conversation had taken. "Well, not at the moment. No."

She looked at him, smiling, waiting for him to continue.

"I mean, I am looking, I guess?" He wanted to bring up Patrizia, but that seemed premature. Should he lie? Certainly not. The truth was he had no girlfriend; he was alone.

"Well," she interrupted his thoughts. "You are a very good looking young man. I'm sure you won't have a problem finding her." She sat back in her chair and smiled. "Maybe I can find one for you!"

"No," he quickly replied. He felt awkward at the thought of Pernille Bjørn setting him up. "I'm okay. I'll find her when I'm ready."

"Don't you worry," she ignored him. "I'm very good at this. I will find her and you will thank me. I promise. Besides," she laughed, "if all else fails, there's always our little mime friend."

Alex just smiled and shook his finger at her in mocking reprimand.

They would stay at Cin Cin for the rest of the evening, talking and enjoying the music. They discussed the talk show and the Italian translation of her book. She explained that she'd taken Italian lessons in Denmark and had hired a tutor in Rome as well.

Finally, after three drinks, two additional sets from the jazz singer, and far too many samplings from the buffet, they decided to end the night.

"Let's do this again when Teddy is here," Pernille said while ducking into her waiting taxi.

"Of course. I look forward to meeting him."

"I can't wait," she said with a wave. He shut the door of her taxi and watched it pull away into the night and went back into the bar.

"American Boy!" Patrizia's raspy voice came from behind him. "Having a late evening, are you?"

Alex turned with a smile. "Ciao, Patrizia." He placed his empty cocktail glass on the silver-laced bar and then proceeded to lean back against it. "I didn't think you were working tonight. In fact, I haven't seen you in a while. Are you not here in the mornings?"

"Oh no, I haven't been," she stated as she set a stack of violet napkins in the holder in front of her. "Have you been coming back steadily? I'm sorry I missed you."

"Yes, I wasn't lying when I said I'd be here every morning. And you haven't been here."

"Well, I'm here now." She walked out from behind the bar. "What are you doing now?"

"Nothing, I suppose. I was just about to leave."

"Good." She grabbed her coat from behind the bar. "I just finished my shift. Care to join me for a late-night stroll?"

Alex didn't know how to respond. Should he join her? What was her story?

"Why not?" he finally blurted out. "I hear Rome is beautiful late at night."

"It is." She smiled, winked, and slowly hooked her arm under his.

Alex and Patrizia wove their way through the cobblestone streets, over a footbridge, through Campo de' Fiori, and into the uncharacteristically quiet Piazza Navona. She led him to a marble bench by Bernini's fountain at the square's center.

"I like seeing Rome this late at night," she said as she stared at the water gushing down into the glowing basin below.

Alex, too, explored Bernini's creation. He remembered reading about it. Each flowing stream appeared to be guided by one of four burly statues representing a river god: The Nile, The Danube, The Ganges in Asia, and what was the other one? He couldn't remember. He proceeded to stare at the tall Egyptian obelisk rising above, which represented the wealth and power of the Papacy.

Oh! The coins! he thought. The fourth river represented the Americas: Rio de la Plata. That was the fourth river.

"There's very few tourists out tonight," Patrizia interrupted his thoughts. "Hardly ever any vendors, and it is so quiet. It makes me feel like I own the city."

Alex found himself staring at her profile as she spoke. Tonight, she looked like a model from the 1920s. She had on very little makeup, but her eyes looked as sultry as a flapper's. Her brown-black hair was now finger-waved and reached just the bottom tip of her pale ears.

"Did you cut your hair?" he broke their silence.

"Oh! Yes." She blushed. "But I don't like it. It will grow back fast, I'm sure."

"Well, I think it looks nice."

"Thank you, Alex," She turned back to watching the flowing water. Her arm still hooked in his. She rubbed her hand along his upper arm. Alex turned to her again, watching her watch the water. He leaned in closer and kissed her.

CHAPTER 7

IT WAS EARLY morning. Alex rolled out of his bed and avoided waking Patrizia. He didn't want to open the shutters and startle her with sunlight, so he searched his dark room for last night's underwear with no success. Rather than put on a new pair, he just threw on the pajama pants he found hanging randomly on the armoire by the door. He went into the bathroom, splashed water on his face, and proceeded into the kitchen to put on a pot of espresso.

Sipping the warm coffee, he opened his laptop at the living room table and scrolled through his various social feeds. On his way back into the kitchen to refill his coffee, he found his underwear hanging from the ceiling light in the tiny foyer. How the hell they'd gotten up there, he couldn't remember. As he reached up and grabbed them, his pants slid to the floor.

"Well, *buon giorno*, Alex," Patrizia said, leaning against the doorway, watching him stretch to the ceiling, underpants in hand and pajama bottoms around his ankles.

Red in the face, Alex quickly bent down and fumbled to grab at his pants, causing him to drop his cup, trip forward, and fall at her feet, naked. It was from this position on the floor that he noticed she was wearing his striped button-down.

"Are you okay?"

"I'm fine." He lay there and pulled up his bottoms, laughing as he reached for his espresso cup, still intact. "Coffee is in the kitchen. I'm okay, go ahead."

She laughed and walked over him, revealing that she wore nothing underneath his dress shirt.

"I hope it's okay that I threw this on," Patrizia said as she joined Alex in the living room. "I don't know where my underpants went."

Alex realized he was still holding his own underwear and threw them into the dark bedroom.

"We'll find them soon enough," he replied and sat on the green sofa. He patted the empty space next to him. "Come. Sit down."

"I can't," she sipped her coffee and smiled. "I should get home."

"Already?" He followed her into the bedroom and turned on the light.

"Well, to tell you the truth," she replied as she searched for her clothes. "I'm a little embarrassed."

"Embarrassed?" He opened the shutters and leaned on the windowsill facing her. "Don't be embarrassed. We had fun. At least, I hope you did."

"We just met, Alex." Her face was turning red, but she was still smiling. "I don't know what came over me." She reached around, feeling for her bra underneath the sheets. "I shouldn't have done this."

Alex spotted her pink lacey underwear in the far corner of the room. He handed it to her. She smiled, a bit sheepishly, and went into the bathroom to dress.

"I wish you wouldn't be embarrassed," Alex said through the door. "I like that this happened."

"Of course you do," she replied from the other end and laughed.

"No," he continued as she opened the door. "I mean, I'd like to see you again . . . "

"You will," she replied as she walked past him and slid into her shoes, which she had found wedged underneath the sofa. "At the café."

He cocked his head and smirked.

"You are very handsome," she chuckled and kissed him on the cheek. "I must go."

"That's it?"

"For now." She winked as she closed the door behind her. Alex stood in the foyer, holding up his pajama bottoms and staring at the closed door, confused.

CHAPTER 8

AFTER PATRIZIA'S SUSPICIOUS and confusing exit, Alex spent the rest of the morning cleaning up the place and trying to forget what had just happened.

Why had Patrizia rushed off so quickly? Should I have run after her? He thought it was probably best to give her space to figure out whatever it was she had to figure out. And because he realized he wasn't living in a romantic comedy.

He ate some leftover prosciutto and mozzarella he had found in his fridge and sat on the couch to think. He knew he would see her at the bar. But now he felt maybe he should keep his distance. He wasn't sure what to do. He had to clear his mind. He showered, dressed, and went for a walk.

He crossed the river and again found himself at Largo Argentina. He leaned on the railing and peeked into the pit of ruins. Remains of what were once a temple and a theatre lay inside. Alex remembered it was the supposed spot where Julius Caesar had been assassinated.

Large columns jutted out from the pit. And it was there he caught sight of a curiously large black cat luxuriating in the shade. Through the columns behind it, a second cat—white with gray spots—popped up. To the left, another was balancing on a stone wall that ran along an opening in the ground. Just below the platform, a gray-striped tabby, who looked as if he'd seen better days, ate from a metal bowl.

Alex walked along the railing, watching the cats in the ruins. He reached a large white sign with a description of the ruins. In reading it, he learned that the area had been turned into a sanctuary for stray cats. Apparently, volunteers regularly fed the cats that gathered and frolicked amid the ruins in the gated area. There was even a veterinary office on site where volunteers cared for the lonely felines' health and well-being.

Amazed by this organized care for strays, Alex sat on one of the stone benches and enjoyed the show. After a while, he began to recognize the cats' disparate traits and abilities, even personalities. The gray tabby was lean but agile, able to jump from one wall to another, sometimes skipping over a partition, without a problem. The white spotted cat was gentler—he seemed to enjoy sneaking through small openings in the ruined walls to surprise his cohorts.

The large and lazy black cat that he'd first spotted in the shade, however, remained stretched out, pulsing his tail against a stone. The other cats roamed around the black cat at a distance. He was like a little feline emperor waiting for something to excite him, occasionally offering a disappointed yawn. Although his playful acquaintances surrounded him, he seemed solitary. This cat wasn't just bored or unimpressed; Alex felt certain that the Emperor was lonely.

After spending some time lost in the imagined lives of otherwise ordinary cats, his thoughts returned to Patrizia's odd departure earlier that morning. Of course, he had been surprised to find himself in bed with her the night before; it all seemed to have happened so quickly. Too quickly, maybe. But it was casual, fun; it just seemed to happen naturally.

When he had kissed her in front of that fountain, she had responded with passion. Influenced by alcohol or by his own loneliness, he'd reciprocated, and what followed was a bit of a blur.

And the morning had brought nothing but confusion. Patrizia seemed to have woken up in a good enough mood—flirting with him and sipping her coffee—but then claiming poor judgment, she'd rushed out of the apartment.

Buzz. Buzz. The vibrations shook Alex from his thoughts. He pulled out his phone and read the text:

Take 25% off your next visit . . .

He rolled his eyes, deleted the spam, and noticed an unread email in his inbox. Had he missed a message from Eleonora? His palms began to sweat. He tapped the icon to reveal, instead, a message from someone he hadn't seen or heard from in years. But the subject next to the name shocked him even more: *I miss you.*

CHAPTER 9

Boston—early 1990s

Freshman Year of College

ALEX TOED THE back of the blue theatre seat in front of him with his black Chuck Taylors, waiting for orientation to begin. The lecture hall was nearly full, and the multiple introductory conversations happening around him echoed in his head. He adjusted his new backpack on the floor between his feet and took inventory of his fellow freshmen seated nearby. A group of three giggling girls with outdated, teased hairdos chatted two rows in front of him. To his right sat a threesome of awkward boys, accidently touching elbows but refusing to converse. Alex introduced himself to his closest and least frightened looking neighbor. The boy turned toward him with shaky hesitation. Then, after assessing Alex for what seemed like an eternity, he smiled and burst forth like a fountain with an abundance of babble.

Conspicuously, Alex scanned the rest of his section, trying not to seem inattentive to the sudden chatter; the boy hadn't yet stopped to breathe. At the far end of the section, just a few rows ahead of them, Alex spotted something a bit more interesting: a girl with long red hair. He debated picking up his backpack and moving closer to her, but he didn't want to snub his new acquaintance, who had since welcomed a scrawny, morbid kid on his right to listen in.

Alex decided to make his move. He grabbed the top of his backpack with his left hand while positioning his right on the armrest. He planned on a quick lift and retreat. He waited for babble-boy to turn his attention again to the scrawny kid and, when he saw his chance, lifted himself quietly off the seat of his chair. He'd only gotten halfway up when the loudspeaker announced the commencement of orientation. Alex noticed the boys watching him, so he made as if he was just getting more comfortable and smiled at them, defeated.

The dean went on for over an hour about dormitory policies and graduation requirements while the listless audience shifted in their seats. The dean's words were swirling around Alex, but he couldn't pay attention. He was focused on getting a better look at the redhead through the slumped bodies of bored freshmen that separated them. The sunlight beamed through the window, and it made the hair cascading down her back seem like it had transformed into a lighter shade of strawberry-blonde. She, too, ignored the dean at the podium, her head turned toward the blonde girl sitting next to her, wearing a black brimmed hat with a giant purple flowery thing that flopped as she animatedly spoke. The blonde yammered on in a loud whisper while the redhead occasionally giggled.

Finally, the students were dismissed and the girls rose to their feet. Alex stood to leave but paused at the aisle, letting others file past him toward the exit. He watched as his girl marched up the aisle, still listening to her bubbly friend. As they approached, Alex got a better look at his mysterious redhead.

THE LOVE FOOL 59

Her orangey-red mane was thick and wavy. She parted it in the middle and allowed it to cascade past her face, reaching her thin waist. She wore a green plaid wool sweater that hung off one shoulder, exposing a white flowery blouse. Her wide-legged jeans were ripped at the hem and showcased the black and yellow plaid laces of her purple Doc Martens.

Just before she passed him by, he stepped into the aisle. She looked up at him, her bright green eyes sparkling amid the sea of freckles on her structured face. Her expression was coy but intrigued.

"Hi, I'm Alex."

"Hi," the blonde girl spoke first. Alex had forgotten she was even there.

"Nice to meet you," Alex offered to the blonde, all while his gaze remained fixed on the redhead. "And you are?"

"Emily."

Her voice was soft but raspy. Students continued to push past them to the doors at the rear of the auditorium, but Alex felt like he was transported to a quieter place. No one was around but him and Emily. Emily. He liked the sound of her name. It completed the package perfectly. She was made for him; he knew it. Alex shook Emily's hand and smiled.

"Come on," the hatted friend coaxed Emily toward the door. "We're going to lose our group."

"Oh. Right." Emily let go of Alex and followed her friend.

"It was nice to meet you," he shouted. He didn't want her to get away so quickly. After all, he had just found her. "I'm sure we'll see each other around?"

Emily stopped at the doorway and looked back. The sunlight shone in around her.

"Of course," she replied and then exited the building. Was she smiling? He couldn't tell.

The swarm of freshmen dispersed outside on the theatre hall lawn. Each small group stood by small tables with white signs indicating the separate majors. Alex scanned the lawn for both the science table and for Emily. He spotted her rifling through a notebook as her floppy flowered friend waited. He couldn't help his wide smile when he noticed they stood by the white sign that read Bio/Chem.

"So, fellow science nerds, are we?" he said to them nonchalantly as he checked in with the group leader. "We're getting off to a good start."

"You're funny," Emily replied with a smirk. "But yes, I suppose we'll be struggling in lab together."

"Great! Looking forward to it."

"Well, I'll see you around then." Emily closed her book and started to walk off.

"You're not doing the tour?"

"Oh. No. I've already seen the place. Besides, I have to be somewhere. I'll see you in class then, okay? Bye." She waved as she disappeared through the crowd.

Alex waved back and despairingly turned to join the group.

The following day, Alex walked into his first biology class, hoping Emily would be there. He scanned the sea of students with no success. Finally, he settled on a seat up front and waited for the lecture to commence. As the professor began his introduction, the door in back opened and in walked Emily. She quietly took a seat in the back of the hall without interrupting the introduction.

Alex had planned to chat with Emily after class, but she had immediately bolted out of the room before he even rose from his seat. Did she know he was there? Maybe he hadn't seen her after all. He hoped to catch her in other classes, but she seemed to be on a different schedule.

In the classes that they shared, Alex strategized to sit closer to her, but because she was typically late or showed up just as class started, she ended up sitting somewhere on the other side of the room.

He concluded that she really wasn't interested in sitting by him or getting to know him.

CHAPTER 10

EVERY ANSWER ON the biology midterm had come quickly to him, so quickly Alex worried he was missing something. He combed through his completed exam, searching for trick questions that might have tripped him up, traps he might have unwittingly fallen into. Then, lest he second-guess himself and start changing correct answers, he dropped his pencil onto his desk with a satisfied sigh, packed his things, and handed his papers to the professor.

Feeling good about his exam, Alex decided to take himself out for a treat. Maybe he'd buy a new CD. He loved walking into music stores like the one he used to work at back home. If he could make time here in the city, he thought, he would apply for a job. In the meantime, he'd explore the different shops around Boston and see which best suited him. He made his way from Beacon Hill, through the Common, toward Back Bay. He wanted to check out Newbury Comics and buy the new Stone Temple Pilots CD while he was at it.

The early snowfall from the previous day had been half-heartedly shoveled on Boylston Street. Pedestrians sloshed their way down the sidewalk, avoiding splatter from the passing cars as best as they could.

When Alex reached the Prudential Tower, the puddles forced him into the path between the famous building and the luxury apartment complexes around it. Rounding the corner of the winding walkway, he noticed a girl by a side exit of one of the condo buildings. She was wearing an oversized gray wool hat that flopped as she struggled with something by her feet.

As he got closer, he realized she was trying to free her beige coat, which had apparently been caught in the back door. Alex quickened his pace.

"Do you need some help?"

"What?" The girl turned to face him. It was Emily. "Oh, hi! Alex, right?"

Although inside he was jumping for joy to have encountered Emily, Alex kept his exterior emotion straight by focusing on looking concerned about her problem.

"Oh, hey! Here, let me grab this." Alex held the bottom of her coat, allowing her to rest from her struggles.

"Thank goodness you walked through here," she held on to the free section of the coat, keeping it from hitting the dirty ground. "Hardly anyone ever does. I don't know why I bothered to go through this back exit. And would you know I let the door lock shut with my coat still in it? Of course, it doesn't open from the outside."

"Is someone coming down to open it for you?"

"No, my friend went back to work. And this literally just happened."

"I'll go around and open it for you. Where's the main entrance? On the Boylston side?"

"Yes, but you can't get in. You need an ID, but I don't have one. It's for residents only and I don't live here. I was—I was visiting someone." She blushed. "Would you mind holding my coat while I go around to get someone to open this door? It would only take a second."

"Sure. Of course."

Alex held the coat as Emily wiggled herself out of it. She smiled with relief.

"Thank you. I'll be right back."

While Alex stood there awkwardly with her coat in hand, held aloft from the slush below, he thought it could be a perfect beginning to a romantic story. Emily would consider him her hero, saving her from her predicament. People walked by looking at him with curiosity. Alex began to feel foolish. Did he look like an idiot, left to stand there for who knows how much longer, holding a woman's fancy winter coat?

The door finally opened and Emily emerged, quickly putting on the newly freed coat.

"Thank you so much for your chivalry." She hugged him.

"Not a problem at all." Alex realized he was probably blushing. This was the moment to ask her out, but he didn't know how. He searched for something, anything to say. "I almost didn't recognize you with your hat."

"My hat? Oh, yeah." Emily reached up and pulled off the floppy wool hat. "I just got my hair cut, and I'm not sure I like it."

Alex saw that her hair was much shorter than he remembered, reaching now only to her shoulders. It was no longer wavy, but still thick and tangerine red.

"Wow." Alex couldn't stop smiling. "You look great. I love it."

"Thank you." Emily looked down as if embarrassed by the compliment.

"You really do look great," Alex repeated. Emily smiled in return.

"Are you free to grab a coffee?" he blurted with much hope.

"I suppose I could grab a quick one," Emily responded after a small pause. "Maybe to-go? I'm running late to meet a friend."

"Sure, sure." Alex nodded, but really he could barely contain his excitement.

"And it's on me," added Emily. "As a thank you for your help with my coat and all."

"Agreed," he replied. He'd take what he could get, as long as he could spend some time with her. And a short walk to the coffee shop was better than nothing at all.

They made their way onto Newbury Street, down one block to an empty coffee shop set below street level. They stepped down into the doorway, avoiding the low ceiling. The tiny café was walled with wooden panels from which hung black-and-white photographs for sale. It was quiet except for the low hum of Miles Davis coming from the speakers. Emily ordered two lattes to go, paid the barista, and led Alex back outside.

"Thank you for the coffee," he said.

"Oh, you're welcome. I mean, you saved my beautiful coat."

They sipped their coffee and continued down Newbury Street back toward the Public Gardens.

"So, Alex. Tell me . . . why *Alex*?"

"What do you mean?"

"I mean, why do you go by *Alex*? Why not the full name? Which is Alexander, I presume."

"Um, I don't know. I mean, why does someone go by John and not Jonathan?"

"I'm sorry," she laughed. "I know my question sounds strange. I'm taking this psychology course as an elective, and I'm supposed to come up with a theory about character traits or something. I don't really know. I thought maybe names or what people prefer to be called says something . . . maybe? I don't think I'm cut out for Psych," she explained.

"Well, I mean . . . " Alex wanted to reassure her in the matter. He'd try anything to keep her wanting to talk to him. "I suppose you do have some point there. I mean, you're right. Why Alex and not Alexander? Right?"

"Or Xander, for that matter," Emily added.

"Xander?" he repeated with a face that expressed his disapproval. "No, I don't think I'd like that. No."

"Why not?" she laughed again. "It sounds cool." Alex wasn't sure if she was teasing him or not.

"Because . . . isn't that a character from *Buffy the Vampire Slayer*? No, thanks."

"Yes!" she seemed happy he knew that. "You watch it too? I love that show."

"No," he replied too quickly. "I mean, I'm not saying it's a bad show. I'm sure it's good. I mean, it's no *X-Files*, which I'd prefer to watch."

"Oh, yes. That's a good one too," she said slowly, in between sips.

Again, Alex was ecstatic. He seemed to have found something in common with Emily. He hoped it would entice her to see more of him. They reached Arlington Street at the end of Newbury and faced the park just across the way.

"Alex, I'm sorry to leave you, but I'm running super late." She pressed the button for the walk signal. "Thank you again for your help. I'll see you in class?"

"Uh, yeah. Sure. No problem. Yes . . . in class. See you there," he replied and then watched her cross the street.

CHAPTER 11

Rome

Present

STILL SEATED ON the white marble bench overlooking the ruins-turned-cat sanctuary, Alex stared at the *I miss you* in his inbox, and at the name in bold just above it: Emily Whitehead. Thoughts of their first encounter and the early stages of their friendship always made him smile. But it was what eventually happened between them that still angered him.

Why was she emailing him? What did she want after all these years?

Sure, Emily had reached out to him before, but he'd been able to avoid her. After the awful final argument years ago, he didn't want to ever speak to her again—and so far he'd been successful. Alex wanted his past with Emily to remain behind him. Why couldn't she just let him go? Why couldn't she let him move on as she so clearly had done?

His thumb hovered back and forth over "Delete" and "Read." He didn't know what to do.

"All right," he said to himself as he looked up and locked eyes with the black emperor.

"You. Big cat. Miniature panther. Whatever you are. I like you. You seem to be the decision maker around here. I get you. You get me? Yeah, I know you do. I will count to three. If you stand up and move around, I open the email. If you stay where you are, I delete it." He closed his eyes and counted: "One . . . two . . . three!"

Alex opened his eyes and stared at the cat still laying there, still flapping his tail. He looked down at his phone, discouraged. It was decided; he was to delete the email. He didn't want to, but his furry friend had made the choice. He looked back at the cat and suddenly noticed something moving behind it. Alex leaned closer, squinted, and examined the movement. It was another black tail!

The second tail was pointing straight up, floating around the columns behind the lazy black emperor. Suddenly, a slender black-and-white cat popped up through the columns, making the emperor roll toward it before slowly raising himself from the ground to exchange a kiss. Or rather, a sniff, as cats do.

That's it, Alex thought to himself. The emperor had moved. That other cat had made the emperor move. The two creatures proceeded to climb down the side of the temple and disappeared into the maze of walls. Alex hovered his thumb over the "Read" button, but hesitated. He felt like he was standing in front of a firing squad. With a flinch, he opened the email.

Hi Alexander,

I bet you're surprised to see my name. I hope this email finds you well. I am following your posts about Rome and I'm excited and super happy for you. I want to talk to you. Let me know when you're online and we can chat or IM.

Miss you – Emily

The note was short, direct, and surprisingly painless. In the time since they'd cut ties, he'd only felt anger and resentment. But now, having read her email, Alex began to truly feel the loss of their friendship for the first time. He'd been denying that loss all these years, until that fat black cat made him re-open the heavy door to his past.

As much as he didn't want to feel what he was feeling, he was glad to have received the note. It had been a very long time since Alex had thought about their roller coaster friendship and the issue they'd never managed to sort out. Maybe it was time to grow up. To rekindle the long-lost connection.

CHAPTER 12

Boston—early 1990s

CLASSES RECONVENED AFTER winter break. Alex found Emily again in their Intro to Biology II class and immediately claimed the seat to her left. They sat quietly during the lecture. At one point, Alex looked over at her desk and noticed her hand resting on top. He stared at it and its many freckles. His eyes followed the freckles up along her arm, then tracked the path, he imagined, that continued underneath her green wool sweater before they appeared again on her soft neck. The trickle of assorted spots crept up along her red hairline and splashed across her blushing cheeks. The trail led him to her green eyes, which sparkled, as always. When had he begun falling in love with Emily? He couldn't recall the precise moment, but clearly that's what was happening. At the very least, he felt something unlike anything he'd ever felt before. And still he hadn't asked her out. Well, aside from that coffee stroll last semester.

At the head of the classroom, the professor lectured about the blood levels in frogs, while in the seats, Alex made his move.

"Emily," he whispered.

"Yeah?"

"I'm thinking of heading over to Harvard Square after class. Want to join me?"

"Sure."

Could it be that easy? He was ecstatic.

After class, they took the red line train over the Charles River into Cambridge. Emily led him to the Garage—a tiny indoor mall with a ramp reminding its patrons that, at one point, it had been an actual parking structure. As they browsed the racks of CDs at the music store, Alex and Emily chatted about their favorite music—the Smashing Pumpkins, Morrissey, Souxie and the Banshees, The Cure, Garbage—and their shared love of WFNX, "Boston's *only* alternative radio station."

They strolled the grounds of Harvard University onto Broadway toward Kendall Square. Their mission was to find a used clothing store that had been heavily advertised on WFNX, but that neither of them had ever visited. Once they'd found it, they hunted through racks of plaid and flannel until finding just the right shirts to add to each other's college wardrobes. On their way out, Emily stopped at a different rack.

"Ooh!" Emily exclaimed as she held up a flowery black baby doll dress. "I think I need to try this on."

"Go for it."

Alex continued rifling through the men's bin, while Emily closed herself in the draped changing room.

"Well, what do you think?" Emily opened the drape and twirled in front of the mirror. The short, frilly dress revealed pale, milky legs, also covered in freckles. Alex was silent. He could not stop staring.

"I'd wear it with black tights," Emily added.

"You look lovely," Alex finally said. "You have to buy it."

"Thanks! I will!" She closed herself back behind the drape and changed. Through the curtain she added, "We should probably head back and do our homework. We have that killer biology test tomorrow morning and I have no idea what the hell I read last night."

Alex agreed as he placed his new shirts, wrapped in the shop's purple plastic bag, in his backpack. Alex was struggling immensely that spring semester, and even more in the quiet and sterile lab sessions. He followed Emily to the T stop and together they made their way back to the university library. It stretched three floors underground and its study rooms were typically full, but they managed to find an empty one on the quiet bottom floor. They closed the door, sat next to each other at the table, and opened their books to make sense of their biology notes together.

As they worked, Alex couldn't help but glance over at Emily's hands again, this time resting on the table. Why he was so fascinated with her hands, he didn't know. He examined the orange freckles that smothered her long, thin, fragile-looking fingers. He wanted to touch them. His eyes again followed her arm up to her speckled neck. When his gaze reached her green eyes, he realized they were looking back at him.

Alex smiled. Emily blushed and turned back to her book, but Alex reached his hand out to hers, forcing her to look back up. He leaned in and softly kissed her. She kissed back, but made no move toward Alex. She seemed nervous. He pulled away carefully and sat back in his chair, still managing to keep his hand on hers.

They sat together, alone, on the quietest floor in the library. Alex looked up through the small rectangular window of the study room door and saw no movement outside. No one else seemed to be on this level of the library. He looked over at Emily, whose eyes were cast down at the table, and he gently squeezed her hand. She smiled. Without a word, they leaned in to each other and kissed again. This time the kiss grew stronger, and after some time, they slipped to the floor in each other's arms.

Under the guise of once confirming the "all clear" at the window, Alex pulled away again to regain his composure. Emily buttoned her shirt, fixed her hair, and returned to her chair. Tucking his shirt neatly back into his jeans, Alex turned to face her.

"We should probably go," she suggested with a smile as she stuffed her book back in her backpack.

"No one saw us," he reassured her.

"Thank god," she laughed. "Imagine someone coming in to study and finding us under the table going at it?"

"And so what if they did?" He picked up his bag and opened the door. "Who cares?"

"Alex," she followed him to the main room. "I don't think these rooms are meant for that."

"Well, they are now," he snickered as she playfully swatted at his arm.

CHAPTER 13

Boston—early 1990s

ALEX SPREAD THE blanket he had packed in his backpack earlier that morning. Put off by Emily's initial hesitation to join him for an early spring picnic lunch, he remained silent as they set down the spread. He was trying to deduce the reason behind her not jumping at the idea. Could she have been upset with him? Disappointed, maybe? Or maybe because it was still a little too cold for a picnic.

Emily smiled as she reached across his lap for the sandwiches. She gave him a coy look, and he blushed, reminded of their library study session from the day before.

The pair sat enjoying the scenery over lunch, but Emily still seemed distant. Alex kept trying to pull a conversation from her about anything—music, movies, TV—but she replied with short answers and, for the most part, remained quiet.

"Are you okay?" he finally asked.

"I'm sorry, Alex," Emily awoke from her thoughts. "I just have a lot on my mind today."

"Anything I can do?"

"Oh. No." Emily wiped crumbs off her thigh. "I'm just worried about the exam."

He sensed she'd used the exam to deflect from her real concerns. He began to worry that she felt they'd made a mistake, that she wasn't interested in any sort of relationship with him.

"I had a lot of fun yesterday," he blurted out. He hoped he didn't sound desperate.

Emily looked at him with a smirk and blushed.

"Oh. No. Not that—," he continued. "I mean, *that* was fun, yes. But I really meant the whole day. Not just the library . . . " He realized he was babbling.

Emily laughed and leaned in, placing her hand on his.

"I had a lot of fun too," she said. "The whole day *and* the library." She laughed again, sipped her tea, and scanned the activity in the park. Alex smiled to himself, relieved, and observed the park life alongside her.

The rest of the lunch was quiet. The two sat on the blanket reviewing their class assignments. Alex moved in closer, so his arm touched hers. Emily didn't move away. She put her hair behind her ear and smiled. He leaned in and kissed her on the cheek. She smiled again and kissed him back, on his lips. As he leaned in for a stronger kiss, she pulled away.

"Alex. Not here." She smiled and pointed to her book. "Come on. We should get to this biology stuff."

"Oh, come on."

"No, *you* come on," she replied, lightly tapping his cheek. "You need to get this. You need to focus. Don't you want to pass this class?"

"Yeah, but—"

"Okay. Well, you want my help, don't you?"

"Yes."

"All right. Let's focus then."

"Then we can make out?"

Emily turned to him with a playful, scolding look and laughed. And that's how he knew she was genuinely interested.

Throughout the semester, Emily continued to tutor Alex, and more than studying happened during their sessions. In class, she sat next to Alex, rubbing her leg against his and occasionally touching his hand on the desk.

"Let's do something this weekend," he whispered in her ear one day. He felt it was time they had a special night together to solidify what was happening between them.

Emily looked at him and quietly said, "I can't. We need to talk."

They sat across from each other in a coffee shop. Alex waited for Emily to speak first. He didn't want to press the issue, because he feared what she'd say. Emily put her tea down and leaned forward.

"Alex, I like you." Her delivery was reserved, almost sad. *She's going to end this. I've done something to upset her.*

"I like you too." He didn't know what else to say.

"I'm enjoying the time we're spending together." She looked around the coffee shop as if making sure no one was listening. "But I have to tell you something." She looked down.

"You're not interested," Alex guessed. He wanted to know; to rip off the bandage and be done with it.

"No, I mean, yes . . . " She took a deep breath. "Alex, I have a boyfriend."

"What?"

"We're going through a rough patch. Well, we've been going through a rough patch for a while now. I know I should probably end it, but I haven't. I think spending time with you this semester gave me a welcome escape from it. It gave me a taste of what it would be like without him—with someone new, maybe. But then I realized none of this is fair to you."

"Wait," he interrupted. "What? You mean this whole time, this semester, you've been dating both of us?"

"Well, no," she stumbled upon her words. "I mean, yes. Well, not really."

"Well, what is it?"

"He's been away this semester. And I thought I'd take a chance . . . I don't know. I'm just so confused."

"What's so confusing? If you're done with him, then end it."

"Right. I suppose. I guess I just need to think a bit."

"So, we're over? You don't want to hang out anymore?"

"No, I do. I would love to keep hanging out with you."

"I'm interested in you," Alex continued. "I want to continue this. I want to be with you."

"I like you too, Alex. And I wish I didn't do this. Being with you has been fun. I felt free. I really enjoyed our time together."

"I don't understand what you're saying."

"I think it's best," Emily continued, "at least for the moment, to remain only friends."

Despite his discomfort, he managed to accept that they would remain no more than friends, tutor and student. As they finished their drinks in uncomfortable silence, he felt sure this was a moment that would haunt him.

* * *

Rome
Present

Alex awoke from his memories and brought his mind back to Rome. He leaped to his feet and shoved his phone in his pocket. He couldn't think about Emily now. Instead he ran his errands and made his way back home to prepare for Pernille's big TV debut.

Emily would have to wait.

CHAPTER 14

Boston—early 1990s

Sophomore Year of College

A CRISP OCTOBER breeze blew a small pile of leaves across the pavement. Alex warmed his hands on the disposable cup of bitter coffee he'd bought at the bookstore café. He sat with Emily on the steps of Harvard's library, searching her gloomy expression for some hint of what ailed her. After she'd admitted to having a boyfriend last spring, Alex stopped seeing her. It wasn't until classes started up again in the fall that they renewed their friendship—and that's all it was, a friendship. He never asked her about her boyfriend because he wanted to pretend the guy didn't exist.

Alex had tried cheering Emily up all morning, but she'd remained distant. Finally, on the steps, she revealed to Alex her latest news.

"I wanted to let you know that I no longer have a boyfriend." She kept her eyes on her own coffee cup as she continued. "We went away for the summer and it wasn't all that great.

I think we both knew it was coming. It's a relief, I suppose. To leave that behind me for good. I feel silly now, letting it stretch on all those months."

She had finally pulled the trigger. The obstacle blocking the path to what Alex was sure was true happiness had at long last been eliminated. And yet, in place of what should have been bubbling joy, he felt a sickening sense of dread. Alex was inexplicably afraid and, in the wake of that fear, he made a decision that he would regret for years to come. He interrupted her.

"Emily . . . " He tried not to stumble on his words. "I wish I had known." He paused his lie, and then quickly regained the thread of his story. "I've met someone."

What followed was a tall tale about a pretty girl in his English class named Alison. He described this imagined love interest in detail. He saw resignation on Emily's face. He had succeeded.

"I've got to tell you, Alex." Emily looked at him squarely. "I was hoping this conversation would turn out differently. I am surprised you're telling me this story."

"Story? What do you mean? Emily, listen. You knew how I felt about you when we first met. That moment in the library; we had something, I get that. But you made your choice back then. You made yourself very clear. You had someone and you stayed with him. I respected that." Alex sipped his coffee and let the dried leaves from the nearby trees collect at his feet in the breeze. "Did you expect me to wait on the sidelines for you?"

Emily didn't respond. She shifted her legs and quietly sipped her coffee. He could tell she was upset—that the flush in her freckled cheeks had nothing to do with the chill in the air. Her eyes began to tear.

"Emily, I'm sorry." He knew he was being a jerk. He felt like a jerk. This was his one chance to be with Emily and he was being a total dick. Emily had opened the door for him and stood waiting at the threshold, and, like a fool, he'd shrugged and walked on by.

* * *

Boston—early 1990s
Junior Year of College

Alex hunched over his class notes. He was seated at a corner table on the library's main level; he never studied in the basement these days. Second semester junior year he found himself loaded with coursework, but since he switched his major to marketing, he'd felt himself hitting his academic stride. He had confidence in his work.

Emily's molecular biology textbook lay open across from him on the table, riddled with stripes of yellow highlighter and copious notes in the margins. Their friendship had been strained for a time after that day on the Harvard Library steps, but when Alex had left his biology major behind, he'd also put some much-needed space between them. That break had eased the tension, and their encounters were becoming more frequent again.

As he scratched out yet another potential topic for his brand management thesis, he heard Emily returning from the vending machines. She plunked down two waters and then pulled a cassette tape from her bag. She handed him the mixtape and returned to her studies. Emily worked at a local record store and had access to the newest music. This unexpected compilation of Emily's consisted of vampire themes and gothic/alternative stuff. She never named the collections, but years later, as technology advanced, Alex would digitize this cassette and title it: *A Valentine from Hell.*

"Alex, I have something to tell you," she said in a throaty whisper.

He hated hearing those words. She never followed them up with something good. He held up a book and pretended not to hear her. He didn't want to respond. She gently pushed his book down onto the table and repeated herself.

"What's that?"

"I met someone, and I think you'll like him."

"What?" He acted confused.

"We met on the train platform," Emily continued as if Alex had asked her to.

"Oh, that's nice."

"His name is Vic. He's from London. He's just finishing up his master's program . . . "

Emily continued to describe him, but Alex had stopped listening. He thought, *. . . and he is successful, handsome, wealthy, and probably has a big cock. Fuck him.*

"Alex?" Emily was looking at him, waiting for his response.

"Huh? What?" *Did she ask me a question?*

"I said," she repeated, "I was waiting for the train and he came up to me and complimented my hair and, well, asked me out. *Bam!* Just like that." She paused.

Alex still wasn't listening. Lie. He was hearing her. He just didn't want her to go on. As the words fell out of her mouth, he felt an imaginary knife slowly plunging into his soul.

"Anyway, I admired his boldness," Emily continued, twisting the imaginary knife in his heart. "So, I said yes. Anyway, I'm hoping you'll meet him at some point."

With this news, Alex got a taste of his own medicine. She really had moved on, and he was not happy. He foolishly thought he could keep Emily dangling on a string until *he* was ready. He realized now that he'd toyed with the idea for too long. His chance with Emily had slipped away. Again.

For a time, Alex doubted Emily could ever be serious with a guy named Vic. He had hoped that at some point she would end it with him and Alex could finally make his move, but Emily's relationship with Vic flourished.

While Alex studied abroad in Milan the following semester, Emily and Vic's relationship continued to thrive, despite the regular mixtapes Emily would post to Italy. They stayed together clear through the year with Alex never even meeting the mysterious grad student.

But when graduation finally rolled around and Emily announced that she and Vic were moving to London and "really hoped Alex would come visit," Alex capitulated. He would eventually go see her in England. And for years after that visit, he would wish he had punched Vic upon their first introduction.

CHAPTER 15

London—late 1990s

ALEX HAD PLANNED a two-day stop-over in London on his way to Italy, where he frequently visited family. After graduation, he hadn't really heard from Emily much. He focused on his new job at a small marketing firm that specialized in publicity for public television programs. There he met his good friend Penny, with whom he had eventually shared his whole story about Emily.

Not a day went by that he hadn't thought of that day on the library steps in Harvard Square. All the possible ways he could have told Emily how he felt constantly haunted him. The wonder of *what if* had been for years swirling around his head.

After talking it out with Penny, he had finally decided to visit Emily. Deep down, he wanted to see if she truly was happy with Vic. He had hoped, really, that Emily would drop her life in London and run away with him. Penny was sometimes able to bring Alex back down to reality, but ultimately it was no use. Alex had made up his mind.

He checked in at the hotel by the airport and took the Tube to Richmond, where Emily and Vic had been living since graduation.

He stepped up out of the underground and onto the wet sidewalk; proof that rain showers had just passed by. The sun was now shining through the clouds, reminding Alex that it really was summer in London. An old man walking his small white dog passed, distracting Alex as he motioned to cross the street. He was startled by a loud honk of the black taxi rushing by. He looked both ways again very cautiously before stepping off the sidewalk and crossing the street. He consulted his map and headed toward the pharmacy where Emily was working part time.

The shops along the street were differentiated by assorted colors. The lavender one was a perfume shop; the blue, a tie shop; and just after that was the green pharmacy. He walked through the doors and found Emily saying goodbye to her boss. She turned and ran to Alex, hugging him with such force that he was sure she had truly missed him.

"It is so great to see you," she whispered in his ear. "I'm so happy you came. Come on." She eased up and led him out the door.

"We have the whole day together, and then we're meeting Vic later for dinner," she informed him, her red hair blowing in the breeze. "It means a lot to me that you've come. Really."

"I know you've been here a while, but I still can't believe you live in London. I'm so happy for you." The lie hung in the air until he continued, "So, what are we doing today?"

Emily went on to describe a typical tourist itinerary, ending with a dinner with her boyfriend in the Covent Garden area, and Alex took this opportunity to fully examine her for the first time since his arrival.

Her voice was just as wonderful as before. Did it always have a slight sultry rasp? He couldn't remember. Her eyes were as brilliant as ever. Her hair was the perfect shade of red with just a hint of blonde. And her freckles. There were those freckles.

They spent the day strolling through London and talking about nothing in particular, just simple conversation like old friends. But already Alex was beginning to doubt the wisdom of this trip. Already it was torture.

Alex knew he had to say goodbye to his friendship with Emily, but so far he'd never had the courage to do it. He was predicting that dinner with Vic would change that.

"I should warn you," Emily softly said as they walked toward the restaurant. "Vic has always been skeptical of our friendship. I've explained to him that we're just close friends. He really wants to meet you. And I think when he does, he'll understand."

"I'm sure he does," Alex replied.

And there he was: a tall, thin man in a smoke-gray business suit, leaning up against the doorway to the restaurant. His designer sunglasses sat on top of his bald, shiny head. Emily ran up to him and gave him a peck on the cheek. Vic stared at Alex as he embraced her, and once he confirmed that Alex was watching, he moved in for a full-on kiss.

Alex walked up to them and interrupted.

"Well, it sure is great to finally meet you, Vic." He offered his hand and waited. Vic forced a smile and shook his hand.

Alex followed the couple into the French restaurant Vic had chosen. The interior was casual, with dark oak chairs and square tables covered in simple white cloth. Emily sat across from Alex while Vic took the seat to his right and immediately ordered wine for the table.

As Alex was browsing the menu, Vic leaned over and said, "I want you to taste some of my favorite dishes." He closed Alex's menu. "You like escargot, don't you, Alex?"

"Vic. No," Emily interrupted. She looked at Alex. "You don't have to eat them. Vic is just teasing."

"What?" replied Vic. "It's a delicacy."

"Actually," Alex spoke up. "I am curious to try them. Let's do it."

"Good man." Vic patted Alex on the back of the shoulder. Alex smiled in return and noticed Emily disappointedly shaking her head at Vic, who sipped his wine with a smirk.

"So, Alex," Emily changed the topic with a cheerful tone. "What are your plans? You mentioned marketing?"

"Marketing, eh," Vic chimed in. "What do you market?"

"Oh, um, it's television," replied Alex. "The company I work for promotes cooking shows."

"So, like, old lady shows?"

"Vic!" Emily slapped his forearm. "I'm sorry, Alex."

"I'm also thinking frogs' legs," Vic changed the subject. "Emily, what about you?" Emily looked uncomfortable and very nervous.

PERNILLE BJØRN'S NORDIC FEASTS
SEASON 03, EPISODE 08
"Fishing in Aland"
SCENE 01

FADE IN:
ON A MOVING FISHING BOAT
PERNILLE stands on a fishing boat, holding on to the ropes. Her hair is tied in
a messy bun. She wears a blue rubber rain
jacket over white jeans and red rain boots.
The sunlight and spots of misty rain make
her squint as she smiles to the camera.

> **PERNILLE**
> Today, I'm visiting the Aland
> Islands—off the coast of Finland—
> with my dear friend Valterri.

The camera pans to a burly blond
man in a yellow rain coat. He's
controlling the fishing boat as it
bounces on the water.

> It's a bit wet here. But Val-
> terri assures me that we should
> have clear weather and calm wa-
> ters ahead.

The soundtrack's tinny music gets louder as
the black-and-white fishing boat is shown
against the vast blue backdrop of the Bal-
tic Sea. Cut to the boat as it comes to a
standstill. Valterri points to the horizon
as Pernille looks on. The music's volume is
lowered as Pernille's voice is heard again.

> **PERNILLE**
> The Aland Islands are located
> between Sweden and Finland. Just
> beyond, you can see a hint of
> the Swedish coast.

A shot of the horizon with a faint strip of
the coastline can be seen.

> **PERNILLE**
> Although a Finnish territory,
> the locals of Aland also speak
> Swedish. Throughout history, the
> sovereignty of these islands has
> much been disputed.

The music crescendos again, drowning out
the voices and sound of the fishing boat's
motor. Valterri raises the net, displaying a catch of large brown fish with yellow
spots. Pernille puts on rubber gloves and
helps Valterri and his crew unload the net
into large white basins. The music is low
again. Pernille picks up one wriggling fish,
holds it up to the camera.

> **PERNILLE**
> This is the one I'll be cooking
> for you today.

Music up again and shots of the fishing boat
returning to land.

CHAPTER 16

Rome—October 2011

Present

ALEX SAT AT the table in the living room watching another episode of Nordic Feasts. Fortunately, Pernille speaks English in the series—a tactic for broadening their market. Alex tried concentrating on the show but occasionally found himself just staring at the computer screen. His mind would not stop thinking about Emily. So much time had passed since he'd last communicated with her. He turned back his focus to the episode to preoccupy himself.

Within minutes, he opened the chat window and noticed the green button by Emily's name indicating that she was active and online. Suddenly, her message bubble appeared, initiating a conversation between two friends who hadn't spoken in a very long time.

Emily: Hello old friend.

Alex: Hi there! I got your email.
Sorry I haven't responded yet.

E: Well thank you for replying now.

A: All OK with you?

E: Yes. Thank you for asking. I just
well, I just miss you. And when I
saw you moved to Rome, I was so
happy for you. And I got to thinking
about you... about us.

A: Aww. That's sweet of you. I appreciate
that. What time is it there?

E: It's 8pm.
You talked about moving to Italy
so many times, I remember. What
made you finally go?

A: Well, I lost my job.
And I wanted a change.

E: I'm proud of you.

A: So, what's going on? How are you?

E: I'm well, thanks. I live in San
Francisco as you may remember.

A: Right. And are you still with...
Whatever his name is...

E: Yes.
So I wanted to see how you feel
about me coming to visit you?
I have a lot of vacation time racked up so I
thought I would use it to reconnect
with you. I really miss you.

A: Right. So, you saw that I moved to Rome and you want to take advantage of the opportunity to come and visit.

E: Well, yeah! Ha! But it's more than that. So much has been going on lately and it's times like these that I wish I still had you in my life. Why can't we be friends like before?

A: You know why. Ha! Why come visit now?

E: Because I miss you. And I want to talk to you.

I understand that it's forward of me. I just thought I'd ask. Because I want to be friends again.

Alex didn't know how to respond. This was the moment he could end it. This was the moment he could reply with a simple decline. He was, again, at a pivotal fork in the road, but which direction would he take? Why was Emily contacting him after so many years? Why would she travel that far to see him? What was up her sleeve?

He had closed the door on her a long time ago. He typed nothing. He wasn't sure what to say, how to decline. Then he realized maybe there was a possibility of rekindling. But he didn't know if he wanted to let her into his life again.

E: Alex?

A: Hey. Sorry, I had a phone call. Um, I think it would be awesome if you came to visit. I would love to have someone to show around.

E: Really? I mean I don't want to
make anything awkward for you.

A: For me? No way. I don't see
why you shouldn't come. When?

E: GREAT! Next month?
If that's OK with you.

A: Yes! That works. Will you be OK if I have
to work some of the days? I'll see if I can
take the time off, but may not be possible.

E: Oh, of course! You have a job?!
What are you doing there?

CHAPTER 17

Boston—Summer 2000

ALEX TOOK THE foil-wrapped burger from the unfriendly woman at the fast food counter and joined Penny at a white metal table in the food court.

"So, are you sure you want to go to this wedding?" asked Penny as she sipped her iced tea. "I mean, Alex, *how*—no—*why* would you even want to go to Emily and Vic's wedding? I mean, let's get serious here. She's gone. She's moved on. Something you should have done years ago, I might add. And you know that."

"I know all that," replied Alex, his mouth full of over-cooked ground beef and stale bun. "But we're friends. We're close friends." He saw Penny roll her eyes and continued, "How would you feel if one day I decided I wasn't going to talk to you anymore? That I was just done?"

"Alex." she put her hand on his shoulder. "I would never have led you on like that. I mean, I'm not the one who wanted to be with you, then didn't follow through with it. The one who flirted with you, inappropriately might I add, while in a serious relationship with someone else. I'm not the one who is getting married yet still wanting *you* to be there to see it all. That's like friggin' torture, and you are doing it to yourself. You know it."

Alex put a fry to his mouth to avoid having to respond, and Penny rolled her eyes again in silence.

"Penny," he finally said with a sigh. "You're right. And you're not telling me anything I don't already know. I realize I'm an idiot. But how can I just walk away from a friend like that? And maybe being at the wedding will help me realize it's done. In any case, I want her in my life, even if it is just as a friend."

"Do you realize that you have a ton of girls who want to date you," she put her fork down, "and you refuse to give them the time of day? I would be more lenient with you if you went out with one of them, gave someone else a chance for once. What about that Janet girl? You liked her, didn't you?"

"Janet?" he scoffed. "God, that girl from accounting? We went out twice and she never spoke to me again."

"I imagine she noticed you weren't taking her seriously." Penny was getting angry. "Listen, do what you want, Alex." She shook her head and bit down into her chicken. "I, for one, am tired of this topic. It just goes in circles and you refuse to change. And it's going to ruin you. Whatever," she laughed. "At least I get to see England."

"I hate you," he joked. Alex knew Penny would always speak her mind. He appreciated her advice and opinions and knew she had his best interests at heart.

"But do you see what I mean?" she continued. "You are letting your life pass you by while pining for a woman who is marrying someone else. I just don't understand."

He nodded as he chewed the final bite of his burger. "I know. I'm an idiot."

"Stop it."

"No," he clarified. "I mean, you're saying everything I need to hear. I try telling this to myself, but I need to hear it from someone else. Someone who knows me—knows me like you do. So, thank you."

Attention passengers, the female voice called over the loud speaker. *British Airways flight 212 to London Heathrow departing at 5:55 p.m., now boarding at Gate 33A.*

"Come on," Penny smiled and grabbed her bag.

* * *

England—Summer 2000

Alex turned the door handle to the hotel room, and Penny rushed to the tiny suite's bathroom sink to wash her face from what she called airplane morning junk. Alex set the suitcases down by the oversized armoire and claimed the bed closest to him. Penny emerged from the bathroom, her face slightly blushed from all the scrubbing, and plopped onto the other bed.

"What a beautiful country," Penny said with a yawn. "The rolling green hills. The sheep everywhere. The cottages. The thatch roofs. It's like a picture postcard here. What's this village again? Where are we?"

"What?" He wasn't really listening to Penny. She repeated herself and he replied, "Chipping Campden. That's the village. The region is the Cotswolds."

"I'm lying here exhausted, but looking out the window, listening to the birds and the village life, it's just so . . . I don't know how to describe it."

"It really is," Alex replied automatically. His mind was still swirling from thoughts of regret. Why had he come to the wedding? Maybe it was a mistake. Maybe Penny wouldn't mind if he suggested they fly back home to Boston.

"Washing my face didn't help," she interrupted his thoughts. "I think I'm going to take a little nap, refresh, and then we can go out and explore?"

"Sure. Sure."

Penny rolled over and instantly fell asleep. Alex lay on his bed, also exhausted, but his mind kept spinning over the reality of what brought him to England.

He awoke with a start. Where was he? *Oh, right*, he thought. *It's real. I'm in England.* He stared at the ceiling and tried to mentally prepare for the big event to follow.

"Oh good." Penny came out from the bathroom with a toothbrush in her mouth. "You're up too. Shall we go see the village? Get a bite to eat?"

"Let's do it." With a struggle, he forced himself off the bed, washed his face, brushed his teeth, and followed her out.

The stroll around the village was like a blur to him. He just followed Penny around as she nodded and pointed at her discoveries. He obliged as she excitedly stood by a pony that was looking over a short-stoned wall, positioning his head practically on her shoulder.

"Oh look!" Penny rushed up to a wooden gate. "It's a footpath! I've read about this in the guidebook. Apparently, we're free to roam the countryside by way of these footpaths. Let's go."

"Erm. There's a flock of sheep on the other side."

"Yeah, so what?"

"Well, is it wise to just walk around in sheep shit?"

"Oh, shut up!" Penny pulled him by his camera strap. "You're coming with me. I need a cool photo. Besides, they don't bite."

Alex struggled to put on a smile, allowing Penny to take a quick photo. Then they quietly moved on.

"Cheer up, moody," Penny commanded over the pint and chicken pie sitting in front of them. "This place is gorgeous. Thank you again for taking me as your guest."

Alex prodded at his chicken and leek pie, forcing a smile on his face.

"You're not upset about the sheep, are you?"

"Seriously?" Alex looked up at Penny, who expressed sarcasm in her look.

"No, not seriously, you idiot. Alex, again, I'm going to ask you: Why did you come here? I mean, look at you. You're a dud. And you're ruining my vacation." With that last remark, she laughed.

"Ha-ha," he replied sarcastically. "Very funny. But, you're right. No need to be a heavy weight."

"Really. It's like we're attending a funeral," Penny remarked and looked again at her guidebook.

A funeral, Alex thought. Yes. That's what it was: A funeral for the idea of getting Emily back. As of tomorrow, that idea would be dead, gone, over.

CHAPTER 18

A WARM BREEZE wafted through the church in Chipping Campden. Alex remained calm as he watched the flower girls and ring bearer make their way down the aisle. Though, when the double doors opened to reveal Emily in her pale wedding dress, he wanted to die.

The sunlight shone around Emily, giving her an angelic appearance, like some blessed creature come down from the heavens. The crowd whispered and sighed as the violins produced a melancholic sonata. Alex watched as Emily began her slow, sad march to the biggest mistake she would ever make.

As Emily passed his pew, Alex noticed she was shaking. He could here snuffles from the crowd. A woman behind him sobbed. A faint bark of a dog from outside could be heard between the sad throngs of the violin. He felt like he was dreaming or, more appropriately, in a nightmare.

"She's beautiful," whispered Penny. "Too bad she's making a big mistake."

"Shut up," laughed Alex.

"I mean, look at him," Penny continued through her a fake smile. "He even *looks* like an asshole."

"Shh . . ."

Emily approached the altar and stood there looking frail. Vic removed her veil, looking as if he was officially claiming her as an asset—not a life partner. *In the movies, what does one say when they speak up against a marriage?* Alex wondered. He looked around, but he ultimately did nothing.

Two of Vic's pompous-looking friends finished their readings and handed the proceedings back over to the priest. The rings were exchanged. Alex couldn't look. He fixed his eyes on a yellowish-green apple in a religious scene on the stained-glass window behind the altar. *Is it yellow or green? Is that what they call chartreuse?*

Suddenly, he felt those around him standing and clapping. He jumped up to join the crowd and found the couple exchanging their kiss. His legs were numb. He felt like he was going to fall over. His false smile was killing his cheeks. He wanted to run. He needed air. He needed to get away. He wanted it to be over. He felt Penny's arm around his shoulder.

"Just gorgeous," she said with tears in her eyes. "That was just plain beautiful. Too bad he's a dick."

Alex stared as Vic quickly led Emily out of the church and into a white antique car. Penny pushed Alex onto the shuttle bus headed to the cocktail reception.

"Wipe that fake smile off your face," said Penny. "You look crazy."

"What?" He shook his head and awoke from his thoughts. "Oh. Do I?"

"Sit down," she laughed. "And stop it before someone notices the foolish faces you're making. Seriously."

The bus pulled up to a cozy cottage that was housed on a massive landscape of beautifully manicured gardens. High tables adorned with white and blue fabrics were scattered about the terrace.

Alex and Penny ordered drinks from the quieter of the two bars that served specialty cocktails and local wines. They walked up to a group of three Americans and introduced themselves. Penny instantly began a deep conversation with a woman who was fascinated by her dress. Alex sat quietly looking around the terrace. He noticed Emily weaving through the crowd and heading straight toward him.

"You look beautiful," he said. "I'm so happy for you." He hugged her and noticed again that she was, in fact, shaking. Her face looked pale, but she still seemed to radiate beauty. She smiled, but sadly.

"Thank you," she replied. "It means a lot to me that you're here." She climbed on the barstool across from him. "Mind if I sit for a moment? I'm exhausted."

"No." He was confused. Why had the bride chosen to sit in the corner of the terrace, away from the party, when she should be making her rounds greeting everyone? Alex continued, "This is such a beautiful place."

"It is," Emily replied as she put her flowers on the table. "When I first saw it, I just couldn't believe the gardens. I wanted to have the wedding ceremony out here, but his family was adamant on a church." She rolled her eyes.

"You have a lot of people here," Alex continued.

"Oh, I know," she shifted her body slightly to the right to block the sun from her eyes. "These are mostly friends of his family that live in town. We couldn't invite them all to the formal reception, so they decided to host this special cocktail party."

Alex felt that Emily wanted to talk to him about something other than the wedding reception. She seemed stressed, and he was touched that she found her safety right there with him.

"I'm really happy you came," she said. "When I invited you, it sounded like you weren't sure you could come."

"Oh, right." He hadn't wanted to come, of course. "I just wasn't sure I could do it, financially. But I worked it out. I *needed* to be here."

"Thank you," she smiled. "You know, I wanted you to be one of the readers in the church. But after you told me you weren't coming . . . "

"You did?" How would he have possibly managed that? He'd barely managed watching the ceremony from a pew. "I wish you told me that. You could have asked. I had no idea."

"I guess," she replied, looking down at her flowers. "I was thinking that you just didn't want to come. That you were angry with me."

"Well—"

"Hi, guys!" A couple joined the table just in time to save Alex from saying something he shouldn't. It was Emily's brother and his girlfriend. "Lovely wedding, sis. You look gorgeous."

"Thank you," she smiled at him and looked at Alex.

"Now isn't that sweet brotherly love," said Alex, grateful for the subject change. "How about we get a photo of the two of you?"

Emily was eventually pulled away to complete her duties as hostess, and Alex didn't get to talk to her again that evening. He and Penny enjoyed a lovely gourmet meal and pretended they knew ballroom dancing. They said their goodbyes as soon as the cake was served, packed their clothes back at the hotel, slept briefly, and woke up early to catch their flight.

Alex returned to Boston to start a life without the idea of Emily. She was married and he would have to rebuild, not knowing that she'd one day reach out to him again.

PERNILLE BJØRN'S NORDIC FEASTS
SEASON 01, EPISODE 04
"Smørrebrød (Open Sandwiches)"
SCENE 03

FADE IN:
INT. PERNILLE'S KITCHEN — DAY
Wide shot of the kitchen. PERNILLE is wearing a light blue linen shirt. Her platinum blonde hair is flat ironed at a medium length, just below her shoulders. She's holding one fresh salmon filet in both hands. The camera zooms in to the salmon as PERNILLE speaks.

> **PERNILLE**
> As I was saying, one of the most popular smørrebrød toppings is gravlax. This is the salmon I caught earlier with my fisherman friend Oskar.

The camera pans out.

> **PERNILLE**
> Oskar lived next door to my family growing up. As children, he and my brother teased me mercilessly. Boys.

Pernille rolls her eyes with a smile.

> **PERNILLE**
> Thankfully, Oskar has grown to be quite a gentleman. He's al-

ready removed all the bones from
our filet. Now, I've shown you
how to slice off the excess fat.
Next, you'll place your salmon
onto parchment paper or baking
paper in a tray. And sprinkle
with salt.

PERNILLE demonstrates as she instructs. She
picks up a wooden bowl, removes a pinch of
salt, and lifts her hand above the salmon.
Her delicate fingers dance above the fish,
releasing large grains of white, hail-like
salt. She repeats this action with sugar,
ground fennel, and dill.

PERNILLE
Cover the salmon with more paper, then cover in plastic wrap.

PERNILLE demonstrates tightening the thin,
transparent plastic wrap around the whole
fish.

PERNILLE
Just leave in refrigerator for
about three to five days—depends
how much flavor you want your
salmon to have.

PERNILLE swaps her salmon with another tray
that was already in the refrigerator and
winks.

>   **PERNILLE**
> With the magic of television, my
> gravlax is complete. First, you
> must scrape off all the herbs.
> Then scatter fresh dill. My fa-
> vorite!

PERNILLE sniffs the fresh dill with excitement. She then chops it finely and sprinkles
it all over the salmon.

>   **PERNILLE**
> When slicing your gravlax, it
> must be against the grain. This
> will ensure a tender slice, full
> of flavor. Place your slices di-
> rectly onto the rye bread, or in
> a platter.

PERNILLE takes the fifth slice, tilts her
head back, and dangles it above her mouth.
She drops the fish into her mouth and looks
forward into the camera with a flirtatious
smile.

CHAPTER 19

Rome

Present

AFTER MANY MEETINGS with Pernille Bjørn's team and several phone calls with the talk show producer, Pernille's big Italian TV debut had finally arrived. Alex waited outside of her dressing room, ready to escort her onto the sound stage.

The dressing room door opened to reveal Pernille wearing a low-cut, flowy, royal-blue blouse with sailor-style white trousers. Her blonde hair was tied in a ponytail that hung down her left shoulder. Alex was almost blinded by her vintage hoop earrings, which matched the gold necklace playfully dangling around her cleavage.

"I know what you're thinking," she said. "I'm cooking in white pants."

"Well," he replied. "You'll have an apron."

"True." She seemed nervous. "You're right. I'm good." She turned around. "Is this shirt too much?"

"You look lovely." He hoped a compliment would calm her. "Beautiful. And you know what to do. You've done this plenty of times. Just be yourself; you'll be great."

"It's the Italian—"

"You'll be fine." He held her gently by her shoulders. "You know enough Italian for this simple interview. Just smile and be yourself, okay?"

"Right, yes," she agreed. "Just as we rehearsed. You got it."

They stood off to the side of the set, watching the sweet Italian cooking hostess, Clara Mucci, instructing her young assistant, who had no clue what he was doing. In fact, he looked like a male model hired to just stand around, mix anything in a bowl, and look handsome. Clara asked her co-host if he had ever been to Scandinavia before introducing the live audience and Italian TV viewers to *La Cuoca Scandinava* (the Scandinavian chef).

As the audience applauded, Pernille gracefully walked onto the set, hitting her mark behind the counter between the proud hostess and the model/assistant. Clara welcomed Pernille, and the two ladies shared introductory pleasantries while the assistant fumbled under the counter for an apron to hand to their guest.

Pernille deftly turned their attention to the Nordic dish they were about to create for the audience, when the model sidled up to her, unnecessarily wrapping his arms around her waist to tie her apron. He hammed it up for the camera, hugging Pernille's curves and making her visibly uncomfortable. She suffered a smile. Alex turned to the show's producer.

"Control that man, will you?!" he whispered.

Pernille continued to smile uncomfortably as Clara broke to commercial.

Makeup assistants ran to the stage for quick touch-ups, Alex close on their heels.

"It's going great," he said, hoping she felt the same.

"Yes, except for the horny boy." She laughed.

"Ha, yes. I am not happy with that. I just spoke to the producer; he's taking care of it." He gestured to the producer, who was scolding the model. Suddenly the crew flew off the set and Alex followed. The countdown began and the cameras rolled once more.

The rest of the interview went well. Pernille showed Clara how to make gravlax while being flirtatious, fun, and approachable. Clara seemed to like joking with Pernille while barking orders at their handsome sidekick "sous chef." "Slice this! Chop that! And *behave* in front of our beautiful guest, *per favore!*" Clara exclaimed.

Pernille talked about her love of Italy and how excited she was to bring her recipes from across Europe to share with a new audience. The crowd cheered Pernille at every accented Italian utterance.

At the close, the stud displayed the Italian translation of Pernille's *My Scandinavian Kitchen* like a game show model. Pernille walked off the set triumphantly waving goodbye.

The feedback was phenomenal. In addition to charming the live audience and the show's host, Pernille made a positive impression on the viewers and the press. Eleonora's inbox quickly filled up with inquiries about "that beautiful chef" and the publication date of the Italian translation of her next book, which was set to release the following month.

As Eleonora focused on the details of the Italian book release, Alex focused on setting up a marketing campaign, including photo shoots, book signings, and press interviews. Alex secured advertising in magazines and newspapers, on billboards, at bus stops and subway stations, and in bookstores.

He also helped Eleonora finalize the distribution of samples from *Pernille Bjørn's Spuntini Danese*—the Italian version of her best-selling cookbook *Danish Snacks*.

October flew by; Pernille had become an instant hit. Seated at a restaurant by the Zero Otto offices, enjoying a light panino and a soda, Alex perused his file of press clippings: mostly interviews he had arranged for Pernille with Italy's popular magazines. Many spoke of her appearance on *Chiacchiere del Cuoco* and her upcoming Italian-translated cookbook. He had already read some of the articles online, but he loved seeing his hard work manifested in print.

Alex had given the publications many photos of Pernille cooking to choose from, but in practically every Italian article he looked at, the photos were zoomed in to focus on Pernille Bjørn's perfect face or to accentuate her incredible body. Although it bothered him, Alex hoped the enhanced photos would at least entice people to read the articles and interviews that highlighted her work and culinary expertise.

Alex placed the magazines and newspapers in his bag and scrolled through the emails on his phone. When he saw the response from the producers of *Chiacchiere del Cuoco*, he smiled. They'd confirmed Pernille Bjørn's return to the show for a meatball competition, which would be filmed offsite on the Spanish Steps.

Alex had known it was a long shot, booking Pernille on the episode, but he had somehow talked the producers into finding a space for her. The timing was essential, as her second Italian translation would be released the day prior. He headed back to the office to prepare, convinced that Pernille Bjørn's second television appearance would catapult her fame.

* * *

Pernille's second television appearance had done just that. The second book was an even bigger hit. Almost immediately following, Pernille was invited to attend fashion shows and movie premieres. Her face appeared on billboards, buses, and in TV ads. Everywhere she went—stepping out of Fendi or just strolling the streets of Rome—photographers followed her. The paparazzi were falling in love with Pernille, which encouraged the Italian public to love her too.

* * *

It was late on a Thursday evening at the office. Alex shut down his laptop and packed his messenger bag. Through the glass walls he watched Eleonora bend over to turn off her desktop lamp. As she turned around, he quickly looked up at her eyes and smiled. She wore a look of accomplishment as she grabbed her large black leather purse and walked over to his desk.

"I have great news for you, Alex." She smiled, set her heavy bag on the desk next to his, and pulled up a chair. Alex sat back down. "I was just on the phone with Pernille's publishers and producers. We've just officially agreed to promote her third book and the accompanying TV series *Trek Scandinavia*." She leaned in closer. "Which means, Alex, that I can officially offer you a contract for full-time employment on this project." She smiled.

"Wow." Alex was excited. He would have a real job with Eleonora's company. He was satisfied. He finally felt that moving to Rome had been worth it. "Thank you! How long would the employment contract be for?"

"It would probably be for four to six months, to start. We'll work out all the details next week—salary, hours, and termination date—once I've had the paperwork drawn up." She stood, returned the chair, and swung her heavy purse onto her shoulder. "In the meantime, you've completed your hours for this week—you should go. As for next week, there isn't much happening, so you might take some time for yourself. Of course, if we finalize this deal with Pernille Bjørn's team, I may need you."

"Well, I'll be seeing Pernille tonight anyway. She's introducing me to Teddy—her fiancé."

"Oh, great," she added as she fumbled for her car keys. "Then you'll be hovering over the project anyway."

"Exactly."

PERNILLE BJØRN'S TREK SCANDINAVIA
SEASON 01, EPISODE 04
"My *Mormor*'s Table"
SCENE 05

FADE IN:
DINING ROOM
With her apron hung loosely, PERNILLE sits
at the dinner table displaying warm apples and cream, inspired by her late grandmother's recipe. In one hand, she holds a
light blue teacup embellished with leaves
of gold. In the other, she holds its com-
plementary saucer.

PERNILLE
Now that my *mormor*'s winter dinner is complete, it's time to
bite into my delicious dessert.
But first, I'd like to prepare my
warm *kaffeepunch*.

PERNILLE sets the cup and saucer down and
picks up a small coin from the table. She
holds up the coin to the television camera.
It is silver in color with a hole at its
center.

PERNILLE
This is a Danish krone. Of
course, you can use any curren-
cy you'd like. But being that I
am Danish and this is a Danish
tradition, I will use my krone.
Gently drop the coin into your
empty cup—like so.

The coin makes a light clink as it hits the
bottom of the teacup.

> ### PERNILLE
> That sound reminds me of my *mor-
> mor*'s home in Southern Denmark.
> It was a lovely red house with
> a blue door. She had a large
> field and a lot of sheep. I loved
> playing with the sheep.
>
> Next, you must use a strong kaf-
> fee. You must sweeten the kaf-
> fee to your liking. Typically,
> a little sweeter than you would
> normally like your coffee.

PERNILLE takes hold of the coffee pot sitting on a crocheted doily and holds it up
to the camera. Then demonstrates as the
camera zooms into the cup.

> ### PERNILLE
> This kaffee here is already
> sweetened.
>
> Now, pour just enough of the kaf-
> fee until you no longer see your
> coin. Of course, the stronger
> and thicker your kaffee, the less
> kaffee you would use. When the
> coin is no longer visible, stop
> pouring.
>
> You can see there is only about
> a third cup, or maybe less than

a third of the liquid. That is
all it takes.

PERNILLE places the coffee pot back onto the
doily and picks up a bottle of liquor sitting beside it. She holds the bottle up to
the camera.

PERNILLE
Of course, the next ingredient is aquavit—the Scandinavian
elixir of choice.

PERNILLE tilts the bottle of aquavit and
slowly pours it into the coffee.

PERNILLE
Pour until you begin to see your
coin again. That is when you
know it is enough. The stronger
the coffee, the more aquavit you
will need. This is why I use a
stronger kaffee.

PERNILLE stops pouring, looks
up at the camera, smiles, and
winks.

CHAPTER 20

Rome

Present

ALEX STEPPED OFF the bus in Largo Argentina. He walked by the ruins-turned-cat-sanctuary and noticed the Emperor, usually lazing out in the half-temple, sauntering along the site's fiberglass perimeter. Alex had the uncanny feeling the creature was following him. He stopped and watched the cat, who took the moment to sprawl out on the ground and yawn. Alex sat on the marble bench, fixated on his feline friend.

The late afternoon sun was still burning bright, but the cat had claimed a shaded spot close to Alex. It stretched its left paw underneath the fiberglass that separated them and left it there. Then it slowly blinked its eyes and surveyed the ruins below. As if hypnotized, Alex remained on the bench for a while, eyes focused on the cat, thoughts elsewhere.

He felt confident Eleonora appreciated his work and had fought to convince her partners to award him a full-time contract. He badly wanted to show her she'd made the right choice.

He'd been working many unpaid overtime hours, determined not to mess things up.

Eleonora had said that after the TV appearance, she expected a slow work week. Alex didn't know that was possible. He had so many balls in the air. So much to do. So much to prove. All while entertaining Emily. *Ha!* It would be a miracle if he survived the week at all. And he had yet to understand Emily's true motives for visiting in the first place. He supposed he'd have to wait until she got to Rome to uncover that mystery.

The lazy cat came back into focus. Alex watched as it stretched its body and let out another long, showy yawn. It then rolled itself upright with tremendous effort and sat facing Alex, flapping its tail against the ground and staring at him with an expression he could only interpret as disdain.

"What are you looking at?" The cat just stared. "Tell me what to do, cat. She'll be here soon and I have no idea what she's expecting."

The cat remained still with its eyes partially closed. Alex reached out his hand to pet it but bumped up against the wall. The cat opened its eyes at the sound and walked again along the perimeter, rubbing up against the fiberglass. Alex looked for an opening in the wall and found a gate two partitions to his right. He walked over, crouched down, and clicked his tongue to get the cat's attention. It slowly crawled through the gate, sniffed Alex's hand, purred loudly, and finally let Alex stroke its surprisingly soft fur.

"You are one cool cat," Alex continued. "And you'll need to make this decision for me. What do I do about Emily? Do you think she's coming to rekindle something? Do I try to win her back? But I hate her, cat. I really do."

He knew that latter part wasn't true. And so did the Emperor. The cat, in seeming exasperation, rose from his position and strutted back behind the gate. There, it met up with the slender black-and-white cat. They ran around the ruined walls and disappeared in the shadows of the evening sun.

Alex was so lost in his thoughts that he didn't realize he'd walked by the café until a blast from the jazz trio's trumpet woke him with a start. He doubled-back to the open-air entrance and found a lively crowd sipping cocktails, listening to the same Danish band from his evening with Pernille. The tables had been rearranged to produce a small open space at the center of the room, and the statue of the embracing couple now found itself on the left of the newly minted dance floor. Specks of colored light floated on the statue's marble surface, giving the impression that the romantic figures were dancing along to the music.

"American Boy!" called a voice from inside. "Are you joining us this evening?"

Patrizia wore a silver beaded mini dress with purple tights and black boots, and her hair was neither futuristic ponytail nor flapper bob, but voluminous and curly. She offered what looked like a perfume bottle filled with an emerald green concoction to a sophisticated woman seated by the entrance. The woman brushed a wisp of white hair from her forehead and tossed her purple feather boa over her shoulder before accepting the drink and returning to her conversation.

Alex hesitated on the threshold of the café for just a moment. It appeared they would not be acknowledging her abrupt departure when last they were together. No less intrigued, he continued into the bar.

"Patrizia! I haven't seen you here in a while. Where have you been?"

"I've been away, but now I'm back," she replied, brushing off the question with an energetic smile. She scanned the back wall of tables and then turned her attention back to Alex. "I'm so glad you've come by. Follow me." She took his hand and led him across the makeshift dance floor, her touch a gentle reminder of their intimacy. They reached a plush green velvet high back chair by the back wall. "This is a good spot for you." She proceeded to clear off the dirty cups from the vintage oak coffee table. "So, tell me, what drink?"

"How about an Americano?" he replied, leaning back on his velvet throne.

"Of course." She put her hands on his shoulders and leaned in close. "An Americano for the Americano."

At this proximity, Alex noticed a smattering of freckles on top of her nose and across her cheekbones that had eluded him before. And her brown eyes were actually lighter than he remembered. Were those flecks of green in her irises or just the lighting? Suddenly, she winked and stood straight up, waking Alex from his trance.

"I'll be right back," she said as she twirled toward the bar.

Patrizia fussed around behind the counter, busily mixing drinks, occasionally glancing back in Alex's direction. But every time he caught her looking, she would avert her eyes. Was she watching him? Teasing him?

She placed a mismatched assortment of glasses on an antique tray, which she then gracefully lifted to her shoulder. Alex watched as she weaved around the room, delivering the colorful cocktails. Finally, she made her way back to Alex.

"Ecco, Mr. Americano." She leaned down, exposing her faint freckles once again as she handed Alex the glass. "Will I see you dance tonight?"

"Dance . . . Uh . . . ?" He shook his head, waking himself from yet another trance. "Oh . . . maybe?"

She smiled and slowly walked back to the bar. Alex knew she wanted him to watch her, and he obliged.

Buzz. Buzz. His cellphone slapped him back to reality. He reached into his pocket and saw Pernille Bjørn flashing back at him. He looked back up at Patrizia, who was now busy handling the patrons at the bar, and read the text message:

Pernille: Hello Friend. Teddy and I are on our way. Please join?
Alex: Where are you?

PB: We are coming to your neighborhood. Maybe to that beautiful bar near you.
AC: I'm already here—please come.
PB: Fantastic! Walking in now.

Alex looked up at the entrance and saw the Scandinavian blonde arm-in-arm with a tall, well-dressed man who exuded confidence. Alex stood up and waved them over. The debonair Teddy held Pernille's hand as they made their way to his table.

As they got closer, Alex took in the apparently perfect couple. Pernille wore a dark blue dress with a thin orange belt that hung askew on her curvy hips. Her golden hair hung in front of her right shoulder. Teddy wore white trousers and a pale-green shirt, the two top buttons unfastened, under a light-brown blazer. He had wavy, sand-colored hair and lightly tanned skin. On his pinky, Alex noticed a gold ring with a signet. They were like two perfectly assembled dolls fresh from their packaging.

"Alex!" Pernille hugged him. "Alex, this is Teddy—my fiancé. Teddy, this is Alex—my Italian babysitter." She laughed.

"Pleasure to finally meet you, Alex," Teddy replied with a posh British accent and a perfect smile. He shook Alex's hand with his right, while embracing Pernille with his left arm. He seemed incredibly pleasant and sincere.

"Of course," Alex replied. "It's a pleasure. She's doing fantastic here."

"Thank you, Alex," Pernille responded. "Teddy was concerned that our joining you would turn into work for you."

"Oh, not at all." Alex turned to Teddy. "Pernille and I look out for each other. We are a team."

"Great." Teddy said, genuinely relieved. "I'm glad to hear that. She was nervous about Italy, but, as you probably noticed, she gets nervous for about five seconds and then takes over like a professional." He kissed her on the cheek and continued, "Shall I get a round?" He pleasantly waved a waiter over to their table. "Ladies first."

"Yes, I'll have an Aperol-spritz." Pernille turned to Alex. "I'm just loving those."

"All right," Teddy nodded. "What are you having there, Alex?"

"An Americano," Alex said to the waiter, who seemed to be smiling underneath his long and ridiculously shaped beard before turning back to Teddy and nodding in gratitude.

"I'll have one of those as well, thank you," he said to the waiter, who responded with an exaggerated bow and then danced across the room, bopping to the music coming from the stage, before disappearing through the dark oak door that glided on its crooked railing.

Alex, Pernille, and Teddy exchanged glances and laughed.

The band headed off the stage, making room for the next band. A softer music was piped into the room through the sound system. Pernille shifted in her seat and withdrew something from her handbag.

"Alex, have you seen this?" She handed him a folded newspaper and watched him over the lip of her cocktail glass.

"Darling, I thought we agreed, no work."

"Oh, this is something exciting," she replied after a sip. "Alex will want to see this."

Alex opened the paper and saw the photo from the talk show followed by a short snippet about *La Cuoca Scandinava*—as they referred to her. It was an announcement about a special event for her third book.

"Oh, I didn't realize they would announce that so soon," he replied. "Well, that's great! I wasn't expecting early publicity."

"Yes, I didn't remember this on the list you had given me."

"No, it wasn't," he replied, handing the paper back to her. "But I'm not surprised, considering how much they liked you and the great feedback they received from their audience."

"I enjoyed it." She sipped. "Aside from that odd fellow on set, I thought it went well."

They proceeded to chat about the photo shoot scheduled for the next day. Since it was to take place not far from his luxury hotel, Teddy planned to join and watch.

"Excuse me." Pernille elegantly rose from her chair, prompting Teddy to politely stand. "I'll be right back," she said to him. "I just want to make myself pretty for dinner with my lover." She put her hand on his forearm, leaned in, and kissed his cheek. He smiled back at her as she slowly removed her arm and walked away.

Both Teddy and Alex watched Pernille Bjørn nimbly maneuver her way to the back of the room, deftly avoiding the stares of the patrons who drooled over her. Teddy finally sat back down and returned to his cocktail.

"Tell me, Alex." Teddy leaned closer and said, "Who is that adorable girl in the silver dress over there? She keeps looking your way."

Alex looked over at Patrizia, who leaned with both hands on the bar. As Alex caught her eye, she quickly looked toward the bandstand where the new musicians were setting up their instruments. Patrizia's coworker joined her from behind the counter and tickled her waist. They embraced, laughed, and danced until another drink order came to them. Alex turned back to Teddy.

"Beautiful girl," Teddy continued. "Maybe you should explore that one."

"Maybe," replied Alex. "But she seems like she has someone exploring her already." He didn't want to tell Teddy that *he* had already done some exploring himself.

"Well, you never really know, do you?"

"No, I suppose not." Alex's words hung in the air as he watched her dance with a barman.

"Teddy Hume! Well, I don't believe it." A shrill British voice came from the embracing statue. Out from behind it appeared a shrieking woman with short, curly red hair. Her black dress trailed behind her as she approached the two men. Teddy stood up and smiled stiffly.

"Hello, Tess," he said as she kissed him lightly on both cheeks. "This is Alex."

Tess nodded toward Alex and quickly returned her gaze to Teddy.

"How wonderful to see you here." She continued to stare as Teddy gestured for her to sit. "No, thank you. I was just leaving. We were sitting just around the corner. How did I not see you? What a small world. Well, you know when I saw you, I just had to come over and say hello."

"What brings you to Rome?"

"Oh, just a girl's weekend, you know," she replied as she slowly took the final swig of her drink. She put her empty glass on the table and continued, "Unfortunately, Miranda couldn't make it."

"How is Miranda?"

"Oh, she's holding up." Tess looked away and lowered her voice. "As best as she can." She leaned in closer. "I see you're still sowing your oats or whatever."

"Tess." Teddy leaned back and grabbed his drink. "Behave." Tess turned to Alex and explained, "Oh, he's driving his family crazy." She turned back to Teddy. "You know you'll break her heart in the end, Teddy."

"Tess!" the group of women hovering at the door called to her. "Come on."

"You should go," added Teddy.

"Right." Tess gathered the back of her black dress, preventing it from dragging on the floor. "Well, it was nice bumping into you. I'll tell Miranda you asked about her."

"Please do."

As Tess joined her party and walked out the door, Pernille returned to the table.

"Even the bathrooms are enchanting," she exclaimed. "There are old wooden pocket doors. The mirrors have gold and silver borders, hung at angles, of course. I love this place!" She sat and sipped her drink and noticed Teddy's face was a bit serious. "Are you okay? Who was that?"

"No one, love." He kissed her. "We'll discuss it later."

The three finished their cocktails in silence as the new band took over the small stage. The band was made up of three men with exaggeratedly slicked back hair, their black jeans rolled up to reveal colorful socks and shiny boots. They each wore white T-shirts under unbuttoned plaid or striped shirts.

The blonde one on the left, in a black porkpie hat trimmed with a red satin ribbon, grabbed the upright bass and began to sound a rhythm. The one with the black horn-rimmed glasses slowly joined in on the drums. The third fellow, the more rugged of the three, raised the yellow strap of his green guitar over his shoulder and sang into the microphone.

The room filled with lively rockabilly jams and a rocking crowd. The place transformed from a cool jazz cocktail lounge to a dance hall. Pernille clapped along.

"This is fun music." She turned to Alex. "Do you like this music?

Alex nodded, trying to look preoccupied by the band and not, as was the case, their odd encounter with Tess.

"It's getting late," Pernille had to yell over the loud guitar riffs. "We should probably get to dinner, no?"

Teddy nodded in agreement, stood up, adjusted his blazer, and took Pernille's hand. "Alex, are you staying? Would you like to join us for dinner?"

"Oh, no, thank you," Alex replied. "You two need some quality time. I think I'll stick around here a bit more."

"Very well," replied Pernille, still moving to the beat. "But we have an early start tomorrow. Don't have too much fun."

She followed Teddy, dancing her way out the door.

PERNILLE BJØRN'S TREK SCANDINAVIA
SEASON 01, EPISODE 05
"Dessert with Nature"
SCENE 06

FADE IN:

KITCHEN INTERIOR

Pernille is wearing a white fluffy blouse with colorful embroidery, covered by a navy-blue apron. Her hair is tied up in an evenly organized but casual bunch. She's at the cutting board slicing the skin off a golden apple.

> **PERNILLE**
> Today's dessert is one of my favorites because, well, I love apples. But also because this is the first dessert I made for my fiancé. [whispers] I think it's the dish that won him over.

She holds an apple up to the camera.

> **PERNILLE**
> This golden delicious temptress will be made into warm, sweet æblegrød. To begin, we cut away the skin like this. Then, we cut the apple into chunks or cubes and put them into a warm saucepan.

Pernille puts the chunks into the saucepan that's sitting on the stove to her right. She turns on the heat and covers the pan.

> PERNILLE
> Heat the pan until the apples
> are soft, about ten minutes.

Cut to ten minutes later, or when the apples
have softened. Pernille removes the lid.

> PERNILLE
> Once the apples are soft, we
> take a potato smasher and smash
> the apples.

Pernille smashes the apples, then grabs a
small bowl of sugar.

> PERNILLE
> Now add some sugar. Maybe one to
> two tablespoons. But really it
> depends on how sweet you like
> your dessert. I always taste as
> I make it.

Pernille adds about two tablespoons of sugar
into the pan and mixes it into the smashed
apples.

> PERNILLE
> Traditionally, we also add cin-
> namon or vanilla. But I like to
> make mine with a Pernille-twist.
> I add vanilla and a little bit
> of cardamom.

Pernille stirs in the ingredients. Then she
takes a glass serving dish and places some
of the smashed apple sauce in. She sprinkles

some more sugar on top of the mound.

>   **PERNILLE**
>   Finally, we finish the dessert by
>   adding a little bit of heavy or
>   whipping cream.

Pernille grabs a small carton of heavy cream
and pours it around the edges of the mound
of apple sauce. She puts down the carton and
picks up a spoon.

>   **PERNILLE**
>   And now, we enjoy.

Pernille eats a spoonful of the æblegrød.

>   **PERNILLE**
>   Yum! Just like my mama's.

                    # # #

CHAPTER 21

THE FOLLOWING MORNING, Alex took a taxi to the St. Regis Hotel in the luxurious Barberini area. He sat on a plush yellow settee in the front lobby, waiting for Pernille and Teddy to join him. He perused the calendar on his phone for Pernille's upcoming appearances and noticed his entry indicating Emily's visit. Her arrival was just around the corner. Had he made a mistake agreeing to have her come?

"Alex!" Pernille greeted him with European cheek kisses. "I am very excited for this photo shoot. It's going to be glamorous." Teddy followed behind and shook Alex's hand. "Great to see you again, chap."

The well-dressed couple followed Alex to the hired car waiting in front that would whisk them off to the serene park of the Villa Borghese. Teddy offered his gentlemanly hand to Pernille, and they all piled in.

"The photo shoot is for SWATCH® Watch Company. They are doing a whole campaign revolving around Italian cinema. Pernille, they are excited to have you involved because you are exactly what they need to recreate a scene from Fellini's *La Dolce Vita*."

"You mean the fountain scene?" asked Teddy.

"Yes, but we obviously cannot use the real Trevi Fountain—it's just impossible to clear that area of tourists," Alex explained. "Besides, the city isn't making it easy to get permits. So the company decided to use the grounds of the villa to capture the glamour of the film."

"Will there be a Marcello?" asked Pernille.

"They may have a model to stand behind you, but the focus would be you, as the *Anita Ekberg* character," he replied as they exited the car and entered the gates of the park.

Alex walked the couple through the manicured park, arriving at a set of light reflectors surrounding a small fountain hidden among tall trees. Just to the left was a trailer. Pernille entered for an hour-long hair and makeup session and clothing change. Teddy sat in the trailer with Pernille while Alex reviewed the shoot with the project manager.

When all done up in a long, black, strapless dress, she looked absolutely glamorous. Her blonde hair was full and wavy. The set designer led her to the jewelry station and placed the silver jewelry with faux diamonds on her ears, neck, and wrist. Finally, she was wrapped in a bright white, fluffy, faux-fur stole. She looked just like Fellini's *Sylvia*.

Pernille was directed to stroll around the small fountain while caressing and kissing a white kitten handed to her just before the photographer announced he was ready. Suddenly, claiming there was "too much fluffy," the photographer ordered the white stole to be taken away.

Teddy joined Alex behind the photographer. He leaned forward, staring at his fiancée, who was slowly twirling in the strapless black dress. The photographer snapped furiously as he followed her around the spitting fountain.

"She is beautiful, isn't she?" Teddy said aloud, keeping his eyes on her.

Alex watched as Teddy gazed at Pernille with admiration, and it put a smile on his face. Their dynamic seemed pure, sincere, and everything Alex dreamed of in a relationship. Everything he'd longed to experience himself. He wondered what he could be doing wrong. Had he been pursuing the wrong girls? His friends constantly hounded him that his expectations for women were too high. But it wasn't true. He wasn't allowing himself to be ruled by some unattainable list of traits, by the nonexistent "perfect woman." He knew all he really wanted was a true, unbridled connection with someone. He'd tried dating for the sake of dating, not stressing about that magical connection, but those couplings never worked out. He was envious of how Teddy looked at Pernille. He wanted what they had. Seeing it in Teddy was proof that the connections Alex dreamed of did, in fact, exist.

"She is very sweet," Alex replied, shifting in his chair. "What I like about her is her way of always finding something to smile about."

"Yes," Teddy, too, smiled. "I love seeing her out there, not worrying herself to a frenzy." He turned to Alex. "She has the tendency to drive herself crazy—living inside her head, constantly thinking about what she did wrong or could have done better."

"Really?" Alex was surprised to hear this about Pernille. She usually seemed like a bubbly, no-cares, life-is-beautiful type of gal.

"Oh, yes," Teddy continued. "You'll soon see that she can be a bit neurotic." He laughed. "She hates it when I say that." He continued, "I love her, Alex. I do. But she needs to relax more. I mean, you, the photographer, the fans, the journalists, you all see fun-loving Pernille. And she is fun and full of love. Please don't misunderstand me. But, frequently, she dwells on things she's done or where she is in life or what people think of her . . . it's a lot of unnecessary stress."

Teddy looked down and rubbed the small ruby on his pinky ring, and Alex could swear he saw a sadness creep into Teddy's eyes as he continued. "She's too concerned about my family, for one thing." He held up his hand to show Alex the ring. "I keep telling her not to be so concerned. What matters is how we feel about each other. And I love her, Alex—but no matter how many times I assure her of my feelings, she constantly seeks approval from my family."

Teddy sat back, crossed one leg over the other, and rested his chin on the hand with the ring. He looked over at Pernille, cooing at the fluffy white kitten still in her arms.

"Take Tess, for example. You remember Tess, Alex—the woman you met at the café last night?"

"Oh, yes. The, um, the—"

"Drunk," Teddy finished the sentence that Alex couldn't bring himself to. "You can say it. Well, what she said was not so far from the truth. I used to be that man Tess described. The *heart breaker*. And as Tess also knows, I was bred to marry royalty, and women like Tess and Miranda—the woman Tess mentioned—they were bred to marry someone like me."

"Ahh . . . and then you found Pernille."

"Yes, and thank god for that," Teddy continued. "And it is true. If I hadn't met Pernille, I would probably have, at some point, ended up with Tess or Miranda or someone like them by default. I'm no longer that person, though. Thanks to Pernille."

Alex felt awkward delving into Teddy's and Pernille's personal lives, but Teddy wanted to talk about it. Alex was unsure if he should ask questions or if Teddy just wanted his ear. Was this too personal? Was he crossing some line of professionalism?

Teddy went on. "It breaks my heart to see Pernille worry about such nonsense. At times, I feel guilty for this burden on her. Then I think to myself: Am I purposefully rebelling against the family? Am I that immature? But it comes down to who I am, Alex. I don't want to be involved in that blue blood nonsense."

"And your family . . . ?" Alex decided to screw professionalism and let his questions out. "Do they disapprove of Pernille? Have they said anything?"

"Well, they are less disapproving of her than they are disappointed in the fact that I'm not pursuing some heir or what-not." He leaned forward with a chuckle. "Listen, had Prince William been a woman, I would've been in line for courtship, for sure. My family would have seen to that."

"So, I'm sitting here with Prince Charming in the flesh. Must be tough." Alex was hoping to get a laugh out of Teddy, and he did.

"Ahh, touché, chap." Teddy smiled. "You're mocking me now."

"I'm sorry," Alex laughed. "I don't mean to offend you."

"Not at all," Teddy laughed. "In a way, you are correct. And I did find my princess in Pernille."

"So, what's the problem?"

"Well . . . " Teddy leaned back, turning his ring again. "Pernille comes from a different class—her words, not mine. She feels like everyone I know looks down upon her."

"And she probably thinks her marrying you would stain your family name." This whole conversation seemed ridiculous and like something out of a fairytale. "I didn't think these sorts of things still happened in the modern age. Again, I don't mean to insult you, Teddy. It's just, from an American perspective—where this stuff exists only in books—it's hard to believe this nonsense still has some role in society. But then again, we do have a wealthy class, which includes celebrities."

"Well, I'm afraid it matters a lot where I'm from." Teddy's sadness returned. "And someone in my position is expected to preserve the bloodline."

"So, you're the embarrassing rogue son, mating with a commoner or however we're referred to these days." Alex laughed. "I'm sorry. I'm just fascinated by this whole . . . life. I've never really been exposed to this type of—"

Teddy laughed at him. "You're mocking me again, Alex. This is why I like you. And this is why I know Pernille is in good hands."

It was now obvious to Alex why Teddy had opened up to him. He had no one to whom he could confide this trivial nonsense. Teddy's own circle of friends would scoff.

"Teddy, how did you meet Pernille?"

"We met last year at a football match in London." Teddy's smile made its way back. "Her cousin is a professional footballer and invited her to the match. I was getting a drink from the bar when I saw her standing by the window overlooking the field. She was just beautiful, sipping her drink and laughing with her friends.

"I was at the match with my mates. Tess and Miranda were there, too. When I saw Pernille, though, I immediately thought to myself: This is the girl who will save me from all this. I didn't know who she was. I didn't care, really. I just wanted to be with her. I hadn't even talked to her yet, but I knew I wanted to run away with her.

"Her friends walked away and I saw my chance. I made my way to her and introduced myself. And I never returned to my seat. After the match, we left the stadium together and have been a pair ever since."

"Love at first sight?" Alex nudged him.

"It sure was," he looked at Pernille again. "How could you not fall in love with that smile? It's contagious."

The white fluffy kitten was eventually taken away as Pernille posed with a slew of bright white SWATCH watches pinned together to create an alternate white stole. Just then, the photographer called for a *Marcello*. Out from the green tent, located at the other end of the fountain steps, emerged a tall male model in a gray suit, white shirt, and thin black tie. As the model stepped closer to the fountain, Alex realized, to his chagrin, that it was the model assistant from *Chiacchiere del Duoco.*

"What is he doing here?" Alex asked himself out loud.

"You know him?" asked Teddy.

"Yes, and I did not expect him," Alex replied as he angrily stepped off the chair. "Excuse me a moment, Teddy," he said as he stormed over to the project manager by the trailer.

"What is he doing here?" Alex asked the project manager.

"Matteo?" she replied nonchalantly. "He is the *Marcello* for the shoot."

"Why him? You told me it would be a male model."

"Matteo Pozzi *is* a male model. In fact, he's one of the most popular in Italy."

"Exactly," he added. He'd needed a reason to get Matteo out of the shoot and away from Pernille, and the project manager had just handed it to him. "But we specifically agreed that the model would not overshadow Pernille. We agreed to this photo shoot only if Pernille would be the focus—aside from the product, of course. Adding him changes the whole agreement."

"But we *did* receive approval to use him," she replied as she handed Alex a form. At the bottom was Eleonora Persini's signature. "We spoke to your boss last week. She agreed with the idea."

Alex looked over at Pernille, who remained professional as she happily posed with the watches alongside the handsome Matteo. Alex returned to his seat by Teddy and kept a close watch on Matteo, making sure he didn't attempt anything inappropriate.

"Is everything all right, Alex?" Teddy asked.

"Oh, yes," Alex replied, keeping his eyes on Matteo. "I apologize. I wasn't expecting *him* to be the model. That's Matteo, the guy from the talk show."

"Ahh," Teddy leaned forward to also monitor the pair's dynamic.

After the shoot, Alex and Teddy waited for Pernille to come out of her trailer. She finally stepped out, embraced Teddy, and lightly kissed him on the lips.

"Well," she said to Alex. "That was a bit of a surprise, wasn't it?" She seemed fine, but Alex was embarrassed to have put her through that.

"I apologize, Pernille," he replied. "I didn't know he'd be involved. The approval went over my head. Had I known, I would never have agreed to have him here."

"Oh, it's all right," she replied. "He behaved very nicely this time. He didn't even say anything to me, really. Just said hello and did his job, thankfully." She put her hand on Alex's arm. "No need to worry. It all went well."

"Yes," added Teddy. "And you looked absolutely gorgeous."

Alex noticed Matteo walking in their direction.

"Well, we should go." He rushed the couple off the lawn and onto the walkway. "I have to get to the office, and you two should enjoy the rest of your day."

The three quickly walked down the curvy and luxurious via Veneto, successfully avoiding Matteo.

CHAPTER 22

Boston—2004

Alex picked up the mail he had dropped on his coffee table coming in from work earlier that evening. He flipped through and saw an envelope with Emily's return address. They hadn't spoken since her wedding. He kept his distance, moving on from what never had been.

He dropped onto the couch and let out a sigh. Curiously and quickly, he ripped open the envelope and read:

Dear Alex,

I write you this letter because I miss you. I miss you, Alex. I miss us. Years have gone by since we last spoke, and I didn't think I would still be thinking about you after all this time.

Vic and I are not doing well. In fact, I don't know why I did it. Why I married him. It's been four years, and I've been playing the role of wife to a man who

I don't feel is in the partnership 100%. Then again, neither am I. What did I do?

I think Vic is having an affair. Well, I accused him of having an affair. He claims he's not. But why, then, is his old girlfriend constantly contacting him? And if nothing is wrong, then why did he have a problem when I mentioned you? I think I was, or I am, looking for an excuse to get out. I'm not happy, Alex. I've tried to make the marriage work. He agreed to make the effort to rekindle what we once had, but I really don't think I can do this anymore. I need to talk to you. I need to see you. I need my friend. I know we haven't spoken in years, but I'm reaching out to you because, well, I don't think there is anyone else out there who understands me like you do. And you may find this hard to believe, but I still think about you and what could have been between us. Why am I having these thoughts?

Please accept my letter for what it is: a cry for help. I will be in Boston for a couple of days soon and I hope I can see you. I want to see you.

With Love,

Emily

Alex sat in his chair, jaw dropped and heart pounding. The letter had come along with another one of Emily's mixtapes (now in the modern form of a burned CD). It was a compilation of songs by some of Emily's favorite artists, and it had a clear message: each and every song spoke of lost love.

He replied by email:

Emily,

Thank you for reaching out to me. It's been so long. I am so sorry for what you are going through right now. Your letter scared me. Are you okay? Know you can call me to talk. When you are in Boston, let's meet up. And thank you for the CD, I love it. :)

Always your friend, Alex

He set about making her a mixtape in response with selected songs of his and her favorite artists. It would be shamelessly packed with messages of love finally returning, dreaming together, finding each other, and adoration. He would hand it to her when they met.

In addition, he wrote a four-page letter of all his thoughts from the day they'd met; all the things he'd never gotten to say to her, all the feelings and thoughts that had gone through his head at her wedding, all the regret he'd felt for not doing anything. He told her he wanted to be with her.

It was a sunny day in May when the two finally met up in Government Center. Alex waited eagerly outside of the subway exit for his friend to arrive. What caught his eye first as she approached was her sad face through her flat red hair, and then her drab, wrinkled clothes. She sank into his arms, defeated, and cried. Alex comforted her as they walked toward the park.

They sat on a bench while Emily collected herself. She fumbled through her bag and pulled out a tissue.

"Thank you for responding to my letter. It meant a lot to me. You mean a lot to me. You stopped talking to me and I hated you, but I understood."

"Emily," he replied, shocked at her admission. "What is going on with you? You seem all over the place. What's happened?"

"Please don't hate me," she replied with a whimper. "I can't bear for you to hate me more than you already do. I've done it. I don't know what I was doing with him. I am so disappointed with myself."

"Done what? What happened?"

"It's over. We're over. We're getting a divorce. He wanted to work things out; he tried, but I just wanted out. I'm done. I'm not happy. I wasn't happy. How could I have married him? What did I do to my life? To you? To us? Alex, he wasn't you. That's what it came down to. I kept looking for the you inside of him and it wasn't there."

Alex didn't respond. He was taking it all in. What was she saying?

"So, I found you in someone else." Emily continued.

Alex was shocked. "What do you mean?"

"I had an affair!" she sobbed looking away from him. She wouldn't look back. "Say something. Please."

Alex wanted to walk away.

"I don't know what to say," he finally replied. "Why are you telling me this? Why all the drama with the letter, the mixtape, the *I want to see you* bullshit? Are you with this other guy now? What is going on in your head?"

"I don't know!" She turned to him. "Don't you see? I'm scared. It's unlike me. What am I doing with my life?"

"Why did you contact me?" He was angry now. "Why me? You have plenty of other friends you could have called. Why the fuck do you come to me? All the time. You do this to me all the fucking time. I'm tired of it. Now what? Where do we go from here?"

"I didn't want any of this to happen. Besides, you and I never had anything. You never made a—"

"Don't point fingers at me. Don't you get it? You keep trying to pull me back in. This was *your* relationship that *you* chose to pursue. And *you* fucked it up—as expected, I might add. Clearly, you didn't love him. I don't know how the hell you could have stood up there and married him."

"I did love him."

"Right."

"You don't know about my relationship with him."

"No, I don't. And I also don't know why the hell you chose to drag me into the mess that you've created."

She didn't respond. She looked away, wiping her eyes.

"Why did you want to meet up today?" He sat back down on the bench. "What was your intention?"

"I don't know," she replied quietly. "I don't know."

They sat silent avoiding each other's eyes. Alex reached into his pocket and pulled out the yellow envelope containing his letter and mixtape.

"You see this?" He held it up to her. "This is my response to you. Four pages of my heart poured out on paper, all for you."

She reached for the packet, but Alex pulled it away.

"I was ready to give this to you because I thought you were here to finally be with me. You led me on, and you know it."

"I'm sorry," Emily replied. She sat quietly looking at Alex, waiting for him to speak again.

"Emily," he finally said. "You said in your letter you needed a friend. And I came out here because I care for you. I was worried about you, that you were going to hurt yourself or something."

"Oh, Alex," she reached out to him as he pulled away.

"Everything I originally came out to say to you today means nothing now," he continued. "Emily, I'm done." He stood up and walked away, leaving Emily on the bench in tears.

It had been a heavy blow, but he had to do it. He had to cut ties. After that day, he'd avoided Emily's emails. They hadn't communicated until the email she sent to him in Rome seven years later.

CHAPTER 23

Rome

Present

ALEX HAD FORGOTTEN the pain he felt on that dreadful day with Emily in the park years ago. He had succeeded in pushing Emily out of his life. He had avoided her phone calls. He had received her letters, but fought hard not to open them. It was very difficult at first, but he finally got into the habit of throwing them directly into the trash. He was done. He needed space.

Any sight of her name reminded him of his foolishness. How could he have thought she had left Vic for him? Never would he have suspected her of adultery. She knew how he felt about her. She knew he was there for her. Why would she have done what she did? And what had she expected Alex's reaction to be? What had she wanted on that day in the park?

Alex was lost in his thoughts as he trudged toward the bus stop at Largo Argentina, where the Emperor ruled the ruins. Eleonora gave him a few days off to spend time with Emily.

The memories of that day in the park kept swirling. An uncertain feeling crept inside of him. It was not hatred. Nor was it embarrassment. It was almost like a sense of betrayal. Was that what he felt when they last spoke? Why betrayal? He and Emily were not together at that point, and she was married—to Vic. It was Vic whom she had betrayed. Not Alex. But Alex couldn't help but feel that Emily's actions had betrayed him too. Had he made a bad decision to let her come visit?

As he waited for the bus that would take him to the airport, he looked in on the ruins and spotted his cat laying in the shade, flapping his tail. Alex was so entranced, he nearly missed seeing the bus that drove by with a Pernille Bjørn cookbook advertisement on its side, complete with her face and book on a lime-green backdrop. In bold, white letters, the text read: MEET PERNILLE IN PERSON AT THE VILLA BORGHESE.

Although he had purchased the advertising space himself, seeing the ad still surprised him. His hard work was bringing success to Pernille, who had made a name for herself in Italy. He hoped he'd also benefit from his hard work, but he had still not seen a contract from Eleonora. He was beginning to doubt a contract would ever be produced. Was Eleonora stringing him along? Or maybe she was still not convinced Alex was right for the position. Was Eleonora not happy with his work? But he knew he had done all the work expected of him and he knew he did it well. He was overthinking it. He felt foolish. The bus he was waiting for finally arrived.

He stood up and shook the thoughts out of his head. Eleonora and Pernille would no longer serve as distractions from Emily's pending visit. The day had come. He had nothing left to do but go meet her at the airport. He stepped up, stamped his ticket, and sat by the window, watching the streets of Rome go by.

Alex stood behind the barrier, holding the small bouquet of flowers he'd decided to purchase when he walked into the airport. Why he had done so, he did not know. It was automatic—his head was preoccupied with memories. Nervously, he waited for Emily to walk through the customs doors. He held on to the thin bunch of flowers with sweaty palms, still wondering why he had purchased them. He sat on the seats to the left of the gate. He needed to collect himself.

Staring at the sad flowers, his cheeks began to flush while his mind flooded with the possibilities of what this visit could bring. Here he was, greeting her again, pathetic heart in hand, and what would she give him in return? An announcement of an engagement? A marriage? A pregnancy? His stomach dropped.

He smelled a wet cigarette coming from the old man seated next to him. The stench brought Alex back to the matter at hand. The customs gates opened, releasing the first of a slew of passengers.

He stood and crossed up to the barrier to get a closer look at the luggage tags on the passengers' bags to see if they had been on a flight from the United States. An elderly woman struggled through the doors with a tattered brown suitcase, a red Air Canada tag flapping on top—not Emily's flight.

His heart began to pound harder. His breathing grew rapid.

The phone in his front pocket buzzed. Alex fumbled as he reached to see the text message. Was it Emily? He looked down at the phone, sighed loudly, and rolled his eyes. It was from Pernille.

"Not now," he said to himself. "I can't. I love you, Pernille, but not now." He clicked the button anyway and read the message:

Waiting for Teddy. I have big news! Do you have a moment to talk? Call me.

Alex monitored the exiting passengers once more, but there was no sign of Emily's flight yet. He reluctantly selected "Reply" on his phone and typed:

Talk later? Sorry.

Immediately, he regretted it. What if it was an emergency? What if she called Eleonora instead? How would that look? He decided he could make a quick call.

"Hi, Pernille! I was able to free up a few minutes. Sorry, I can't talk long though."

"I apologize for disturbing you," she replied, "but I have big news and I had to share it with you!"

She revealed that the Danish company producing her cooking series decided to keep her in Rome as a correspondent for a Danish news show, which would require her to shoot onsite. His PR firm would take advantage of her time in Italy and try to get her more exposure in the market. This meant more work for Alex.

"Isn't that great?" she exclaimed.

"Wow," he replied with a genuine smile. "That is amazing. For both of us!"

"Precisely! I am so happy!" she practically screamed. "I'll see you soon. Okay?"

"Of course!"

The timing was perfect, as far as Zero Otto Marketing was concerned. Pernille's correspondence gig would allow her more time to promote her latest book in Italy. And she made his job so easy. The Italian public already loved Pernille. She constantly accepted invitations to events, and photographs of her were everywhere. It all seemed to be working out. But again, the news reminded Alex that he was still waiting for his full-time contract.

The flow of passengers dwindled around him. He glanced up at the arrivals monitor, confused: NEW YORK DELAYED 20

MIN. The waiting was unbearable. He wandered into the terminal bookstore in search of a distraction.

He browsed the travel books, cookbooks, and other food-and-travel writing. He always monitored what was available in international markets. Of course, airport bookstores only offered a limited stock, but it was a good sample of new releases. As usual, he started in the English language section and then moved on to the native language.

He noticed that none of Pernille's books were on the shelf. He would reach out to the publishers when he was back at work. Clara Mucci's *Dolci Semplice* was prominently displayed on the shelf, facing forward, allowing shoppers to spot her genuine smile behind a display of cookies and cakes. Alex took the book from the shelf and perused the pages. He noted the high-quality paper, gorgeous photographs, modern font, and overall perfect size for a cookbook to sit on a bookstand on a kitchen counter. Impressed with the production, he moved on to other books. The next book he handled was a smaller size—more like the size of a novel. The dust jacket was well designed. He opened the book and noticed again, like a novel, the paper was rough, the font was basic, and there were no photographs of the recipes. Disappointed, he returned the book and moved on to the next.

As he continued down the shelf, he hoped he could get a project with a local cookbook or travel author. He wanted to see better book production, crisper photos, and cleaner layouts—like the ones Clara Mucci managed to get. For some reason, most of the cookbooks he examined lacked quality production. He knew the cookbook offerings in Italy were of higher quality than the shabby production he was seeing at the airport. And he didn't want to believe cookbook production was moving toward the simple novel-like format. He put the last book back on the shelf and noted that he'd continue his research when back in the city.

Alex checked his watch and realized he had been in the bookstore for over thirty-five minutes. He quickly walked to the arrivals monitor and saw Emily's flight had arrived within the last five minutes.

He rushed back to the customs doors once more and found a large group of people waiting for family and friends. He weeded through the chaos until the next group of passengers burst through the doors. Alex spotted the luggage tags and the bold, black letters LGA, which he knew stood for LaGuardia Airport.

No turning back now. He kept himself on guard, watching all the passengers. Emily should come out any minute.

The phone in his pocket buzzed again. Alex wanted to let it go to voicemail. He didn't want Emily to find him distracted on the phone when she walked through the doors. He had it all planned out. He would open his arms and she would run to him with tears in her eyes. The urge to kiss her would be insufferable.

He pulled the phone from his pocket and looked at the text message. It was from Emily.

Turn around.

CHAPTER 24

EMILY WAS WEARING a loosely fit, flowery blouse over skin-tight faded jeans, cinched with a shiny teal patent-leather belt. Her legs and black flats bobbled about like a graceless ballerina as she wrestled with her bright red suitcase.

Amid her struggle, she glanced around the terminal and found an opening through the crowd. She quickened her pace toward Alex. He caught her in his arms, raising her up as she tightly embraced him.

"It's so great to see you," he said. He couldn't do it—he couldn't kiss her. He realized in that moment, for Emily, it probably would have come out of nowhere. "After all these years, we finally meet up in Rome, of all places." He kept his hands on her shoulders and smiled.

"I know," her voice cracked a bit. Were there tears in her eyes? "I'm so happy that you agreed to my visit." Her eyelashes fluttered as her green eyes struggled to hide the fact that she was staring.

"I was glad—shocked—that you emailed me, but I'm happy you came." He grabbed the handle of her suitcase and led her out of the airport.

They sat on the train toward central Rome. Exhausted from the flight, Emily leaned back in her seat with her eyes closed. Alex sat across from her, staring out the window, quietly thinking. The whole kissing idea was blown out of the water. He didn't do it. However, if he wanted to kiss her, he still had the twenty-minute train ride into the city center to try. The key, though, was to build up the courage to stick with his decision. A kiss would be a good way to find out if romance was her reason for this visit.

"Well, Alex?" Emily's voice awoke him from his thoughts.

"Yeah?" He straightened up and nodded to the window as if pretending the view had mesmerized him, which he knew was ridiculous because the landscape was a bunch of gray buildings.

"You looked like you were in some strange daze," she laughed. "Did you hear me?"

"What?" He smiled and laughed along—to what, he had no idea.

"I mentioned I was hungry. Was wondering what we're going to eat." She smiled, leaned back in her seat, and closed her eyes again.

"Oh," he replied. *How did I not hear her? I must have looked like an idiot.* "Yeah, well, we're in Italy. I mean, pizza, of course. Right?"

"Mmm," she replied satisfyingly. "Yes, of course." She kept her eyes closed and moved her face into the sunlight coming from the window. Her lip-gloss made her mouth glisten. Alex wondered what it would taste like to kiss her. But instead of making his move, he looked out the window again. This time there was an actual landscape, although it quickly turned urban once again. Emily had dozed off. Alex's gaze now focused on her reflection in the glass. He wondered what it would have been like if they had actually worked it out in the past.

Alex led Emily down the narrow cobblestone walkway from the bridge toward his apartment building. Emily was smiling as she admired the scenery and architecture surrounding her.

"It's just like the movies," she said. "It feels like it's not real. So beautiful."

"Oh, it's real. And just up here is my favorite café bar. I've been coming here practically every morning and even after work on occasion."

As they approached the café, Emily's eyes lit up. He knew what she was thinking.

"I know what you're thinking," he said. "It's as if you're looking through Alice's looking glass." He remembered Emily's affinity for that story. She had made him read both *The Adventures of Alice in Wonderland* and *Alice Through the Looking Glass* so they could discuss the imagery and theory, which Alex never understood.

"Yeah . . . " she replied, amazed. "I feel like I'm walking through a dream."

"Well, there's a lot more to see, kiddo." He pulled the suitcase as they continued down the street to his apartment.

"We have four flights of stairs," he told her. "But it will be worth it—trust me."

Alex carried her luggage up the marble staircase, relieved that it wasn't as heavy as it appeared. Emily followed him through the bright red apartment door and gazed at the living room, taking it all in.

"Wow. You really lucked out," she said as she followed Alex through the rooms. "This is such a nice place."

"Wait till you see the view." He led her to his bedroom and opened the window that overlooked the river.

As she peeped through the window, he began to feel awkward about leading her to his bedroom. Would she think him too forward? It hadn't been intentional.

Suddenly, he felt his body pulled by two lanky, freckled arms toward the window and her pink, glossy lips on his. He couldn't think. He felt her kiss trickle through his body, causing a euphoric, dream-like state that numbed him all over. He was powerless to stop himself. He kissed her back. The spell was broken when she pushed him away.

"I'm so sorry." Emily looked down and rushed out of the room. Alex, in somewhat of a shock, couldn't really think straight. What just happened? He followed her back to the living room.

"It's okay . . . " he said automatically. His brain still hadn't processed what had just happened by the window.

"No." She turned to him, tears in her eyes. "No, I shouldn't have done that. I'm sorry. I don't know . . . I'm jet-lagged . . . " Leaving that as her excuse, she opened her baggage and nervously fumbled around in it, looking down, avoiding him. He wished he could just press pause and evaluate what had occurred. Why did she kiss him? What was going on in her mind? Did she want him back? Was it wrong to throw these questions at her when she appeared to be shaken? Space was probably the best thing for them both, he decided.

"Emily, stop," he replied. "Why don't you go to the guest room and relax for a bit? There are towels in there. Feel free to shower, freshen up, and you'll be fine. We'll just go to dinner. We'll pretend that never happened. Okay?"

She nodded as she followed him through the kitchen to the tiny guest room. She chuckled, "I'm so embarrassed."

"Don't be," he replied as he closed the sliding door between them.

Alex rushed back to the living room, plopped down on the couch, and let out a long, hard breath of disbelief.

CHAPTER 25

EMILY FINALLY EMERGED from her room dressed in tight blue jeans and a soft pink blouse, her damp hair cascading down the front of her left shoulder.

"That shower was much needed," she said as she sat in the green armchair by the bookcase. "Sorry I took so long. I did a little bit of unpacking. Some of my clothes were wrinkled so I hung them up. I might need to iron them later."

"No problem." Alex sat up trying not to look frazzled from the kiss earlier. "Let's go eat, I'm starving." He went into his bedroom and grabbed a light jacket. "You may want to grab a little something to bring with you—it can get chilly as the sun goes down."

"Good idea." She rushed back into her room.

Buzz. Buzz. Alex took out his phone and saw a text from Eleonora.

Please check email when you can.

Could this be good news about his contract? He quickly opened his laptop and read her note:

Hello Alex,

Thank you for your work on the photo shoot at the park. I understand your concern about Matteo, but I felt it would make the campaign more effective having a face that is known to the Italian public.

As for your contract, I have some news for you. I should have papers finalized next week when you report back in the office. For now, don't worry about work. Be with your friend and enjoy your holiday!

A presto,

E. Persini

Alex fired off a quick reply and shut his laptop. Emily returned from the guest room with a lightweight, hot-pink rain jacket.

Alex stared at Emily. She looked down and patted her jacket. "What? It looks cloudy out." She noticed he was still looking at the jacket. "Don't you like it? It's new. Very light and girly."

"That's the thing," he replied as he grabbed a small black umbrella. "I'm just surprised by the hot pink. It's so . . . not what I remembered about you."

They walked down the stony steps through the heavy, carved wooden door and took a right toward Trastevere's main piazza. Once again, they passed by the quirky bar. The place was quiet, aside from a small band setting up for the evening's entertainment. There was no sign of Patrizia. Emily curiously peered inside as Alex rushed her past the café.

"Should we just go here?" Emily tried to slow him down.

"I do like this place a lot . . . " But he edged her on. He wanted alone time with Emily to maybe approach a discussion about the kiss. A longer walk would suffice. "But they don't serve much for dinner. We can come back for a cocktail later if you're not too tired."

He led her across the paved main street, stepping over the trolley tracks and down another narrow cobblestoned pedestrian way. The street was lively with tourist eateries and shops. Restaurant owners stood in doorways calling people into their establishments. Tourists strolled like wandering sheep and pointed left and right, up and across.

Alex wove Emily around the tourists, focused on finding a quiet space to talk. By the time they reached the end of the loud street, he changed his mind and decided not to ask her anything, not yet. Besides, he was hungry and he wanted pizza.

He led her into the open piazza with a large fountain, empty of water, sitting in the center of it. To their left and right lay outdoor eateries that, again, appeared to be ready to gouge the tourists. Directly across from them, past the fountain, sat an entrance to a huge church. An old woman was kneeling on the ground, holding a platter and pointing to anyone walking by, preaching that she couldn't get a job because she wasn't able to walk. Alex remembered seeing that very same woman, walking perfectly fine, by Largo Argentina earlier that same day. He thought it was awful to pretend to have a handicap for money. How bad was this woman's life that she had to resort to that? It hurt him every time he saw someone sitting on the street with his or her hand out, asking for help. He wanted to know why they did it. Did they really need the help? Or are they being forced to do it? What situation is that person in?

Shouting from around the corner broke his train of thought.

Another old woman appeared, yelling at the kneeling beggar to leave the area; this was her turf and the other woman had no right to take stake close by and take her income. The first woman shouted back and stood up, grabbing her belongings.

The second woman continued to shoo her away with her wooden cane. As the first woman trudged off shouting back, the second woman knelt in that same spot, acting as if no one around her had witnessed the scene.

Emily, ignoring the spectacle, had slowed her pace to enjoy the view of the piazza. Alex held her hand and pulled her past the beggar, down another narrow street. Along the way lay more small eateries with outdoor seating—some with awnings and some without. Alex, however, knew exactly where he wanted to take Emily, so he led her to another small square.

"It is so beautiful here," she broke her silence. "I'm just in awe of this place. It really is like the movies."

"I know. That's why I chose to live here."

"Of course," she laughed.

"Here we are." He walked her into a pub that served only pizza and beer. It was filled up with people. To the left was a long oak bar serving local artisan beer on tap and in bottles. They squeezed their way through the patrons, reaching the hostess at the cashier. After a few minutes, Alex and Emily were led up three small steps and past the open pizza oven to an area of wooden tables.

"In Italy," Alex was explaining the menu to Emily, "they typically order small fried appetizers before their pizza."

"Really?" replied Emily. "That sounds heavy before chowing down on a bready meal."

"I know. All these years I've been coming to Italy and eating pizza with my friends, I never really noticed that we did always start out with fried appetizers. Sounds strange, but it's typical."

"Well," she shrugged with a smile, "when in Rome."

"You are so cheesy," replied Alex, and they laughed. "So for an appetizer," he continued, "we should start with the *supplí*. It's a typical Roman appetizer."

"Okay." Emily was excited. "What's in those?"

"They are breaded rice croquettes with melted mozzarella in the center. Almost like *arancini*, but shaped long."

Alex continued to explain the menu, and Emily decided on her pizza—a simple margherita with fresh buffalo mozzarella. Alex got the same. The waiter asked what beers they typically liked, and then recommended a local brew. When the appetizer arrived, Alex explained the *supplì*.

"So, the full name for these is *supplì al telefono*—meaning telephone-style *supplì*—because when you break them apart like so," Alex broke one of the three *supplì* and slowly pulled a half from the other, allowing the mozzarella center to stretch into a long string, "they resemble a little telephone, the mozzarella as the cord. See?"

"Oh my god." Emily sat amazed. "That is so clever. Leave it to the Italians." She took a bite of the half Alex had placed on her plate and moaned. "This is incredible."

"Glad you like it," he smiled. "Wait until you taste the pizza."

The waiter returned with two warm pizzas. As he set them down, Alex and Emily were hypnotized by the sweet aroma of the fresh tomato sauce combined with the tangy, deep scent of buffalo mozzarella and the refreshing fragrance of basil.

As the waiter explained, the last two ingredients were placed immediately after the pizza was removed from the oven, allowing the torn bits of buffalo mozzarella and the peppery basil to keep their shape. Alex watched as Emily examined her pizza with wonder.

"Wow," exclaimed Emily. "People told me the pizza in Italy is incredible, but I never imagined it to be like this. I haven't even bit into it and I feel like I'm in heaven!"

"Wait until you taste it." Alex continued to share his knowledge of Italian food. "The mozzarella is made fresh daily in regions south of Rome, just above Naples."

"And pizza is from Naples, right?" added Emily. "That's what is said in the books and travel shows."

"Correct," replied Alex as they both cut into their pizza. "Well, Rome has its own style of pizza, which we will have sometime this week. This type of pizza—the round disc and the simple ingredients: tomato, mozzarella, and basil—originated in Naples. It has the colors of the Italian flag, and it was named after Margherita of Savoy, once Princess of the kingdom of Naples.

"Legend is that she wanted to try the people's food. So, during some procession or festival or something, she took a bite of this particular pizza and exclaimed her love for it. I'm no historian, but I assume the people rejoiced and honored her by naming the pizza Margherita."

Alex watched as she took her first bite, closed her eyes, and enjoyed the flavors. She kept her eyes closed and softly moaned, like she was in ecstasy. Alex kept his eyes on her as he ate his pizza, waiting for her to mentally return to the table.

"This is incredible!" she cried. "It's even better than it looks. I cannot believe a simple pizza can be so good! Damn! I forgot to take a photo." She quickly reached for her mobile phone and snapped a photo. "Remind me to take photos," she ordered Alex. "I don't ever want to forget this trip."

Throughout the rest of the meal, Alex told Emily about his job, his first client, Pernille Bjørn, and how he liked living in Rome.

"And what about yourself?" he asked. "So I saw on your Facebook page that you're seeing someone new? Is this new guy sticking around?"

"Yes. He's back at home, holding up the fort," she replied, keeping her eyes on her plate and picking up the crust of her pizza.

"So, I have to ask you," he sat back. "What brings you here really?"

She looked up at him, confused and a bit startled.

"I mean," Alex cleared up his intention. "Don't get me wrong—I love that you came to see me. I've wanted a visitor to take around Rome. I was just surprised when *you* asked me if you could come visit. I mean, we haven't spoken in years, and . . . " He faltered. This hadn't been the right time; the right approach. He struggled to right this sinking ship. "I was just surprised, that's all."

Emily was about to respond when the waiter returned and cleared the table. Alex smiled awkwardly and focused his attention on paying the bill.

They stepped onto the cobblestones, now wet from the rain that had fallen while they ate. The sky was dark and the air brisk with a crisp after-rain scent.

"Are you tired?" he asked her, hoping to further distract her from his question in the restaurant. "Or shall we go for a stroll?"

"I'm okay, I think. I'm open to whatever, just not too late. I'm starting to get a little groggy."

"Okay, we can head back—maybe stop in that café you wanted to see. My favorite one, you know. *Wonderland*. It's closest to the apartment."

"Oh yes!" she perked up. "I definitely want go. Maybe a tea or something?"

Alex put his arm out, allowing Emily to latch on, and led her back through the main piazza, now filled with even more people.

"So, you asked why I came to Rome," she said abruptly. "I came to see *you*. I miss my friend, Alex. Well, what I really miss is my friend Xander."

"Oh, man," he replied, nostalgic and smiling. "I haven't heard *that* in forever. Feels weird when you say it."

"Why doesn't anyone call you that anymore?"

"Um, *no one* called me that ever. Just you. Well, you tried to anyway, but it didn't stick."

"Yeah, to be honest, I'm kind of glad it didn't. I don't even know why I thought it was so cool."

"Because you're an idiot."

He said it with such conviction that they both laughed all the way back to his neighborhood.

CHAPTER 26

THE CAFÉ WAS as lively as ever. The live band Alex had seen earlier was no longer playing, instead popular Italian '60s music by Adriano Celantano was bopping through the speakers. The room was filling up behind them, but Alex and Emily managed to find a spot for themselves on an empty, plush, blue couch.

Alex scanned the room and noticed that the staff had mixed up their costumes and makeup. Some maintained a beatnik '60s mime look, while a few of the women seemed inspired by Audrey Hepburn.

Alex spotted Patrizia in the corner, attempting to dance the Charleston with some male patrons. She wore a form-fitting, black dress with beaded fringe dangling from it. On her head was a platinum-white wig with an extra-long, bright-green feather that flopped as she danced. Her colorful costume jewelry sparkled in the soft lights.

Alex wished he could talk to her, but so much time had passed since their date that he felt awkward bringing it up. He watched her dance. She laughed as one of the customers grabbed her by the waist, pulled her onto his lap, and gave her a peck on the cheek. She embraced him and they pecked again.

"Eek!" Emily let out a shriek, making Alex turn back to her rescue.

One of the beatniks had apparently appeared from behind the couch. He remained silent, holding on to that mime act. His right arm was painted with black and white stripes and extended around Emily's shoulder holding a menu. Alex rolled his eyes, took the menu, and ordered two teas. The mime rolled over the arm of the couch and landed in front of them with a bow. The red papier-mâché mask that covered only his eyes tumbled to the floor. Embarrassed, he quickly picked it up and scurried away.

"I'm sorry. I was not expecting that!" Emily said laughing. "This place is lovely! I feel like I'm in a dream."

"Yes." Alex sat back in the sofa. "And they definitely make sure you feel that way." He was usually enamored of the quirky barmen, but tonight he only felt annoyed. Emily continued to quietly admire the space.

The waiter returned, this time without the mask or the theatrics. With a defeated look, he delivered a silver tray with mismatched teacups and saucers and a round silver teapot. Also on the tray was a small dish of cookies and a little note card that read: *My apologies for the disappointing performance.*

Alex looked up at the waiter, who avoided eye contact by looking at the ceiling. He was clearly determined to make Alex smile. Alex took the cookie dish from the tray and complimented him for a wonderful recovery, hoping it would boost the performer's confidence and rid him from their table. The waiter smiled, stretching his thin, curvy mustache. He placed the empty silver tray under his arm, bowed, and gleefully twirled back to the bar.

"Emily," Alex began again. "I apologize for all the distractions. So, you were telling me what made you come, that you missed my friendship. I hate to be forward, but I have to be honest: I don't believe that's the case.

He'd caught Emily mid-sip. She raised an eyebrow in confusion.

"But that *is* why I came here," she replied, returning the cup to the coffee table in front of them. "I've missed you."

"I think you're lying."

"Excuse me?" The quizzical look on her face had shifted to a defensive skepticism.

"I think you came here to check up on me."

"What on earth do you mean?"

"I think you came because my moving here means you may have lost me. It bothered you that I've finally moved on." Feeling accomplished, Alex dipped a cookie in his tea and ate it.

"Is that really what you think?" she asked.

"Yes. That's what it is. Isn't it?"

Emily sat back in the chair in silence. She grabbed a soft, maroon pillow and clutched it on her lap. Alex looked away as he placed his tea down on the table.

"Why are you being so harsh?" Emily asked, incredulous.

"I'm not being harsh." Alex touched her arm. "I just think it's time you and I have this talk. I think we need to end . . . this . . . whatever it is we have or don't have between us. It's not healthy for either of us."

Emily sipped her tea silently. Alex hoped she wouldn't break down dramatically.

"Listen," he continued. "I'm so glad you came here. I really am. I just think you owe me some type of explanation."

"Explanation?" she replied. "And just what do I have to explain?"

"Emily." Alex was getting tired of her questions. He wanted answers. "You flew across a continent and an ocean to visit me. In one of the most romantic cities in the world, I might add.

Surely, like me, your new boyfriend must wonder why. I mean, what did he say when you planned this?"

"He didn't think anything of it," she said, shaking her head. "He knows you're a close friend and he trusts me. Besides, it doesn't matter what he thinks. I'm here to spend time with you. I wanted to reconnect with you, my friend who I missed."

"Right," Alex replied. He sat back in his chair and looked at the coffee table. "You want to know what I think?"

"You just told me what you think."

"Yes, but there's more to it," Alex explained further. "You see, I think my moving here bothered you because in Boston, you knew where I was. You could imagine me there, like a toy sitting in its box waiting for you to take it out whenever you felt down. But when you saw that I had picked up and moved to Italy, you freaked."

"What?" Emily attempted a denial, but Alex continued.

"You freaked because you realized I'd moved on. I wasn't waiting for you anymore. Our story might really be over, and that bothered you. I imagine what probably bothers you more is that what I do means anything to you at all."

Alex could see Emily was uncomfortable. She stared at her teacup, avoiding eye contact with him.

"Emily," his tone was softer now, almost consoling. "I apologize if I sound like I'm attacking you."

"Alex," she finally looked at him. "Maybe my coming here was a bad idea. Would you feel more comfortable if I went to a hotel?"

"Don't do that," he scolded her. "Emily, I'm so happy you came here. So much time has passed without ever addressing *us*. I'm done with whatever it is that hovers over us like a cloud. It's like we haunt each other. Now, you can sit there and tell me it's not true, but you know I'm right and that this isn't working for you either.

"We also both know that you and I will never be together, but for some reason—and I speak for myself here now—I always have that thought: *Why am I not with Emily?*" Alex felt relieved to finally say the words to her. Although he probably shouldn't have attacked her with such a heavy discussion on her first day, he was glad he got it out of his system and out in the open.

"Why me?" Emily broke the silence.

"What?" Alex was caught off guard.

"Why me, Alex?" she repeated herself, adding nothing more. She sat back staring at him, this time with less confidence.

"Don't do that, Emily." He felt himself growing frustrated. "Why you? Really? Emily, I could ask the same of you. Why me? Why the hell won't you leave me alone? But that's not what this is about. We *both* have to move on. In fact, I moved on a long time ago, but again, you decided to wiggle your way back into my life."

"Alex," she replaced her teacup and crossed her legs. "If you had a problem with me coming here, why didn't you just say so?"

"You obviously don't want to talk about the matter at hand."

"What do you mean?" she leaned forward. "We are talking right now."

"Stop it." He felt he was losing control of the conversation. "You're talking, but you're avoiding my questions. You keep harping on the idea that I'm uncomfortable with you being here. Well, Emily, I'm sorry to disappoint you, but I'm not uncomfortable. I am not nervous around you. I wanted you here to have this conversation and end this bullshit that's forever ruining our lives. I want it over. I've moved on. I'm done. You can't keep crawling back in to check on me and to keep me pining for you. It's been quite some time since I thought about you like that. Can we please just move forward and put this behind us?"

Emily didn't respond. She just looked down at her hands resting on her lap. She stretched out her fingers as if she was examining her clear, glossy nail polish, but Alex knew she was processing her response.

"Alex," she finally looked up at him. "Please don't say that. I know you don't mean it." She paused, but Alex kept quiet. He wanted her to go on. "It's true. I did come here to check on you. Well, not *check on you*. But . . . well, Alex . . . I don't want you to leave me. I miss you. I miss my *friend*. I feel so lonely. I know I can count on you to be there for me. For some reason, just hearing your voice or reading your emails, any response from you, puts me at ease, no matter what I'm going through. And I miss laughing with you. The fun we used to have together."

Buzz. Buzz. Alex's phone vibrated in his front pocket. He tried to ignore it, but as he stared into Emily's face he saw that he might, in fact, be getting his wish. That this all might be ending. He decided to take the call.

"I'm sorry," he took out his phone. "It's been buzzing since we sat down. It could be about my job. They mentioned I might be needed this week." He stumbled as he explained and looked down at the phone: three missed calls from Eleonora Persini. He was torn between concern and relief. "I should probably call her."

"No problem," Emily grinned. "I was just going to head to the ladies' room."

He was left alone on the couch to return Eleonora's call.

"Pronto?"

"Ciao, Eleonora," Alex switched on his Italian. "I apologize for not answering my phone earlier; it's been a crazy evening."

"Not a problem, Alex. I apologize for disturbing you. I know you are on holiday with your friend. And I'm sorry for calling you at this hour."

"That's okay. I assume it is something urgent."

"It is. First, I wanted to tell you that Pernille is now officially in demand. The news shows are talking about her. The brands for which she is a spokesperson in Scandinavia are now airing their TV adverts here in Italy. People know her and want to see her.

"As you know," Eleonora continued quickly. "They want her back on *Chiacchiere del Cuoco* at the end of this month. And—before you say anything, Alex—yes, Matteo will be there. He's part of the show. I'm sorry."

"Fine." Alex felt awkward responding to Eleonora like that. He forgot whom he was talking to. But he focused on the success. All the publicity he set up for Pernille was effective and Italy was embracing her positively.

"Alex," Eleonora continued. "I received so many calls today requesting Pernille. Her Swatch ad campaign has been rushed through and a very large ad is, at this very moment, being placed on a prominent billboard on via del Corso and another on via del Babuino. Newspapers are running more adverts than planned for tomorrow's edition. She was just interviewed for a snippet that will appear on tomorrow's news. And—this is why I called you, Alex—she was invited to attend the football match tomorrow evening. I won't be able to accompany her, but I thought you and your friend may like the match. It's the Italian national team against Denmark, just a friendly match apparently to help promote world tournaments.

"You won't have to do much," she continued without taking a breath. "Just sit with Pernille and be there to make sure no reporter gets out of hand. They gave her amazing seats and plan to have the camera come to her and announce her appearance on the big screen. I emailed you the details, but I want to confirm tonight that you can do it.

"Oh, and I am waiting to hear about a possible quick interview there as well. The football organizers want to take advantage of her fame now that she's all over the place."

"Wow, that's great exposure for Pernille."

"And for Zero Otto," Eleonora replied. The sound of a car door binged in the background. "Take a taxi, pick her up at the hotel. Grazie."

"Thank you for what?"

"Oh, sorry. Not you," Eleonora explained. "I just got to the restaurant. They are taking my car. Okay, I will leave tickets for you at the office tomorrow. Just come by and pick them up whenever you can."

"Thank you, Eleanora. I look forward to the match."

Eleonora ended the call.

Emily returned refreshed. She removed her thin, hot pink jacket and placed it on the empty seat by her. She then sat back in her crossed legged position on the blue couch. "Everything all right?"

Alex wasn't sure what she meant. Was she talking about the phone call or were they picking up where they'd left off?

"Oh," he looked at the phone. "Yes, indeed. That was my boss, Eleonora. She gave us tickets to a soccer match tomorrow. I took them. Well, there's a bit of work involved, of course. Pernille, our client, will be with us. She has to make an appearance, wave, say hello, that sort of thing."

"Oh, nice," replied Emily with excitement. "I get to meet this gorgeous Scandinavian cook. And see the master at work." She grinned as she sat back, finishing up her tea.

"Yup," he said smugly. "And you are going to be very impressed, I'm sure."

"Who wouldn't?" she replied, and they both laughed.

"You see?" He felt he needed to close the previous conversation. "Somehow, we manage to push all our bullshit away, like under a rug, right?"

Emily smiled back at him and looked at her hands again. The music had stopped, allowing the live band to take their spots and transition the mood to a slower pace. Three couples had started to dance in the small open area in the center of the room. Alex spotted Patrizia leaning up against a wall, chatting up the man whose lap she'd sat on earlier. She looked up and noticed Alex watching her. She smiled and looked away, as if to prevent her companion from noticing the silent interaction with Alex.

"Well," Alex turned to Emily. "We should probably head back home. You're tired, I'm sure, and we've got some places to visit tomorrow."

"Good idea," she replied as she yawned. "What's the plan for tomorrow?"

"Well, since we are attending the match in the afternoon . . . " He was thinking out loud as they walked out the door. "I have to pick up the tickets at the office. I suppose the Vatican is probably a good spot. You did want to see that, right?"

"Definitely," she replied. "I can't come to Rome without seeing the Vatican museums."

"Another idea," he suggested as they ascended the stairs to his apartment. "We could go to this beautiful park I went to the other day, where we had the photo shoot. I really want to check out the museum there, the Galleria Borghese."

"I'm fine with whatever," replied Emily as she made her way to the guest room, putting her hair up in a casual twist. "Goodnight, Alex."

CHAPTER 27

THE NEXT MORNING, Alex woke up early as usual and lay in bed thinking about the conversation he and Emily had had the night before at the bar. He wanted it to end. It was the first time he had said it aloud to her. He had convinced himself he was over her. She was done and gone, had moved on. Over the years, he had convinced himself to believe it was over. That he had to move on from the idea of them. But the idea of her not wanting to be with him bothered Alex. Was he falling for it all over again? A bird chirped outside his window, egging him out of his contemplation and on with his day.

He rose from the bed and walked into the kitchen in his pajama bottoms. He didn't hear any stirring from Emily's room, so he assumed she was still asleep. As he walked back into the mini-foyer, he looked up at the ceiling light and was struck by a memory of that odd morning with Patrizia. What would Emily think, discovering him in the same delicate position as he was in that morning, arms stretched to the ceiling, pants around his ankles?

He sauntered into the living room and sat at the table with his laptop, the morning sun warming his bare back through the window. Every now and then, he slid a dining chair across the tiled floor or dropped a pen, purposely making loud noises to wake Emily, but to no avail.

Eventually, he went back into the kitchen for his morning espresso, quietly assembling the mini stove-top moka pot. Realizing he was being considerately quiet, he stopped himself, opened the cabinet door in front of him, and slammed it. It was childish, but he didn't care. He finally heard some stirring coming from the guest room. Alex stepped into the living room to await the call of percolating coffee and to greet his houseguest as nonchalantly as possible.

He heard her door slide open. Alex took his seat at the table and shamelessly struck a pose to accentuate any tone on his back and forearms.

"Good morning," she whispered. Alex turned around and noticed, to his delight, a glint in Emily's eye before she averted her gaze. He liked that she was looking. He was realizing that even though he'd asked her to move on, he still wanted her to want him. But why?

Emily was still wearing her gray polka-dot pajama pants and teal tank top. She hadn't put her contacts in yet, so she wore purple-framed glasses.

"Did I wake you?" Alex said as he breezed by her, purposefully brushing his arm against her back while he walked into the kitchen. He turned off the flame from underneath the coffee pot and poured himself an espresso.

"Not at all," she replied from the living room. "I was laying in bed, listening to the morning church bells ring. What a lovely sound. They reminded me of Chipping Campden—" She stopped herself abruptly. After a moment, she continued, "I actually forgot where I was until I heard them. I still can't believe I'm in Rome."

In the kitchen, Alex poured a second cup of coffee into a larger mug and added a light dollop of milk. A bit of the milk

splashed on his bare abdomen. As he wiped, he carefully lowered his pajama bottoms so they rested on his hip bones and
was then instantly mortified by his immaturity. Nonetheless,
he left them low-slung on his hips as he returned to the living
room. He handed the coffee to Emily, who was now sitting in
the green armchair by the sofa.

"Oh, I have church bells on this side of the apartment?" He
sat at his computer again, purposefully flexing his forearms as
he typed. "I didn't realize. I suppose I should sleep there one
night just to experience the other side." He winked at her as
he logged on to his computer. What was he doing? Had she
picked up on it? His face flushed from embarrassment.

"You really found an incredible place." Emily leaned back,
put her feet up onto the seat, and held her coffee mug with
both hands as she rested it on her knees.

"So, aside from the Vatican, is there anything that you
really must see?" He clicked at the keyboard, confirming the
bus route for the day's adventure. He figured they would see
the Vatican before swinging by the office to pick up the soccer
tickets. *I wonder if it's sacrilege to try and seduce someone inside
the Vatican. Wait, am I trying to seduce Emily?*

"Not really." Emily replied. Alex shot her a glance, but she
didn't notice, lost in the aroma of her coffee and the sounds
of the birdsong. "I figured we'd see the typical tourist things.
I mean, it was really cool to see the Colosseum from the bus.
Could we go there at some point?"

"Oh, yes. We will definitely stroll in that direction later in
the week. I sort of threw together a little agenda for us. I hope
you don't mind."

"Oh, let's hear it," she sipped her coffee.

He pulled up the detailed itinerary he'd painstakingly organized in anticipation of her visit, which he then adjusted after
Eleonora offered them the soccer tickets. "I have a Vatican

guidebook here that we can use to allow us to breeze through the museums and look for specific paintings and stuff." He handed her the guidebook and she flipped through it.

"We can grab a quick bite somewhere, stroll around a bit, you know, play it by ear, make our way back here to drop anything off and get ready for the match tonight." He opened Eleonora's email with details regarding the match.

"According to my boss, we have to pick up Pernille at her hotel and then head to the stadium. What about Teddy?"

"Who's Teddy?"

"Oh, Pernille's fiancé. He's in town to visit her. Eleonora didn't mention him."

"Are you sure I should come along tonight?"

"Oh, yeah," he assured her. "I mean, it will be an easy job, and we can enjoy the game in amazing seats. And although Pernille is energetic and a bit out there, she's very approachable and cool with everything."

"Well, I suppose I should go get ready so we can start our day early," Emily said as she put her cup into the kitchen sink and started her morning ritual. "Okay if I shower first?"

As Emily showered, Alex researched restaurants that might impress her. Nothing romantic, he told himself. At least not intentionally. He was just trying to show her a good time, right? If the restaurant he decided on happened to be romantic, well, it *was* Rome. What could he do?

Alex closed his laptop at the sound of the bathroom door opening. Emily was wrapped in an oversized light blue towel, her wet red hair cascading down her back. The light scent of strawberry soap wafted in the air around him.

Emily passed through the kitchen, into her bedroom, and closed the sliding door behind her. As soon as the door slid shut, Alex slapped himself. Hard. He went into his bedroom, threw off his pajama bottoms, grabbed a towel, and took an icy, cold shower.

CHAPTER 28

ALEX LOOKED OUT his bedroom window at the partly cloudy sky. He went back into the living room and grabbed his small black umbrella and the guidebook. Emily had opted to keep her purple-framed glasses on for the day. She also left her hot pink rain jacket in her room, swapping it out for a simple black zip-up accompanied by a loose fitting, lavender beret.

Once outside, he led her across the bridge and into a tiny coffee shop just before the ruins. They each had freshly squeezed orange juice and crispy, warm croissants.

As they waited at the bus stop by the cat sanctuary, Alex peered inside the ruins and found the Emperor sitting up, staring in his direction. Was he analyzing Emily? If so, Alex thought, did he approve? What could he be thinking? After what seemed like forever, the cat got on all fours and walked away. At that moment, the bus had finally arrived.

They walked along the Vatican walls to the museum entrance. Alex was glad he'd gotten there early, avoiding the chaotic line typically found along the walls. It helped that it was Rome's off-season, too.

They quickly passed through the security area, paid their entrance fee, and headed upstairs to the main foyer. Alex noticed a few tour groups gathered around them. He led Emily aside and pulled out his guidebook.

"So, this book is a Vatican museum walking tour," he explained as he flipped through the book. "These three pages will lead us through the Vatican, calling out the main pieces. Of course, we can stop to see anything else that pops out at you, but this will be our guide to get us through quickly."

"That's perfect," replied Emily. "I'm all for seeing the Vatican, but I didn't want to make it a whole-day thing."

"You're so uncultured," he mocked.

"Shut up!" She smacked him on the shoulder as he led her through the first gallery.

They walked through the museums, led by Alex's guidebook, which explained the background of the most popular works in the collection. They finally descended the dark spiral walkway out of the museums and through the maze of rooms leading to the *pièce de résistance*—the Sistine Chapel.

Although they had been among the first to enter the museum, the chapel room was already packed with people staring up at the ceiling. Alex was beginning to feel his claustrophobia kicking in, but then he looked at Emily's face, which was filled with awe. Always amazed at seeing this room, he scanned the walls and the ceiling and pointed out particular sections to Emily. As he spotted a new scene, he leaned into her left ear and whispered descriptions. His lips accidentally brushed her ear. She smelled glorious.

Alex stopped himself. He remembered the crowd again. The lack of space was getting to him. He took Emily's arm and led her to the other end of the chapel where it was less crowded. He continued whispering his descriptions in her ear, taking in her aroma. Emily's neck was exposed as she looked up, admiring all the artwork.

Alex stopped himself again, looked up at the ceiling, and pointed to specific paintings as he softly spoke. He turned to face Emily, catching her averting her eyes from him, red-faced.

"Well," he said as he put the book in Emily's bag. "I guess it's time we visit St. Peter's Basilica. We'll have to go through these doors and hopefully there's not a big line to get in."

As they approached the chapel exit, they inadvertently shuffled into a Japanese tour group leaving at the same time. Not remembering the direction to the church, Alex followed the Japanese tour guide.

At the bottom of the wide steps, he noticed the tour guide speaking with a security guard. She seemed to be getting authority clearance to lead her group in a certain direction. Alex, with Emily at his side, continued to follow the group.

"I've never gone this way," he whispered into Emily's ear. "But I'm sure this group is headed to the church." He noticed they were walking alongside St. Peter's, avoiding the long line entirely. "And I think this is a direct route!"

Alex and Emily stuck with the tour group until they reached the main entrance of the basilica. They looked at each other, smiled, and walked over the threshold. He led Emily directly to the right side of the massive church to look at Michelangelo's famous *Pietà*.

"I heard once," Alex continued to speak softly in Emily's ear, "that this is the only piece Michelangelo had ever signed." They leaned closer to the statue to try and find some sort of evidence. "It's supposed to be on Mary's sash somewhere, but I don't see it." He moved closer to Emily. His cheek brushed hers. He turned his face left to allow his lips to softly touch her face as he continued the story.

"Apparently, he had a bad temper. He once overheard people crediting other artists for the work, or someone had told him that the Pope intended to give credit to someone else. So, he snuck in one night and carved his name across her sash. But I don't see a thing. Must be tiny."

Silence. Alex kept his face close to Emily's. She did not move. He could kiss her now, he thought.

"Are you making this up?" Emily broke the closeness and stepped back, looking skeptical.

"No." He looked again. "I mean, I'm no historian, but I read it in a couple of other places, too."

"Just because it's on the web doesn't mean it's true."

"Ha, ha. Very funny."

They stepped out to the key-shaped piazza. Emily snapped a few photographs of the cathedral's exterior while Alex offered more quick descriptions, this time far away from Emily's warm, freckled ear.

Alex left Emily browsing in a shop by his office building while he ran upstairs to grab the soccer tickets. Eleonora wasn't in, but on his desk, she had left a marked envelope containing three glossy tickets and a note:

Good morning, Alex.

Enclosed are the tickets. Pernille's date is unable to make it. Please take care of her. Thank you again for working today. Enjoy the match!

—E.P.

Outside, he found Emily seated on a bench, her eyes closed, her face angled toward the sun that had finally emerged from the parting clouds. Alex wanted to sneak up to her and kiss her exposed, freckly neck, but he didn't. When she finally noticed his footsteps on the pavement, she put her glasses back on and gathered her jacket.

"Looks like it's warming up," she said as she joined him on the sidewalk. He smiled as he texted Pernille with details for meeting at the hotel.

TABLOID ARTICLE

PHOTO: Pernille Bjørn walking out of the Fendi store. In the photo, she is wearing a loose blue-and-white striped blouse over a short navy pencil skirt. Next to her is Teddy, dressed in a gray wool suit with his light blue shirt unbuttoned at the top. Pernille is smiling and waving to a crowd as the couple steps out of the shop with bags in hand.

CAPTION: La cuoca Nordese Pernille Bjørn fa shopping in Fendi su via del Corso, Roma. [The Nordic chef Pernille Bjørn shops at Fendi on via del Corso, Rome.]

BLURB: [translated from Italian] Over the weekend, Italy's new love Pernille Bjørn was seen shopping at Fendi on via del Corso, accompanied by a handsome man. Pernille is in Italy promoting her cookbooks—now translated in Italian—and filming her TV series, which we hope to see on Italian television very soon. Will Pernille also find an Italian lover? What Italian celebrity would make a good match for this Nordic beauty? Sources say it could be model and *Chiacchiere del Cuoco* TV host Matteo Pozzi.

[END]

CHAPTER 29

THE TAXI ARRIVED at the hotel by Piazza della Repubblica. Alex and Emily stepped into the hotel lobby and sat on two plush red chairs while they waited for the celebrity chef to join them.

"Alex?" Emily picked up a newspaper from the table. "Is this Pernille Bjørn?"

Alex looked at the photo of the blonde chef walking out of the Fendi store. The photo was a paparazzi snapshot. He remembered the article he had pitched to the reporter, but he didn't understand how or when—or even why—the photo was taken. It had nothing to do with promoting the book.

"What the hell is this?!" Alex stormed out of the lobby with phone in hand.

He paced outside of the hotel while leaving a voicemail for the reporter: "Where did this crap come from? And Matteo? What is this amateur reporting?" He practically screamed to the answering service.

He ended the call and punched in Eleonora's number. *Ring. Ring.* He paced to the right. *Ring. Ring.* He paced to the left. *Ring. Ring.* He stopped at the lobby window and saw Emily introduce herself to Pernille. *Ring. Ring.* He hung up, rolled up the paper, took a breath, and calmly strode into the lobby.

He didn't want Pernille to know about the article. He didn't really have any answers for her yet. He felt he could tell her after the soccer appearance. By then he would have spoken with Eleonora, and hopefully she too wouldn't be upset. Maybe she had an answer, he hoped, from the reporter. He dumped the paper into the waste bin by the door.

"Hello, Pernille," he greeted her as warmly as he could.

"Hi, Alex." She jumped up, hugged him, and kissed him on both cheeks. "I'm so happy you're joining me today."

"I see you've met my friend Emily."

"Oh, yes," she replied with even more effervescence. "We were just talking sports. Ha! So, are you rooting for Demark with me?"

Pernille's hair was wavy and set casually just below her shoulders. She wore tight jeans and a red-and-white striped tank under a white blouse tied at the waist. Her fingernails were painted red and white. And on her left cheek she'd painted the Danish flag.

"Do I look like a fan?" She waved the team scarf.

"Well, I don't know," he replied as he led them outside. "It may have to be Italy for me."

"How could we root for opposing teams?" she scoffed and handed him a Denmark jersey. "This is for you. It's my home team and you must follow what I follow. Am I right, Emily?"

"Oh, uh—" Emily stumbled. She watched Pernille hook her arm in Alex's. "Yeah, I think she's right, Alex."

"Fine, fine," he gave in. "Whatever the Great Dane says, I do." He smiled and pulled the large jersey over his head.

"Of course," Pernille winked. "Italy must know I am a fan. But I can't root against my Danes, can I?"

"Wait," Alex broke in. "I heard your brother is a soccer player, I mean *football*. So, you're used to this environment then."

"My cousin," she said with pride. "But not for the national team, so he won't be here today. And yes, I'm very used to footballers and their ilk. So today is going to be easy. No surprises to worry about, I hope."

* * *

The traffic was a bit heavy, but they still managed to arrive at the Stadio Olimpico on time. The crowd was just starting to pour in. Alex and Emily accompanied Pernille through the VIP entrance and up the staircases to a concourse inside the stadium. At the top of the stairs stood a tall woman in a security uniform asking for identification. She waved off Pernille's ID, welcoming her with a smile and a nod of recognition, and instructed the group to proceed down the hall to the indicated lounge.

As Pernille, Alex, and Emily walked into the secured area, a young woman introduced herself as their server and offered them drinks and snacks. Pernille ordered soda water with an orange and then walked over to the glass wall overlooking the bright-green soccer field. Alex and Emily followed and watched the teams down on the field practicing before the big match.

"I've always loved watching football matches," Pernille said, still staring out the window. "Teddy and I try to catch a match whenever we can. Of course, with our busy schedules, it's always so difficult. But I try to see my cousin when I can. Someday he'll play for Denmark."

"So, you are familiar with the sport in case any questions come up?" asked Alex. "Are you okay with the interview? From what I understand, they will interview you in the stands before the match and then announce you and show you on the big screen at some point during the game."

"Yes," replied Pernille. "Just let me know when you need me. Right now, I'm going to enjoy the practice. Can we go down to our seats?"

"Oh, we're not watching from here?" Emily asked. It was then Alex realized that Emily had been virtually silent since Pernille had joined them.

"Pernille has to be seen in the seats down below." Alex pointed out the window, straight down to the right of mid-field. "Our seats should be just down there. See that section there? Closer to the field?"

The fans were beginning to fill the stands as the young waitress returned with their drinks and some crostini. Behind her followed a tall man in his fifties who introduced himself as the reporter for the sports channel. He led Pernille and Alex down to the stands, where she was fixed with a microphone. The cameraman's red light turned on.

"I'm Massimo Diventi at the Italy versus Denmark friendly football match at Rome's Stadio Olimpico. And speaking of Denmark, I'm standing here with the beautiful Scandinavian chef Pernille Bjørn. Welcome, Pernille."

"Thank you, Massimo. Happy to be here. I'm very excited."

"You have become a well-known name in Italian households. It was almost as if it happened overnight. I recently watched you on the popular TV show *Chiacchiere del Cuoco* with Clara Mucci and Matteo Pozzi." He nudged her as he mentioned Matteo's name and continued. "How does it feel to be so famous so quickly?"

"Oh, I don't know about that."

"Yes. And Matteo seems to have taken a liking to you," Massimo flirted with Pernille. "Did I detect sparks on the set?"

Alex's ears pricked up. Pernille just smiled and shook her head with a polite dismissal of Massimo's question. The reporter quickly recovered and asked her why she had come to Italy.

"Well, I love Italy. Always have. I mean, who doesn't? It's a gorgeous country: delicious food, beautiful people. And being in Rome is just enchanting. I love Italia."

"You are wearing a Denmark football jersey, and very beautifully, I might add."

"Thank you." Pernille blushed. "I am hoping my country's team wins today. No offense, Italia!"

"Oh, you don't think Denmark stands a chance, do you?"

"Of course they have a chance, although I'll admit, Italy is one of the best." She smiled sweetly, but Alex could see out of the frame that she'd placed her hand on Massimo's and firmly removed it from its unwelcomed perch on her thigh. "I am so excited for the match today. My seat is just down below there. Look for me cheering for the Danes!"

"We definitely will. I'm sure every man watching the match today will look for you." Massimo winked at the camera.

Alex wanted to jump into the shot, punch the old man, and declare the interview over. And the letch still hadn't mentioned her book. Pernille, as though reading Alex's mind, ignored the reporter's comment and brought her cookbook up herself.

"In my cookbook," she said, "I have a few recipes inspired by my Italian holidays."

"Oh, yes," he eyed her breasts for the fifth time. "Was the holiday with an Italian lover?"

"Oh, Massimo." Pernille readied herself to deflect his question when she noticed Alex appear next to the cameraman.

"I'm sorry to interrupt," Alex said quietly from behind the camera to the befuddled Massimo, "but Pernille is needed for another interview." He stepped back to allow the reporter to wrap up the interview.

"Well, Pernille," Massimo held a forced smile. "It appears we're out of time. Thank you for taking a moment to sit with me today. I hope to see you later."

"Thank you, Massimo. I'm very excited to be here. Viva Italia!"

"Ha! Ha! Yes, thank you." Massimo turned back to the camera and closed the segment by thanking his fans and wishing the Italian team good luck.

The camera light turned off, and Massimo pretended to have an urgent phone call. Alex helped Pernille quickly remove her microphone and threw it on the seat. He led Pernille down the aisle, through the stands, and back to the club box.

"I'm so sorry about that," Alex finally said to her.

"That's okay, Alex," she replied. "It's not your fault. Thank you for stepping in when you did."

Alex was still furious. He grabbed his beer, sat in the plush chair, and stared out the window. He was upset with himself for letting that happen. And he knew that nothing could be done about it. The segment was live, and he was sure that it would be repeated throughout the day.

Buzz. Buzz. Alex rolled his eyes and opened the text message. It was Emily letting him know that she had gone down to their seats.

"Do you want to stay up here a bit?" he asked Pernille. "Collect yourself, relax a moment?"

"Oh, no," Pernille replied, grabbing his hand. "Let's get down to our seats. I want to see the game! And I want to say hello to my players. Besides, don't I have to be down there for the announcement?"

"You have some time. But it's up to you."

"Oh, cheer up," she said. "You look so upset. That interview was not the end of the world. It wasn't that bad at all. And did you hear what he said? I'm famous!"

They found Emily seated, legs crossed, looking nervously around as a boisterous Italian couple attempted conversation with her. Within moments, the enthusiastic pair, Paola and Ennio, recognized Pernille and congratulated her on her newfound celebrity in Italy. Pernille chatted kindly with her admirers, and when the Danes in the crowd sang along to their country's national anthem, she made everyone in the row stand up to join in. Emily found herself hooked arm-in-arm and swaying with Paola and Ennio, who were pretending to sing along. Well, Paola and Ennio were doing most of the swaying. Emily was completely at the mercy of the boisterous football fans, hanging onto them like a dead fish.

Once the anthems had been sung and the referee's opening whistle had sounded, Alex settled in to enjoy some of the match. He noticed Emily following the action on the field quietly, offering little more than a polite smile or nod in the bubbly Paola's direction. He knew she wasn't intentionally being rude to Paola. Something was eating at her. He wondered, a bit smugly, if it might be jealousy over his rapport with Pernille.

Suddenly, the crowd erupted. Italy had scored and Alex had missed it. As the fans around them returned to their seats, the sound of Paola nattering away at Emily's side rose again over the din of the crowd. Alex kept his focus on the ball—this was Emily's concern, not his—until he heard something he couldn't ignore.

"Emily, do you see him? That is a very beautiful Italian man," Paola offered in her thick Italian accent.

"Oh, really?"

"Yes! Forget George Clooney. This is an *Italian* man. Perfect breeding. Look, he is coming here. He is very close." Paola then whispered urgently to Ennio in Italian, "I don't believe it! He's coming this way."

Alex strained his neck to see who Paola might be talking about when he heard an unwelcome voice booming behind him.

"Pernille Bjørn! I'm so very happy to see you here." It was that damn model Matteo Pozzi.

CHAPTER 30

MATTEO—TALL, THIN, AND so very toned—stood with his back to Alex, hand on the railing, greeted Pernille Bjørn. His butt was moving closer and closer to Alex's face, forcing him to lean into Emily. To his right, Alex overheard Paola's excitement as she whispered to Emily.

"So perfect. We can almost touch it." Paola reached out and mocked a squeeze.

Matteo leaned over Pernille suggestively and offered to buy her a drink. Alex wanted to intervene. He stood up with such force, and so quickly, that his pelvis bumped into Matteo's butt, making the model stumble forward. Alex was horrified.

He blushed as Paola and Emily snickered. Ignoring them, he apologized to Matteo, who responded with an exaggerated laugh and casually struck a catalogue-model pose on the banister, legs spread wide, brooding stare directed down at Pernille.

She suddenly jumped up and screamed with excitement along with the crowd behind her. The Danish team was about to shoot a corner kick on the far side of the field. Pernille leaned on the banister next to Matteo. Ennio, Paola, and a few other spectators scolded Alex to sit in his seat because he was blocking their view.

"Really, Paola?" Alex whispered, absurdly, he thought, to a near perfect stranger. "Matteo isn't blocking your view?"

"That's the view I'm trying to see," she said as she nudged Emily. "You see? I told you. A perfect Italian man." Emily, blushing, peeked at Matteo while trying to avoid staring.

Ennio, meanwhile, was fidgeting in his seat as the Danish player kicked the ball into play. It bounced off the head of his teammate, grazed the fingers of the Italian goalkeeper, and flew into the net.

Pernille cheered with the Danish fans. She clapped and jumped while Matteo quickly repositioned himself and caught her in his arms to share in her celebration. Pernille calmed down as the ball went back into play, but remained standing with Matteo's arm still hooked around her shoulder, like he was an animal claiming his prey. Matteo shifted his stance yet again, leaning on his left leg, this time varying his pose for his imaginary photo shoot.

As the ball made its way down to their end, Matteo, along with the rest of the Italian fans in the stands, began to cheer. The Italian players maneuvered the ball around the Danish defense and ended the play with a bicycle kick straight past the opposing goalkeeper. Matteo shouted with excitement, grabbed Pernille by the shoulders, and kissed her squarely on the mouth.

Alex's world suddenly moved in slow motion. He, Emily, and Paola watched with jaws dropped. Ennio, ever the fan, remained oblivious, caught up in his own celebration. Alex instinctively rose to his feet to save Pernille. Hell, to save his job. Emily and Paola tried to stop him, but he was already standing up and again bumping Matteo into the banister. A wide-eyed Pernille looked on in horror. Emily and Paola reached for Matteo, but it all happened so quickly. His sculpted torso and bulging legs slid over the banister and down onto the sidelines. Photographers instantly gathered around with flashes popping.

Alex looked up and saw himself and Pernille on the big screen. Pernille shrieked and covered herself up with her Denmark scarf. Alex, mortified, rushed her past Emily and Paola—who were frozen with shock—and out of the seats toward the VIP lounge. The image on the big screen panned to Matteo laying on the ground, somehow striking another sexy pose despite the circumstances. He welcomed the multitude of flashes with a photogenic smile. Emily, Paola, and Ennio inconspicuously left the scene and made their way up to Alex.

"We need to go. Now," commanded Alex. "Damn it!"

"It's okay, Alex," Pernille said as she sat in the chair nervously picking at her nails. "I'm sure you can turn it around. Use it to our advantage, right?" She stood up and searched his face. His mind raced, thinking of what the next day's headlines would claim.

"Let's go. I don't want the press finding you. More importantly—" He looked at the big screen again. One last shot of Matteo waving to the crowd before the screen switched back to the game still in action. "I don't want that asshole finding you."

"Is there anything we can do to help?" Ennio asked.

"Maybe. Come on."

He led the group out of the lounge. They hurried through the VIP concourse and down to the exit. He scanned the parking lot for a taxi. Ennio led them to the left of the lot and pushed them all in his small black Fiat. The paparazzi hadn't caught up with them yet. Matteo must still have been posing.

Ennio tore out of the stadium parking lot and made his way back to the St. Regis, hopping onto the sidewalk in front of the elegant hotel to the raised eyebrows of the doorman.

Emily crawled out the back seat, then Alex, followed by Pernille. The doorman held the door open, allowing Alex to rush Pernille and Emily inside, before getting into a shouting match with Paola and Ennio. After giving the doorman a vulgar gesture, Ennio pulled off the sidewalk and skidded away.

"Come on!" Alex said to the elevator, pounding the button. Although none had arrived at the hotel yet, he needed to keep Pernille away from the paparazzi.

"Alex, I'll get a taxi back home," Emily said as she stepped back to the door.

"No, wait. I'll be right down. Please, wait for me in the lobby. okay?"

"Okay. Goodnight, Pernille. It was nice meeting you. And don't worry, Alex will take care of this, I'm sure."

"Thank you, Emily," Pernille replied. "Goodnight."

The elevator doors finally slid open. They stepped in and stood in silence as the elevator climbed.

"I can't believe that just happened," Pernille finally said. She seemed to still be in a state of shock. "Was it all on the screen?"

"I don't think so," Alex lied. "I think they just caught the very end of it. Matteo seemed to have gotten more screen time than we did."

The elevator lifted them to the sixth floor. Alex followed Pernille to her hotel room door. She slid her key card in and turned back to him, the door ajar.

"Thank you, Alex," she said. "I appreciate your quick response. But I don't think it was necessary to throw him over the banister." She held his gaze for a moment and then stifled a laugh.

"I didn't throw him over," he laughed in relief. "He jumped over. I barely touched him!"

"Well, whatever the case, I suppose he deserved it." She hesitated at the threshold and then let the door close behind her.

CHAPTER 31

"BY THE WAY, thanks again for signing me up for the group tour today." Emily came out of her room carrying her bag, jacket, and camera.

"I'm sorry I have to abandon you today," Alex replied while typing profusely on his laptop.

"Oh, don't be. I understand. You have to handle this crisis situation. Besides, you've already seen all these tourist sites; I hate dragging you to them all over again."

"But you're only here for a few days, and—"

"It's okay, Alex. We've got a few more days. Do your thing."

Emily looked at her watch. "Ooh, I should go. I don't want to be late. See you this afternoon. Okay. Bye and good luck."

* * *

"Alex, again, I am so sorry for not returning your calls," Eleonora was curt. "I heard the message and immediately set to work. I think I've cleared up the situation." She turned her computer around and showed him a video from the news reports.

There was Matteo on TV, being interviewed on the sidelines. He was telling reporters how he went to reach for a soccer ball and got overly excited and tumbled over the banister. He kept mentioning Pernille's name. A photo from the game appeared on the screen. It was Matteo with his arm around Pernille. The next photo was from afar, of Matteo leaning over Pernille. Alex knew Matteo had been offering her a drink in that moment, but the angle made it appear as though he was going in for a kiss. They looked like a celebrity couple enjoying a sporting event.

"We're very good friends," Matteo said in the video.

"How good?" asked one reporter as the rest snickered.

"Very good," Matteo replied with a sneer. The comment was followed by a clear and focused snapshot of the couple engaged in the kiss.

They went back to a live shot of Matteo basking in the light from the surrounding cameras.

"Fortunately, Matteo's story that he fell trying to catch a stray ball was believable." Eleonora stopped the footage and turned the computer back around. "So, no one is implicating *you* in this mess—or the firm by association. However, I must admit, I didn't know what to do about the kiss! Please explain how the hell that happened!"

Alex repeated the whole story to Eleonora. She remained silent for some time. Alex squirmed in his seat.

"Well," she finally said, "fortunately for Pernille, it worked."

"Worked?"

"She is in practically every paper this morning." Eleanora dropped several newspapers in front of him.

"What do you mean?" Alex picked up the papers and noticed several headlines:

Pernille La Bella

Barbie e Ken

La Cuoca TROVA L'AMORE

"Alex," she explained, "the Italians loved it! Every headline is calling her Italy's new sweetheart. Whatever you may think about Matteo, he made her a star."

"But some of these are really inappropriate." Alex held up a sports paper with a photo of Matteo and Pernille under the headline: ITALIA INVASA LA DANIMARCA, translating to *Italy invades Denmark*. "This one especially."

"They are talking about the match," Eleonora brushed it off.

"Eleonora," Alex stood up and insisted, "this isn't the image Pernille is going for."

"Alex, relax." Eleonora leaned on her desk, looking angry once again, and rationalized. "This is how Italy works. We have them now. Pernille has arrived. Now, I have a lot of work to do. I have requests from many reporters. I need to sort through them. Please, just go and we'll sort it out by Monday when you're back in the office. For now, let me handle this one."

"At least know that I am available," Alex replied.

"Thank you, but I should be okay," she replied, sorting out the newspapers again and picking up her office phone. "Alex," she added calmly, "I know it will all work out. This incident really helped, and I see her career in Italy skyrocketing. Trust me."

"Okay." He was uncertain. "I just feel like she's getting noticed for this stupid scandal and her beauty, not for her talent. And we both know Pernille won't appreciate that."

"Really, Alex?" Eleonora rolled her eyes as she dialed the phone. "Wake up. This is Italy. This is how things work here." She looked back up at him and continued, "I'm meeting with her later this morning, and I'll explain it all to her. Don't worry about it. Now seriously, go finish your holiday. I don't want to hear that you didn't enjoy yourself when you get back on Monday."

Alex left the office unconvinced. He felt somewhat defeated. He was glad that Pernille was getting front-page coverage, but it wasn't for her cooking. It was some cheap, empty paparazzi bullshit. Pernille wanted to be respected as a culinary expert, and this scandal wasn't helping in that regard. To the public, Pernille Bjørn was just a gorgeous television personality, turning into a Scandinavian sex symbol, most likely sleeping with the most famous model in Italy. This was not the type of work he wanted to be associated with.

He pictured Pernille having breakfast at that very moment, seeing her face smeared all over the papers that surrounded her. He felt like he had failed her.

* * *

Alex threw his keys onto his console table by the door and plopped down on the sofa next to Emily. He let out a long breath and put his head on her lap. She didn't say anything. She let him rest as she read her book. She stroked his hair, and he closed his eyes and let her calm him down. He resisted the urge to reach out and touch her.

"How was the Colosseum?" he finally asked.

"Incredible," she said. "I cannot believe how old it is. Just being there, in the footsteps of history, was amazing. I really enjoyed it."

"Good," Alex replied, closing his eyes once again. "I'm glad you enjoyed it." It was the last he remembered before falling asleep on her soft, warm lap.

He awoke to Emily still reading her book. He was thirsty, but too comfortable to move from her lap. She let him nap there the whole time. *How long was I out?* he wondered. Did he really have to get up? He wanted to just remain there in silence, appreciating the closeness with Emily.

"Welcome back, sleepy head," she said as she held his head.

"Hey. Sorry." He sat up. "How long was I out?"

"Not long. Five minutes. Maybe Ten."

"Really? That's it?" Alex got up from the couch. "I'm thirsty. You want some water, juice, anything?"

"No, I'm okay, thank you." Emily smiled back.

Alex came back from the kitchen guzzling a tall, cool glass of water. He barely gave himself room to breathe as he drank. When the glass emptied, he stood with his hand on his hip, catching his breath.

"How about a stroll?" he said. "It'll wake me up a bit."

"Sure. But I'm okay if you want to just stay in."

"Well, we can grab some takeout and bring it back. I just want to get some air."

"All right. I'll just grab my jacket. And maybe an umbrella, just in case."

As they walked across the bridge, Alex felt a light sprinkle of rain on his face. He was relieved Emily had taken the small umbrella along in case the gray clouds overhead decided to grace them with a full-on shower. As they reached Largo Argentina, he was struck by an idea.

"Come on." Alex took Emily's hand and led her past the busy piazza, through the narrow cobblestoned streets, toward the Pantheon. "There's something I want you to see. I want to get there before the rain really picks up."

They entered a piazza that sloped to their left, anchored by the impressive Pantheon. The square was filled with groups of tourists staring up at the ancient temple-turned-church. The rain began to fall harder. One by one, colorful umbrellas opened all around them.

"You need to see this." Alex took Emily's hand, once again, and quickly led her to the entrance of the Pantheon. Fortunately, there was no line to fight and they walked right inside.

The thick walls and marble interior somehow blocked the loud voices outside. An occasional shout followed by whispered admonitions from the guards traveled through the round interior. In the center of the room was a circle of banisters blocking a drain in the floor that collected the water that came in from a round hole in the dome above.

Although the rain was falling outside, the water came through the hole in a spiraling mist that trickled slowly down to the floor. Alex and Emily stared up at the ceiling, watching the slow, enchanting spiral.

"Wow," Emily whispered. "It looks as though a magic spell has been cast down from above. So surreal." She knelt, pointing her camera up to the hole, attempting to catch the beauty. After a few snaps, she stood back up and put her arms around Alex. "Oh, Alex. Thank you."

Alex didn't know what was happening. This was the first time she'd touched him like that since the kiss. In fact, he didn't even realize how close they'd been earlier as he napped on her lap. Was she coming around? Was there something happening between them again? Had he somehow gotten through to her? Was she breaking down her wall and letting it happen? He liked the feeling of having her so close to his body. He felt her warmth. Her breathing.

"This is what I missed, Alex." Her body vibrated as she spoke in his ear, still embraced. "Us. You and me. Having my friend. I don't know why, but this moment right here has made me realize how much you mean to me." She softened her hug and let go, revealing a small amount of water in her eyes. "You are such a wonderful person. You really are."

"Hey," Alex wiped her tear. "Are you all right? I didn't mean to make you cry."

"Sorry, it's just that I really did miss you, Alex. And I don't know if I can handle not having you around."

Alex didn't know what to say. He didn't really understand what she was getting at. Was he was supposed to kiss her? Like in a romantic comedy? He held her by both arms and pulled her in. She lifted her head, closed her eyes, and let him kiss her.

It was a soft, warm kiss. Afterward, they rested their lips on each other for longer than someone would when ending a kiss. Slowly he let go and looked in her eyes. They looked at each other for what seemed like an eternity until Emily finally broke the gaze and fumbled in her bag.

"I'm sorry, Alex. I shouldn't have let that happen. I don't know what came over me."

"Emily—"

"No, please. Stop." She pulled away and left him to explore the circular church. He found her again at Raphael's tomb.

"Are you okay?"

"Yes," she replied quietly. "I'm sorry. I'm being—I'm giving mixed—I just don't know. We just can't, Alex. We just can't. So, please, let's just—"

He was disappointed. He made his move and she turned him away. Was that not what she wanted? Something was going on with her. He had to get to the bottom of it. Why was she resisting him? If it was the boyfriend, then why did she let him kiss her like that? Why had she kissed him upon arrival? The kisses had proved to Alex that there could still be a chance to get her back. He knew he didn't want to come across as too aggressive. He didn't want to pressure her. But her time in

Rome was running out. He had to maintain the slow pace and, maybe, eventually she would let him in.

"Come on." Alex hooked her arm. "Let's go get some air."

"It's raining."

"It's just a drizzle now. It's lightening up." He led her outside, stopping among the columns of the Pantheon's front portico. "See? It's not that bad."

"You're right. Where to?"

"How about some gelato?"

"Yes."

They lost themselves in the thick crowd of visitors and wandered to a quiet gelateria away from all the noise.

CHAPTER 32

"WOULD YOU RATHER stay in town today?" Emily called out from her room. "I mean, we don't have to take this day trip. I don't want to take you away from all this."

"No. No," Alex replied from the living room. "After what happened with Eleonora yesterday, I want to get out of here. Have some space. Let's go away from all this. It's just for the day. Eleonora's got it covered." He grabbed his jacket. "I just hope she's not reconsidering my contract."

"Stop. Don't do that to yourself." Emily joined Alex in the living room, placing her oversized purse on the chair across from him. With her back to him, she bent down to adjust the items inside the bag. "It was out of your control. I'm sure she understands that. And it was a one-time thing. I mean, you're allowed to make a mistake. Besides, you really didn't do anything damaging."

As she spoke, Alex stared at her behind, wanting to reach out and caress it. When Emily shifted, Alex quickly stood up and walked to the other end of the room, attempting to hide his thoughts. She didn't turn around, which meant she didn't notice, maybe. He was relieved.

"You're right," he replied as he grabbed the keys. "We should get going. If we catch the next bus, we can get to Viterbo in time for lunch."

They reached the quiet village of Bomarzo. Emily had requested a trip to the town's Park of Monsters, *Parco dei Mostri*, and, with that in mind, they'd packed a picnic lunch of a baguette, cheese, salami, and a bottle of red wine. As they gathered their things, the bus driver kindly offered directions to the park but warned Alex to be mindful of the time. The town was quite small and buses didn't travel through frequently; he didn't want them to be stranded.

It was lunchtime and the village was deserted. There wasn't a soul in sight and the only sound was the roar of the bus's engine driving away, leaving Alex and Emily to their fate. Alex followed the driver's directions down a steep hill.

"It's too quiet here." Emily walked closer to Alex. "It almost feels like a ghost town."

"A perfect setting for today's adventure, huh?"

"It's creepy, for sure."

"Well, it's lunchtime," Alex offered by way of explanation.

"Oh, right, that siesta thing."

"Well, yes. You don't see much of it in the big cities," Alex explained as he monitored the map on his phone. "I mean, shops shut down, but there's still some movement in the city. It's when you come to these small villages that lunch can become, as you said, a ghost town."

"So, they eat a big meal and they nap?"

"Well, some nap. Some just relax. They have a slow meal. And some use the time to . . . you know . . . have *relations*." He said this last part close to her ear.

"What?" Emily gently pushed him away and laughed. She was blushing.

Alex smiled. "This is Italy. Italians are passionate people. Don't judge."

They continued down the hill until they came to a small stone gate with a carved wooden sign that read: SACRO BOSCO DI BOMARZO / PARCO DEI MOSTRI.

"Well, this is it," Alex pointed down yet another long, steep, winding path. "This is the way to The Park of Monsters in the Sacred Woods of Bomarzo."

"Of course it's down a creepy, winding dirt path into a dark forest." Emily hooked herself under Alex's arm.

"Well, what did you expect, a yellow brick road?" They strolled down the path hearing only birds chirping.

"How did you find this place?" Alex asked. "I mean, of all the places you could see in the area."

"I was just browsing the web when I found it," she replied as they turned the third bend. "I thought it looked cool. And we both have an affinity for the macabre." She raised her free hand like a zombie.

Alex looked back at the long, steep path he knew they would have to climb later. "Look behind us." Emily turned.

Beyond the steep, winding hill, the town of Bomarzo rose up, a cluster of old houses all stuck together at varying heights, resembling a medieval castle. Alex hadn't realized the town was so much larger than what they had first witnessed when they stepped off the bus.

"I wonder what it's like in there," Emily said as she took more photos.

"I'm sure it's just a small piazza," Alex replied, continuing down the winding road. "We can go through that side of town when we head back to the bus stop."

They turned left on the fourth bend and saw a small building with a metal gate that welcomed them to the Sacred

Woods. To the left were picnic tables and a small playground. Aside from a red station wagon and a utility truck, the dirt parking lot was empty.

Alex noticed a woman sitting in a ticket booth reading a book. She explained that the park was open but that it was empty because it was off-season. She handed them a map of the walking path and told them about a shortcut to get back to the village center to catch their bus. Alex and Emily thanked her and walked on. They followed a wall of large green hedges to a stone entrance shaped like a castle's gate. Together, Alex and Emily passed through the gate slowly, as if being transported into some enchanted land, and entered the Sacred Woods.

Emily read from her phone, "According to local legend—or rumor, or tale, or whatever you call it—in the late 1500s Prince Vicino Orsini commissioned the park to express the pain he felt for the loss of his wife, Giuliana Farnese, who was, at one time, rumored to be the mistress of the Pope, incidentally. Orsini had the artists sculpt the boulders on his property into hideous monsters."

"Now, I don't know how much of that is true," Alex responded, "but it is interesting all the same."

Still arm-in-arm, they came upon a stone wall topped with statues of gargoyles, trolls, and fearsome dragons. To the left stood a massive stone sculpture that was about twenty feet tall and had bits of moss growing on it. Alex and Emily's mouths both dropped as they stared at the carefully sculpted giant head of a sea monster. The massive fish head had a wide, gaping mouth full of pointy teeth.

Alex hadn't expected to stand in front of such massive and creepy creations. Between the tall stone wall and the massive sea creature, he felt like he had entered a David Bowie movie, trapped in a labyrinth of magical monsters.

"This place is incredible," Emily said. "I didn't imagine it to be like this at all. I'm so happy we came." She ran down the path to the next opening in the tall hedges.

Alex's stomach grumbled. They had traveled quite some time to reach the hidden forest, and he'd forgotten about the food they packed.

"Shall we find a spot to picnic?" Alex continued along the walking path, looking for an open grassy area or some sort of table.

"Definitely." Emily appeared from behind a gigantic turtle with her camera in hand. She put her camera up to her face and aimed it at Alex, who stood by an empty fountain with a Pegasus perched on top, about to take flight. She snapped the photo and slowly lowered her camera, blushing. She looked away, let her camera hang by her side, and caught up with him.

As they turned the corner, they came upon a structure made into a medieval two-story house that appeared as though it was about to fall. Alex and Emily ran up the stairs of the house like two children reaching a fairytale witch's gingerbread home. The crooked sculpture held four rooms, two on the first floor and two on the second. Bracing themselves against walls, Alex and Emily explored the structure, carefully navigating the slanted tile floors.

"I would suggest eating at *home*, but this doesn't seem practical," Alex laughed. Emily snapped another photo of him as he tried holding himself steady by an open window.

She joined him by the window and looked at the view. All that was visible was the tiny meadow in which the house stood, surrounded by trees. Alex felt at peace in the crooked house. Emily's long red hair danced in the slight breeze, caressing his face.

He leaned in closer and allowed her aroma to hypnotize him. Her perfume exuded a soft scent of summer flowers and a hint of wood. His left hand was leaning on the sill of the crooked window. He swung his right arm around her and placed his other hand also on the sill, almost embracing her. She didn't push him away.

He slowly placed his chin on top of her left shoulder, his cheek lightly touching hers. Her eyes were closed, breathing in the fresh air and probably imagining herself in some other world. He slowly turned his face toward hers, hoping she would, in response, turn toward him. She didn't. She just stood there, eyes closed, lost in a dream. Did she want him to kiss her? He didn't know. He'd thought he'd gotten to her the night before at the Pantheon, but now she seemed to be pushing him away.

He felt foolish. There he was, standing in a crooked house, trying to rekindle a crooked love, offering up his crooked heart once again. He took his hands off the ledge, stepped back, and headed for the stairs.

Alex stood outside the house wondering if it was worth it, having Emily visit. It seemed to be reviving all his feelings, especially those of hurt and failure. Emily finally emerged, and they continued around the back of the house, along a path that wound up a small hill.

Alex wasn't paying attention to the sculptures he was passing. His mind was elsewhere.

He looked up and found himself in another open area of statues lined up on both sides, as if guarding the stone sculpture of a mermaid in the center. To the right, Emily was photographing a statue of an elephant with some sort of structure on its back. Alex stood by a screaming dragon statue, trying to get over the ridiculous emotions that were stirring inside of him.

This experience of discovery reminded Alex of his early days in college with Emily. With a sense of adventure, they had explored Boston and Cambridge after classes. Those days were filled with little moments that led up to his falling in love with her. He remembered the first time they had fooled around in the library, holding hands as they strolled around Harvard Square, and almost getting caught while making out in the Public Gardens. They'd dated and he'd thought they'd be together—until that moment she surprised him with news of her boyfriend.

Alex slowly walked around the screaming dragon while his mind revived memories and the pain that came with them. He shook his head to push the memories away. He didn't want to think about them. He wasn't living in the past; he had moved on. They both had moved on.

Alex emptied his thoughts and found himself standing, again, in front of the sculpture. He looked up at its bulging eyes. Its mouth was puffy, like the sea monster they saw at the park's entrance. It had scales and small wings. Its claws were tiny, like those of a Tyrannosaurus Rex.

"Alex!" Emily was calling him from somewhere around the bend behind the elephant. "You've got to see this! Come over here!"

He squeezed between the elephant and dragon, through short hedges, into another open area where Emily was standing, staring at her discovery: a massive ogre head.

"I think I found our picnic spot," Emily said.

The ogre's eyes and nostrils were hollowed out. Through its mouth, which was wide open, Alex could make out another object.

"What's inside?" he asked.

"I don't know," she replied. "I was too scared to go inside. That's why I called you. Who knows what creatures are lurking in there?"

"Oh, but you want to eat out here in front of it?" he laughed.

Alex stepped up to the ogre for a closer look inside. Its massive mouth was lined with four wide-gapped square teeth. As he stepped closer, the pitch-black interior became clearer. He was finally able to make out the object inside the ogre's mouth. Inside the head were a stone table and bench. The sunlight trickled in through the eyes and the nostrils, giving the head's interior a soft glow.

He turned back out to Emily and called her to come closer. She refused and told him to pose in the mouth for a photo. After a few snapshots of Alex pretending to be eaten by the ogre, he called back out to her.

"Come look inside," he said. "You have to see this."

"What is it?" She finally stepped up to the mouth and peeked inside.

"Well, you were right," he said. "You definitely found a picnic spot."

"I'm not eating in there! With my luck, some insect will crawl on me or I'll get bitten by a rat. Forget that." She stepped away from the ogre and coaxed Alex to continue up the path. "Come on. We'll eat on top of this hill. I'm sure there's something more pleasant than that cavernous place."

They found an open meadow surrounded by several stone shapes including pillars, a gazebo, and a small church. They laid out their blanket and feasted on their picnic lunch. Afterward they lay on their backs and looked up at the sky.

It was quiet, except for the birds in the trees and the annoying sound of a leaf blower in the distance. Emily browsed through her photos on her digital camera, showing a photo to Alex every now and then. He smiled back at her, pretending he cared about her photos. His memories were coming back.

He fought to keep them at bay as he stared at the shapes of the clouds above. After what seemed like an eternity of silence, he spoke up.

"Emily, I apologize for kissing you yesterday," he blurted without looking at her. His eyes focused on the clouds. He waited in silence and added, "I'm sorry." Still no response. He pushed, "And I've been thinking about what you said. I think I feel the same."

"What?" Emily finally replied.

Alex could feel her staring at him, but he didn't want to look at her. He continued.

"What you said. Last night. In the Pantheon. About missing us," he reminded her.

"Oh. Yeah," she said, sounding relieved. She put her camera down. She turned and lay on her back, looking toward the sky, and added, "What about it?"

"I've missed us too. But, at the same time, I was hurt and tired of feeling that loss I felt. When I was with you, around you, when I heard your name—it bothered me. I had to get over it. And the only way to do that, I thought, was to just shut you out. And so that's what I did."

Alex felt his voice begin to quiver. He took deep breaths as he continued. "But, I have to be honest with you. When you first asked to come visit, I hesitated. But I'm glad that, in the end, I agreed to have you come. This time that we've spent together made me realize how much I miss you too."

Emily offered no response. They both lay on the blanket, staring at the sky in awkward silence. Alex was teetering on getting up and moving on or pushing the topic further. He shifted, uncomfortably.

"What did we do wrong?" Emily finally responded.

Alex didn't reply. Although he was the one who'd started the conversation, he hadn't thought ahead. Now that Emily had replied, it was with a question he did not know how to answer. He was flustered. The topic was on the table and he realized he didn't like it. There was no turning back. They had entered a confrontation, and he realized he was afraid to poke further. He wanted to divert the subject. Give himself more time to think it through. What happens from here, he thought, would change their relationship. He could lose her forever, and as much as he had convinced himself he was okay with that, he freaked at the reality of it.

They lay in silence as Alex thought this through. He needed to say something. His mind swirled thinking of ways to end the conversation or to jump in further. Why did she ask him that question?

"Being stupid kids." He attempted a light-hearted response. "Teenagers are stupid and we were stupid. Simple as that."

"Right." Emily sat up, started to pack her bag, and repeated him. "Simple as that."

"Shit," Alex looked at his watch. "We've got to go."

"We do?" Emily immediately packed up her camera and gathered the trash back into her bag. "Will we make it?"

"Yes. I think so." He looked at the map, relieved to have found a way to stop the conversation. "We've seen all there is to see, so we just need to get back to the entrance and find our way to the bus stop. The ticket lady said there was a shortcut we can take, but we have to go now."

They quickly left the serenity of the park by way of a path straight from the small church sculpture back to the entrance gate. The ticket lady gave them instructions for the shortcut through the tiny town. Unfortunately, Alex and Emily still had to make their way back up the steep, windy hill.

The village was still quiet. It was as if no one lived there at all. They found the bus stop with no one there. They sat on a green metal bench and waited for the bus to hopefully arrive.

Finally, they were picked up, and they made their way back to the train station in Viterbo.

"Let's grab a coffee," Alex suggested. "I'm dying to have one."

They entered the bar attached to the train station. There was no one in sight except for the barman leaning against the counter. His eyes were glued to the TV set above the bar. Alex ordered an espresso for himself and a cappuccino for Emily. The barman set down two saucers, dropping the metal espresso spoons with a clink. He proceeded to make the drinks while trying to keep his eyes on the TV.

Alex looked up at the screen to see what it was the barman refused to miss. It was a cooking show set in an open field, and behind the IKEA-style modular kitchen was the bubbly face of Pernille Bjørn. It was her Scandinavian series finally airing on Italian national television. The show was not dubbed. Pernille was speaking in English and Italian subtitles floated at the bottom of the screen.

Pernille was wearing a frilly, lavender blouse and dark blue jeans under a hot pink apron with a print of golden vines creeping along the left, up to her chest. Alex knew it was an old episode. Her hair was longer, clipped up away from her face, giving her an attractive farm-girl look.

She held a large white bowl of colorful berries. She picked out a red fruit, then a blue fruit, and then a yellow one. *As a little girl, I remember helping my grandfather pick these berries from his farm* . . . She proceeded to pick the berries off the stems and scatter them onto a salad of field greens she had just plated.

Pernille turned back to her frying pan for a final flip of the white fish that she was sautéing in butter. She turned off the gas, removed the browned pieces, and gently placed them on top of the greens. She then raised the plate close to her gorgeous face, closed her eyes, and described the "incredible aroma."

She set the plate back on the counter, allowing the camera to show the dish in detail. Finally, from the drawer in front of her, she pulled out a fork and tasted her creation. She closed her eyes again and then explained all the flavors that danced in her mouth.

"*Che bella*," the barman said to Alex. He placed their espresso cups on the counter and said, "*Bellissima*."

"*Sì, certo*," Alex felt like he had to reply, like the barman needed assurance that Pernille was beautiful. The barman seemed happy with the acknowledgment and stepped back from the counter, folded his arms, and continued to watch as Pernille whipped fluffy white cream in a glass bowl.

"Wow," Emily chimed in. "She really is gorgeous. I mean, she looks amazing in person, but seeing her on screen here, she's more than just pretty; she's a successful model cooking fancy food in a field. I mean, *really*? I know I don't look like that when I'm cooking."

"Well," Alex teased her, "she is Scandinavian. I mean . . . those people are all beautiful. It's in their genes."

"Right," Emily replied and gave him a little stink eye.

On the screen, Pernille placed more berries into the fluffy cream and slowly ate it.

The train ride was longer on the way back to Rome because the train made more stops. As they got closer to Rome, more passengers boarded, men and women in their business attire, signaling to Alex that it was rush hour. Emily was leaning back in her seat, flipping through a magazine.

"Where did you get that?" he asked.

"Oh, it was sitting on the seat across from us," she replied and lifted the magazine. "Look! It's the Swatch ad you were telling me about. It's gorgeous."

The black-and-white photo was of Pernille leaning back on the fountain laughing, wrapped in the stole made of pure-white Swatch watches. Behind her stood Matteo in his black suit.

The ad looked classy and presented Pernille in a clean and glamorous way. But, while Matteo stood farther back from the camera, he was staring directly at it, which made him the more prominent figure in the ad. It was as if he was telling the viewer: *Look how I can land a beautiful lady.* Alex wanted to rip the ad to shreds.

Emily continued to flip through the pages. "Oh, look." She sat up and shared the magazine with Alex. "There's an article about her. What does it say?"

The article was accompanied by a photo of Pernille smiling while holding a large silvery fish above her head. It was a publicity photo from her cooking series and her cookbook. The headline read L'ITALIA LOVES PERNILLE BJØRN, LA CUOCA SCANDINAVA.

"At least they got a photo of her cooking," he replied. "Seems like a lovely headline. What magazine is this?" He turned it over. "Oh, this is one of my articles! All right!"

Alex was excited. Finally, he saw a reporter had actually paid attention and followed all of his instructions. The article went on to talk clearly about the Italian debut of Pernille's cooking series and the recent Italian release of her cookbook. It promoted an upcoming cookbook-signing event that was to take place at the Pincio in a week. Pernille would sign her books and then do a live cooking demonstration and answer questions from the audience.

"This article is perfect." Alex was smiling. He knew Eleonora would be ecstatic when she saw it. Maybe he had overreacted about the paparazzi at the soccer match. Maybe it really had worked in her favor, as Eleonora had explained to him. Maybe it wasn't all that bad.

"Congratulations." Emily sat back. "I'm sorry I'm going to miss the big event."

"Me too," Alex replied, almost somber. He realized his time in Italy with Emily was probably going to be his last with her. He knew he had to confront their situation again before she left. He had to come up with the courage before then.

"I'm exhausted. I'm thinking a simple dinner at home tonight," Alex said. "Then, later, we can go meet up with Pernille. What do you say?"

"I think that's a nice idea," Emily replied as she leaned against the window and closed her eyes.

CHAPTER 33

ALEX BUTTONED HIS shirt in front of the mirror that hung inside the large wooden armoire. The bedroom door was open. He heard Emily slide open her bedroom's pocket door, walk into the bathroom, lock the door, and turn on the shower.

The walk back from the train station had felt automatic. He had led Emily to a takeout eatery. They purchased basic pizzas and fried appetizers, and quietly ate them at the dining table back in the apartment.

While Emily showered, Alex finally had some time to think about his newly revived feelings for her. He'd thought he was over her. Or at least he'd thought he had succeeded in moving on from the idea of her. A sudden sense of shame came over him. How could his feelings be coming back?

The feelings were familiar to him. Again. They were feelings that continued to haunt him for many years. All the years he had known or interacted with Emily. The shame. The pain. The rejection. He didn't want to feel those emotions again, but they hit him by surprise in that dreaded park of monsters.

The pop of the lock on the bathroom door brought him back to reality. He heard Emily shuffle back to her room and close the pocket door.

Why had he bothered telling Emily that he missed her, just as she did? Why had he brought it up in the park? Why had he then brushed off the topic? He decided to find out how she felt about him.

The pocket door slid open. Emily came into his room, shaking her red hair dry with a towel.

"I'm still full from that pizza," she said as she held the towel in her left hand. "But, I might be hungry later."

"I agree," Alex replied, halting his thoughts. He shut the door to his old wooden armoire and put on his watch. "There will be passed hors d'oeuvres at the event, I'm sure. These things always have food. They're Italian."

"Of course," Emily smiled and followed Alex back to the kitchen. "That works. How do I look?" Emily stood in the doorway of her small room holding her arms out, showcasing her outfit. "It's the best I could do with what I brought."

"You look fine," Alex reassured her as he placed the dried silverware from the dish rack in the kitchen drawer. "I wouldn't be concerned about the other people there. Pernille said it's a casual club; I doubt anyone is going to be overly dressed. Don't worry about it."

Evenings in Trastevere made Alex smile in spite of himself. The narrow street leading toward Piazza Santa Maria was alive with people. The restaurants that lined the cobblestone pedestrian walkway were full. Alex and Emily passed through without stopping. Their destination was across the bridge, past the busy Campo de' Fiori.

They weaved their way through narrow streets. Alex led Emily to the right, down a street no wider than an alley. They approached a brown door with a well-dressed man standing out front. Alex said the ridiculous password, giving Emily a side smile and an eye roll. The man pulled open the heavy door and pointed them through the velvet curtain. On the other side of the curtain they were greeted by clusters of laughing party-goers and a crowd singing along to Italian classics.

Aptly called La Vespa, the popular lounge was known for playing the classics and hosting karaoke performances and impersonators. It seemed to be a '60s inspired evening, similar to the one at the Cin Cin. The patrons were dressed in era inspired garb and dancing along to Raffaella Carrà's "5353456" when Alex and Emily walked in. Although the women pulled the look off, most of the men looked as silly as Alex: short hair puffed as much as possible with an abundance of pomade.

Alex let Pernille know they had arrived via text. They then climbed down metal stairs lit up in blue with smoke machines working overtime all around them. It was like being on the set of a foreign film. They got to the landing as the sound of Celentano's "Impazzivo Per Te" began blaring from the speakers.

The room was shaped like an amphitheater—a large dance floor, theatre seating, private booths on one side, and three bars. Lights were changing colors as the smoke machines continued to blow out white puffy clouds. The stage hosted a large screen showing Fellini's *Nights of Cabiria*, while the puffy-haired crowd danced, looking straight out of the era.

"Wow, this was not at all what I expected!" Emily guffawed. "I love it."

"Indeed," replied Alex over the crowd. "And everyone seems to be having a blast." He took out his phone and read Pernille's response:

We see you.
Look at private booth at left bar.
See Teddy waving.

Alex looked to the left and saw Teddy waving at them with both hands. Upon seeing them, Alex felt underdressed.

Teddy was wearing a pure white linen blazer with a black shirt and a loosened, skinny, bright yellow tie. Pernille managed to look gorgeous in her teased coif. In it, she wore a lace ribbon tied into an oversized bow. Her sequined purple top sparkled underneath the multi-colored disco lights.

She shimmied out of the booth, exposing her strategic skirt slit and green and yellow heels. She greeted both Alex and Emily with the European double kiss on the cheeks and pulled Teddy's arms around her.

"So glad you joined us," she said, bouncing to the beat of Celentano's hit. "Shall we dance?" With her left hand, she grabbed Teddy and led the group to the dance floor.

Alex was bumped and jostled through the thick ensemble of people. He hated crowds. Pernille sensed his discomfort and pulled him away to an open area, leaving Emily nervously swaying next to Teddy.

"So she's almost leaving, huh?" Pernille said loudly over the music and crowd.

"Yes," Alex replied, but he didn't want to talk about it over the loud music. Besides, it wasn't like she wanted to have a deep discussion on the dance floor. Pernille was just being nice. "She leaves in a couple of days."

"Will you be at the big event? You'd better be there for me. I don't know if I can handle it on my own."

"Of course I'll be there," he assured her. "And you'll be fine."

The switch to Celentano's soft and romantic "Soli" came through the speakers. The crowd around them paired off and began to slow dance, as if at a prom. Pernille grabbed Alex's hands and followed suit.

"So, that's the girl of your dreams, huh?" She was speaking softly now.

"Dreams? No. She's just a friend."

"Well, good, because she doesn't seem like she wants to be in your dream."

"What?" Alex was shocked at Pernille's words. Alex turned them around and saw Emily held closely in Teddy's arms. Her eyes were closed and her head was practically resting on his chest. He, eyes also closed, swayed along with her. Their bodies moved closer and closer.

"Come on." Pernille led him hurriedly back to the booth. "Let's grab a drink."

"Well, shouldn't we, I mean, what about Teddy and Emily?"

"Oh, their dance love affair will end with the song. Don't worry about it. I'm not."

"Alex?" Pernille was waving her hand in front of his face. "Are you all right?"

"Huh? Oh, yeah." Alex couldn't stop looking at Emily and Teddy. She seemed so comfortable throwing herself all over him.

"Do you want to leave?" Pernille had her arm hooked in his.

"Huh?" Alex wasn't really listening to her. "Yeah, you have an early start tomorrow."

"Yes, you're right." She grabbed her sweater. "Let's get those two and go home. We've been here long enough." Pernille ran up to Teddy and tickled his sides. In his surprise, he unintentionally thrust his pelvis forward into Emily and then blushed as he backed away. Emily walked behind the couple as they left the dance floor, embarrassed, with her head hanging low but smiling.

The music had switched to the loud guitar riffs of grunge rock as the foursome left the club.

"Have fun tomorrow!" Pernille shouted from the taxi. "It was very nice meeting you, Emily. I hope you enjoyed Rome."

"I did, thank you," Emily replied. She tried to glimpse Teddy as he followed Pernille into the cab from the other side. "And it was nice meeting you both. Good luck with your event."

"Thank you." Pernille blew a kiss and sat back as Teddy leaned over.

"Cheerio, chaps!" he shouted as he tickled Pernille, making her shout with laughter. "Lovely meeting you," he continued as the window rolled up and the taxi pulled away.

"Wow," Emily said aloud. "He is perfect. I couldn't stop staring at him."

"I know." Alex aggressively waved down a second cab, a scowl on his face.

CHAPTER 34

THE NEXT MORNING, Alex didn't bother checking his emails. He didn't even make his morning espresso. Both he and Emily woke at seven, showered quickly, and set off to enjoy breakfast out. A good way to delay the conversation, thought Alex.

They stopped at the corner café and sat at a small table close to the metal bar run by the barbell-mustached bohemian who wore his typical exaggerated smile. The café was quiet. The staff seemed exhausted and still waking up from the night before. No sign of Patrizia in the place. He'd hoped she would be there. He wanted to see her again.

It was the last full day he'd have with Emily, and he had promised to take her to see his favorite sculptures in Rome. They made their way back to the Trevi fountain and up via Veneto, avoiding the elephant that had been in the room since her arrival.

He led Emily on a serene stroll through the park of the Villa Borghese. They went inside the museum and gawked with awe at Bernini's exquisite marble creation: *Apollo and Daphne*.

Daphne looked frightened, running from Apollo's determined grasp. Bernini had portrayed Daphne in the middle of a metamorphosis; bark was forming on her legs, her fingertips sprouting intricate leaves. Daphne was turning into a laurel tree.

"Isn't it beautiful?" he whispered into Emily's ear, purposefully brushing his lips on her cheek. She blushed and quietly listened. "Daphne was willing to do anything to get away from Apollo. Even pray to be turned into a tree." He stepped away and walked around the sculpture. He shrugged and exited the gallery, leaving Emily to her thoughts.

Alex was standing at another Bernini sculpture—*The Rape of Persephone*—when Emily caught up to him.

"This is incredible," Emily whispered. "Look at his hands. They look as if they're sinking into her flesh. And her face. She is screaming for help."

"Well, he's kidnapping her," Alex added as he walked around the art piece. "I'm just saying. Bernini really captured her fear. Are there tears?"

They examined Persephone's face closely. It was fixed in an expression of abject terror. There were indeed tears in her eyes.

"See how one arm appears to be pushing Pluto's face away while the other reaches up to the heavens?" Alex gently put his hand on Emily's back as he spoke and leaned in to her. He could feel her shaking. His face was close to Emily's. He thought he could kiss her again. She turned to face him, but he pulled away.

"I love this sculpture," Emily remarked. "But it's too intense."

Alex took her hand and led her into another room. Inside, they stumbled upon another of Bernini's famous sculptures. It was of David. His torso was twisted, frozen in the moment, before firing his slingshot.

"Well, now here's an amazing piece of work," Alex commented aloud as he walked around the sculpture. On the other side of it, he caught glimpses of Emily examining practically every inch of the figure's sculpted muscles. "It's amazing how these artists capture the shape and curves of the body. I mean, even down to the fibers of a muscle in action."

"I know," Emily responded in awe. "The sense of movement. And he's all muscular and powerful . . . "

"Obviously compensating for his small size." Alex quipped, and noticed Emily blush at his comment. "Compared to Goliath, I mean." He felt himself blush too. "Come on." He walked toward the exit. Emily followed.

They continued their stroll through the serene park, which was now filled with people enjoying a leisurely stroll. They passed the zoo, the park's Globe Theatre, and an open running track, and then they crossed a busy road into the area of the park known as the Pincio Hill. Around them, kids and adults were riding scooters or learning to rollerblade.

To the right, Alex and Emily heard children cheering. The cheers led them to a birthday party set up outside a small puppet theatre. A large woman in a blue peasant costume and exaggerated makeup came out of the theatre with a boisterous laugh. She was greeted by a stampede of small children, who seemed to know the show inside was about to begin.

Across the way, Alex spotted a stand for renting surrey bikes.

"Shall we rent one?" he asked Emily.

"Maybe later," Emily replied as she continued up the path. "I want to see that view."

Alex followed her to the stone wall that overlooked the city with a clear view of the world-famous dome of St. Peter's Cathedral. To their left was a path to a peach-colored, baroque-style building enclosed by a black gate.

"Oh, this is where the big press event will take place in a couple of days," Alex explained as they approached the gate from the side.

"This is beautiful," Emily said slowly as she photographed the building through the bars.

"We probably shouldn't take photos." Alex slowly pushed her hand holding the camera down. "You never know who's eating on the terrace there. And we don't want any security guys knocking us down for your camera. Ha, ha!"

"Shut up," Emily laughed as they continued to walk around the fence. "Tell me more about the event."

"Pernille is set to do a press event and live cooking demonstration out on the terrace there." Alex pointed through the bars. "I assume here, where the cars are, we'll have chairs set up for the press."

"You mean you'll get to eat here?" Emily asked.

"Well, not really. Maybe?" Alex replied. "I'll be working. Now I'm hungry," he added, taking her hand. "Let's get out of here and grab something a little more up our alley price-wise."

CHAPTER 35

INSTEAD OF NAPPING, Emily spent a good hour packing her bags in her small room. Alex, who had never been able to partake in the Italian siesta tradition himself, sat at the round table in the living room reading emails, mostly from Eleonora. Her first email was to inform him that she had his contract and it was ready to be signed. Alex was official. He was due to report back to a full day's work at the press event in the park. A gentle reminder that his "time off" had to end. In her second note, Eleonora provided a full itinerary for the event: Pernille would arrive early that morning at Casina Valadier to prepare the ingredients and make sure the food was cooked appropriately. Eleonora would accompany her there that morning. Pernille would then return to her hotel to dress for the event, which was due to begin at noon. At that time, Alex would take over, picking up Pernille and escorting her to the press event. Relieved that his job would finally be secure and he could soon put thoughts of Emily behind him in favor of work, he closed his laptop and washed up for dinner.

Alex pulled up his gray slacks, tucked in his pressed white shirt, and added a white-striped blazer, all inspired by the suaveness of Teddy Hume. He then looked through his drawers and around the room to see if he could rummage some fabric for a pocket square, to no avail. He fixed his hair, slicking it to the side as Teddy would do, and met Emily in the living room.

Alex hadn't told Emily the details of their destination. He only instructed her to dress for a nice dinner out, that a cocktail dress would suffice. She wore a black and beige cocktail dress with lace trim and a vibrant yellow belt. Her hair was clipped to the side with a teal satin flower. Her matching shoes were a delicate web of straps and buckles.

"Wow," he said while she twirled. "You really did yourself up nice. And on such short notice."

"Thank you," she replied, feigning a curtsy.

Under an opened umbrella, Alex guided Emily through the bustling shop-lined streets around Piazza di Spagna. The rain began to let up and the clouds quickly dispersed, revealing the last of the sunset reflected in the puddles below.

On the buildings surrounding them, shadows of neighboring structures formed. Emily commented on the beauty of one structure and then the next until they reached the famous Spanish steps. The sun was almost fully set as the tourist traffic died down, leaving the stairway nearly empty.

The amber light faded as they walked halfway up the steps and stopped on the first landing to admire the view of Rome. The city lights had just begun to glow as dusk swept over the skyline. Alex could have sworn he saw a tear in Emily's eye as she stared off into the night.

"This city is so damn beautiful." She placed her elbows on the stone wall. "It seems so unreal."

Alex remained quiet. He too perched his elbows on the wall and watched the people hustling about below. When he finally looked back at Emily, she had turned and was now leaning against the wall, facing Alex with her back to the piazza. Surprising even himself, he wrapped his left arm around her waist and pulled her to him. The kiss was so sudden that his right arm hung out in midair, as if still deciding whether to go along with the rest of his body. He felt her hands on his face as she kissed back. His free hand fell to her upper back and a week's worth of tension melted away. Emily softened her kiss and slowly pulled away.

"What are we doing?" she asked. She looked down and turned back toward the view.

Alex didn't know what to say. He didn't even know if what had happened was real. He smiled sheepishly.

"Sorry," he said. "I got caught up in the moment."

Emily didn't reply. She kept her eyes on the dome of St. Peter's Basilica.

"What are you thinking?" Alex finally asked, breaking a brutally awkward silence.

"Life," Emily sighed. "Just life, Alex." She turned around again. "And us."

"Us?"

"So much time has passed between us, Alex," Emily continued. "We've both been through so much. Separately, that is. It's been years."

"Too many years."

"And look at us." She was shaking her head, as if disappointed in both of them. "I mean, what was that? What's wrong with us?"

"What do you mean?"

"First, I kissed you when I got here. Then we kissed that night at the Pantheon. And now you kissed me again, and I had no problem kissing you back. Just like you had no problem kissing me back when I first kissed you." She was beginning to ramble.

"Emily . . . " Alex reached for her arm, but she moved away, eyes cast down. "Listen, we—"

"We *what* Alex?" She looked up at him with her arms folded. "We are idiots is what we are."

"No." He held her arms. This time she let him. "We are not idiots. We are, well, it's like that saying. I don't know who said it. God, I sound like a moron, but it's something like 'If you don't make a choice, life will choose for you' or something like that. Well, that's what happened to us. We let life choose for us. And now we can finally choose for ourselves."

"Well, I've always felt like you couldn't decide if you wanted me or . . . "

"Or what?"

"Nothing." She pushed away from the wall and started off down the steps. Alex followed.

"What do you mean, *nothing*?" Alex caught up to her at the ship fountain. She reached out to touch the ship's bow. "Emily?"

"Forget it, Alex," she continued, eyes still focused on the fountain. "It doesn't matter." She turned back to him. "Let's go eat. I'm famished."

"No," he insisted. He wasn't going to let her off that easily. She was finally opening up to him. She was beginning to reveal her true feelings. He was disappointed that she stopped herself. "Emily, we can't just let this stupid cloud drift over us. It's got to end."

"Well, it has, hasn't it?" Emily stepped down from her perch on the ship fountain. "I mean, you're here and I'm in San Francisco. So, it doesn't matter. Our lives are separate. Besides, you know as well as I do that you and I never would have worked. You would have gotten sick of me. And to be honest, that would hurt me more than anything."

"So that's it. You decided not to even bother, to push me away all these years because you were afraid of getting hurt?"

"Just like you did. You said so yourself in your letter to me many years ago."

"But don't you see how silly that was?"

"Of course I did. But it's too late. And like you just said: *Life has chosen for us.* We need to move on. And I've been trying to. I want us to see things as they are, and not go on hurting ourselves. And that means you need to let it end as well." She hooked her arm under his and led him away from the fountain. "Now, which way is it to this special restaurant?"

Alex was stunned into submission. Had she just admitted that she, too, felt regret for not pursuing him? What was she saying? And she had easily dismissed the idea as if it were nothing. He could feel her guiding him swiftly across the cobblestones; he was powerless to even slow his own steps. He had been so certain the conversation would go a different way. A sense of shame smothered his insides.

"So, that's it?" Alex regained enough composure to speak up, though not to break the spell of their forward progression on the sidewalk. "It's done?"

"Alex, there's no doubt that you and I have some . . . some connection. I don't know what it is anymore. It's a closeness that I can't explain. But we live completely separate lives."

"But you're here. Why did you come here?"

"To see you. My friend."

Alex stopped dead in his tracks. It was so abrupt that Emily nearly tripped as her arm came free from his.

"I'm sorry, Emily," Alex laughed as he replied. "But don't stand there and think for one second that I believe that you came here to *see an old friend.*"

"Alex." Emily said it slowly, as if warning him not to go too far with whatever he was about to say.

"I mean, really Emily." He stalked off around the corner, not even considering where he was going. Emily followed close on his heels. "Who the hell would believe that? Seriously—"

Rounding the corner, Alex nearly plowed into a well-dressed group of Italians, smoking cigarettes and laughing loudly. He looked up and realized, to his surprise, that they were standing in front of the same restaurant he had planned to take Emily to all along.

"Well, what do you know," he said through a forced grin. "Looks like a happening time inside. Let's check it out, shall we?" He grabbed Emily by the hand and, with grim determination, walked past the cluster of smokers and threw open the door to the restaurant, flooding the street with the sounds of the insistent, frenetic jazz playing inside.

CHAPTER 36

THE MELODY FROM the piano and trumpet grew louder as Alex and Emily pushed their way through the violet velvet curtain hanging inside the restaurant doorway. The dark wood interior reminded Alex of being backstage at an old theatre. The room was square with tables set all around the edges. The floor was made of wide wooden planks. In the center of the room was a dance floor, where three couples performed some sort of jive dance. At the other end of the room sat the band.

Along the walls hung oil paintings of still life with rich, bold colors matching the rest of the room. More velvet curtains hung along the wall, leading Alex to look up and notice a second-floor balcony along the interior border.

The pair stood at the host stand waiting to be noticed.

"I'm going to find the restroom," Emily said softly as she walked along a long row of velvet-topped stools that accompanied the oak bar topped with mini antique lamps. Alex stared at Emily's silhouette lit by a glow of light shining from the kitchen doorway. The conversation on the Spanish steps disappointed him. He was upset with her, but he couldn't keep his eyes off her. He continued to watch until she turned left just before the kitchen doorway and entered the restroom.

He needed to get back into that tense conversation with Emily. He was convinced he was getting through to her. Convinced she may be in love with him. Convinced that he had fallen in love with her, once again. He had nearly gotten her to acknowledge her feelings for him. He had to come up with a plan to break down her wall, but what that plan would be, he didn't know.

Alex was surprised by a bump as a waiter rushed passed him carrying two plates of lamb chops. His eyes followed the server as he brushed around the small round tables and delivered the warm plates to a couple in the corner. All the servers were dressed in crisp white, button-down shirts, pitch-black bow ties, and long black aprons that hung from the waist.

"Welcome," said the returning host. He too was dressed in black and white. He wore round glasses with thin wire frames and a very wide smile. "I'm sorry to keep you waiting. My name is Roberto. Do you have a reservation?"

"Hello, Roberto," Alex replied. "No, we don't. We will need a table for two." It was then Alex decided. The opportunity for convincing her with conversation had passed. It was time for drastic measures. "Roberto, listen. Tonight is a special occasion for us. I want to surprise her. I plan to propose to her later tonight, and I want to make this memorable. Please don't tell her."

"*Che bello*," Roberto replied. "Don't you worry, signore. We will make this a special occasion."

"Thank you. And, please, don't tell her. She's coming now."

Emily joined Alex at the host stand. She looked as if she was trying to hide her nervousness.

"And welcome. Signorina?" Roberto gestured for Emily to follow him toward the dining room.

"Hello," Emily replied in English, grabbing hold of Alex's hand as if he were protecting her from certain danger.

"Very well." Roberto looked at his book one last time. "I have a special table for you." He continued speaking to Alex in Italian while pointing with his arm toward the dining room.

Alex and Emily followed the graceful host away from the bar and into the main dining hall on their left. The music had calmed, allowing the din of conversations to fill the open room. Alex looked up at the balcony that bordered the room. The tables up there were full of people boisterously chatting over cocktails and meals. Roberto seated Alex and Emily on the main floor at a small, secluded table in the far-right corner.

Alex and Emily sat next to each other on the banquette facing the now empty dance floor. Roberto handed them their menus and was gone.

The round table had pure-white table linen and vintage-looking plates and glasses. A waiter appeared, greeted the couple, and poured water into the rose-tinted glasses. Throughout the recitation of specials and taking of drink orders, Alex and Emily avoided eye contact. When the wine was poured, they sat and sipped in silence. This reassured Alex that the tension was still in the air.

He stared at the empty dance floor, but it was as if the kiss and conversation on the Spanish steps was playing out in front of him again and again. The idea of winning Emily over was floating around in the air, but he could not grasp it. He needed to move things forward.

The waiter returned to take their order. To prevent Emily from understanding, Alex proceeded to speak to him in Italian. "Tonight is a special evening and we are very romantic, so we may end up feeding each other." The waiter was overjoyed. He explained that Roberto had advised him and that he would do the best he could to accommodate. The waiter then took their order, winked, and walked away.

"What did you order?" Emily asked suspiciously.

"Oh, a special pasta dish. But, well, it's just the oddest thing . . . " Alex picked up his glass. The rich red wine buoyed his confidence with every sip.

"What's odd about it?" She sipped her wine in kind.

"Well, he told me that the restaurant has a theme tonight." Alex pretended to be confused. "That tonight's dinner has a special twist."

"Yes . . . "

"Well," he smiled. "I ordered that pasta dish. The carbonara."

"So?"

"Well, apparently, the diners are required to feed each other the first course, the pasta dish." He shook his head and sipped his wine. "It's going to come on one big plate. We are expected to feed each other from that same plate."

"What?" She sat back and laughed. "He didn't say that. That's just silly."

"He did. I know. It's, well, it's odd."

Emily looked around the room and, Alex realized too late, didn't see any of the other patrons feeding each other. She turned back to Alex.

"No one else seems to be doing it," she said.

"I know." Alex needed an out. "That's what I meant by *odd*. Maybe it was the specific pasta dish? The carbonara." He had to keep the lie going. It was his only hope.

Emily frowned and sipped her wine. The waiter arrived with a platter of the spaghetti. He set it between Emily and Alex. He then proceeded to remove the silverware, leaving them only one fork.

"Alex," Emily hit him under the table. "Ask him why."

Alex spoke again in Italian to the waiter. He asked him an innocent question about the art on the walls and listened intently as the waiter told him about the landscape paintings and the décor. Alex thanked him and allowed him to return to his work. He then turned to Emily, faced with the daunting task of inventing the story he'd pretended to hear from the waiter.

"Apparently, this restaurant is one of the oldest in Rome," he lied. It would have to come to him as he went along. "According to legend, this building was the home of some poor artist who was in love with a wealthy girl. They met one day as the girl was shopping for art along this street."

Alex didn't know what to say. He didn't even remember what his point was supposed to be.

"I've heard of this story before, but I never knew it was here." He took another long sip of wine to stall and tried to continue. "Anyway, they met and she would come every day, pretending to peruse the art as an excuse. She never bought any. At least not from him. But she always made a stop to visit him."

Emily's head tilted in confusion. Alex continued.

"Obviously, they had some passionate love affair . . . and um . . . then one night, she decided to surprise him. She decided she would run away with him. She packed a small bag, snuck out of her house, and went to his studio. Oh, which was here, I suppose!"

Alex was so proud of himself for remembering to connect his rambling tale back to the restaurant that he almost lost the thread of his own shaky narrative.

"Anyway," Alex continued. The story just kept flowing out of him. "She showed up unexpectedly and found the place vandalized. The windows were smashed, and I believe the art was torn. She found him in the corner all bruised. He hadn't paid his debt, so he was beaten. You know, the typical poor man in the wrong crowd kind of thing."

Emily's eyes were growing wider. She looked around to see if anyone nearby was listening to Alex's fantastical tale.

"So she took care of him. She cleaned him, washed up the place, and fed him, of course. The artist claimed that because of her empathy, he was *revived*. He said he was inspired. He painted a series of landscapes that resulted in major sales and wealth. Then the two lovers finally ran off together. He is remembered to have said that Clara—that was her name, the girl's—fed him life, love, and inspiration. So, the restaurant—which stands in the location of this artist's studio, remember—celebrates his inspiration every month, by making the patrons feed each other."

The silence was deafening. Alex felt a bead of sweat dripping down into his left brow, and he realized that his right knee was jigging up and down so furiously that he was knocking the table.

"Wow," Emily shook her head in disbelief. Then a wide smile grew on her face. "That is so romantic. I mean, only in Italy would they celebrate something so simple."

Alex took an audible deep breath and knocked back the last of his wine, immediately refilling his glass from the open bottle on the table.

"Yeah, so I guess we need to feed each other this plate of pasta."

"Was this what she fed him?"

"Oh, right." *Good idea Emily!* "Yes, this is a typical Roman dish of the poor. So, yes, this was one of the dishes she would have fed him. Yes."

"Who was the artist? Anyone famous?"

"Um, good question." *Shit.* "It's some Pietro something. Some of his paintings are on the walls here."

"Wow. That is beautiful." Emily looked around the room, squinting at some landscape paintings in the far corner. "This place is wonderful."

"Let's dig in." Alex pulled the platter closer to them and grabbed the single fork.

The spaghetti was plated in a beautiful nest of yellow. It was coated in egg and Pecorino-Romano cheese with bits of crispy pancetta. Alex twirled the fork, pulling several strings of pasta out of the dish. He lifted the fork and turned to Emily who was watching him as she held the napkin onto her chest.

"You can't feed me that," she laughed. "That's way too much for one bite. Are you serious?"

"What? It's a good bite. Looks delicious."

"Let me take that. I'll feed you." She gently took the forkful of pasta from Alex and held it up to his mouth.

The cheese coating, thickened by the rich egg, and the salty crisp pancetta swirled on his taste buds. Alex let his tongue wrap itself in the moist and salty pasta, welcoming the sharp heat of ground black pepper on his palette.

He picked up the fork that Emily had returned to the plate, already wrapped in a smaller bite of the pasta. She closed her eyes and let Alex place the sampling in her mouth. Alex stared at her as she slowly chewed the food. He had always liked watching people eat because he felt that the motion of the jaw was similar to the motion of a passionate kiss. As he watched her, a sense of comfort came over him. He liked being around Emily. He was happy she was with him, in that moment, in Rome. The anxiety that had plagued him the earlier part of her visit was melting away. In the years that had passed, he'd forgotten how wonderful it felt to just be next to her.

"So, I know this is going to be hard, but I think it's time we finish our conversation," he said after chewing a second forkful. "I mean, we seem to find ways to approach the subject but never really fully attack it."

"Alex," she sipped her wine. "Let's just enjoy our night. Don't do this."

"I'm not doing anything. I just want to clear the air between us. End this illusion."

"Illusion?"

"Emily," he pressed on absentmindedly, twirling more pasta. "It's hard for me to say this, but I have to say it. You know I do."

"Say what?" She gently wiped her lips with her cloth napkin and sat back.

"All the years we've known each other. You've always denied your feelings for me."

"Alex—"

"I mean . . . " He sat back, holding his wine glass, abandoning the fork. "All the crap you went through with Vic. And over the years, I was there for you. To help you. To catch you when you fell."

"And I love you for that." Emily sat up and touched the hand he'd left resting on the table. "You mean so much to me, Alex. You always have and you always will. You know that."

"But, you do admit you wanted me." He let her keep her hand on his. "Even during your marriage."

"Stop it." She removed her hand, looked down, and adjusted her napkin. "You know I loved Vic. I was wrong for what I did to him, and it killed me to hurt him like that." Emily's eyes watered. She sat back and sipped her wine again. "I don't want to talk about this."

"We have to, Emily. Don't you see?" Alex motioned between the two of them. "This can't go on. You know that. We've been fighting this for years. When you invited me to that wedding,

I wanted to die. I couldn't bear to watch you walk down that aisle."

"I remember you telling me you couldn't make it."

"Well, I didn't want to go."

"I was sad when you told me you wouldn't come."

"But, as a friend, I refused to miss your big day. I'm sure Vic would have preferred I stay in Boston."

"That's not true. He liked you."

"No. Well, he definitely didn't like our relationship—you and I—whatever this is."

"Stop it. Alex, I came here to reconnect with you. I miss you. It's been, what? Seven years? And every now and then, I think of you. I go to a restaurant and think *Alex would love this place.* I hear a Cranberries song and think of that amazing concert we went to. I miss you. A lot."

Alex leaned forward. "Emily, but you are thinking these things while in a relationship with another man. You seem to be doing it all over again. You did this when we first met. We were together and then you decided to tell me you had a boyfriend—whoever it was back then, I don't even know his name—and it definitely didn't come up in the library. It didn't come up during any of the time we spent together in Boston. Not until he had returned from wherever he was."

"Stop it," Emily said again sharply. She dropped the fork she had been fiddling with, looked down again, and flattened the napkin on her lap.

"You did this to your marriage." Alex ignored her. "And now, it sounds like you're doing it again. I mean, why would you come here? Why would you leave him and come here? Just to reconnect with an old friend? That is ridiculous. Just fess up that you're in love with me. Tell me. Tell me you've come here to spend the rest of our lives together. Tell me. Tell me now."

Emily didn't respond. She looked away, took a sip of her wine, and sat quietly. Finally she broke her silence.

"Why me?" she blurted out. She sat back and folded her arms. Alex didn't respond. He was confused by the question. Emily asked again. "Why me, Alex?

"What do you mean, *why you?*"

"You keep implying that over the years, you were in love with me. You wanted to be with me. You missed me." She sat up, arms on her lap. "But not once did you show me that that's how you really felt. It was all words, Alex. You never acted. You never made a move."

Alex was getting angry. "Emily, what are you talking about? Other than the time we were together—while you were with someone else, I will remind you again—you never made it convenient to do so."

"Convenient?!" She seemed at a loss.

"You were always the serial dater." He poured more wine. "You went from one man to another, with no break in between. I didn't want to be that guy, in the middle again. I didn't like it when you surprised me the first time back in college. I never wanted to be that guy breaking up the couple, taking you away. That guy never ends up with the girl."

"Well, *did you* end up with the girl?" She sat back and took another sip of her wine.

"So, is that why you're here?" he asked, almost snapping at her.

"What are you talking about?" She twirled more pasta and then dropped the fork in exasperation, giving up again on the idea of the meal altogether.

He couldn't look at her. He stared into his wine glass.

"Did you come all the way out here to tell me that it was my fault? That our . . . our inability to connect romantically was my fault?"

"No, of course, no—"

"Because a lot of it was you."

"Me?!"

"Yes, you." He sat up straight now, with both hands on the table. "How many times did I have to tell you I wanted to be with you? How many years have gone by that you knew how I felt for you—as you just admitted—and you led me on anyway? With that letter and the romantic mixtapes and . . . and now you tell me that you weren't sure how I felt because I didn't make a move to break up your marriage? That is bullshit."

"Alex, stop." She touched his hand again.

"No. We need to settle this crap. I'm done putting it off."

"Alex—"

"Why do you do this? It's as if you just like being wanted by me. I never imagined you to be so egotistical and shallow."

"Shallow? Alex, that's enough."

"Yes, shallow." He pulled his hand off the table. "It's like, when you feel down or depressed, you turn to me. When things don't go so well at home, you know I'll be there to build you up. Hearing my affection for you, you feel wanted and better about yourself. Well, I'm done. I've *been* done. I'd closed that door between us and you *knew* that, and *that's* why you came here, isn't it?"

Emily was quiet. She just looked at him in silence. Alex went on.

"You came because, why? Maybe life isn't going so well with your new lover? I don't know. But you came here to be sure I hadn't really let you go. You couldn't handle not being wanted by me."

"Alex, stop it."

"It bothered you to no end that I've moved on. And you just couldn't have it. You want me around, for what, I don't know.

If you were truly in love with this latest guy, you wouldn't need me. But you're *still* not sure, you stupid—"

"Alex!" Emily leaned forward and slapped him.

Alex sat back in the booth with his hand to his cheek. The conversation had escalated well beyond what he'd imagined, but underneath the shame, he was glad that he had struck a nerve. He looked around the room. Somehow, no one seemed to have noticed.

After a moment of silent avoidance, Emily sat forward and again placed her hand on his.

"I'm sorry, Alex," she said with a slight tremble in her voice.

"It's fine." Alex took his hand away, continued to avoid her eyes, and sipped his wine.

"Alex," Emily continued, "I need you to stop this. You don't love me. You haven't for a long time. You only think you do."

"What is that supposed to mean?" His reply was sharp as he reestablished eye contact.

In her green eyes, brimming with tears and pleading with him to be reasonable, he saw his answer. Emily was right. Sure, he had loved her at one point, but not anymore. Not on the Spanish steps. Not in the Enchanted Park. Not in the Pantheon. Not by the window in his bedroom when she'd first arrived. He'd known it at the soccer match. He'd known it at her wedding. And he knew it now, mindlessly twirling the fork in the noodles, that she was right: he didn't love her.

It wasn't love. It was a desperate grasp to keep a hold on her. He realized he too was to blame for the constant pull. He needed Emily. He needed her to keep coming to him. It wasn't Emily he wanted. It was what she represented: his past.

He suddenly felt old. Without the protection that his obsession with Emily had afforded him, he saw clearly how much the time they had spent together over the years, those years of promise and potential, had held him strong since.

Through all the defeat and disappointment life had thrown his way. It wasn't Emily he wanted. It was his youth. It was the hope. He had instead lived a life of false hope. Wasting chances for the promise of what would never be. The promise of keeping his past, his youth, alive. Was he dead without it? Was he just nothing now?

"Alex." He finally heard Emily calling his name. "Alex. Talk to me." He wanted to run away.

"Alex," Emily continued. "Are you okay?"

He needed to leave. He stood up.

"Alex, where are you going?"

He couldn't look at her. She was clearly a figment of his imagination. A ghost from his past that he never wanted to see again. A living portrait of a life wasted.

"I think I need some air." The words came out in a rasp. "I'm sorry." He was gone before she could reply.

CHAPTER 37

ALEX PUSHED HIS way through the crowd loitering outside of the restaurant and into the driving rain. The group snickered at him, accusing him of being a staggering drunk. He wanted nothing more than to just walk away, but he had left his umbrella at the table. It was just as well. He couldn't leave her; she wouldn't know how to get back.

He ducked under a portico a couple of doors down from the restaurant. He leaned against the wall, his back to the restaurant, and stared at the rings the raindrops created in each puddle, reflecting the streetlights. More light and a burst of jazz filled the alleyway.

"Alex!" Emily called out. Her footsteps got louder as she approached him, offering him the open umbrella. "Alex, I'm sorry."

"Let's not talk about it." He looked away and lifted the collar of his blazer, holding it tighter around him as if Emily brought a chill with her.

They stood under the streetlight for a moment and said nothing to each other. Emily broke the silence.

"I took care of the bill." She rubbed his arm. Alex shifted away and stood straight.

"Let's get going and out of this rain. I just want to go home." They walked down the street and quickly flagged a taxi.

They remained silent during the ride to the apartment. When they arrived, Alex shook out the umbrella and threw it in the corner by the door. He removed his jacket and walked straight into his bedroom, shutting the door behind him. He didn't bother with the light. He undressed in the dark and lay on his bed. The only light came from the streetlights that crept through the blinds.

He heard Emily slide the door to her guest room shut. He shifted in bed to face the window and stared at the light trickling through, listening to the faint noise of the street below. He could make out the crowds talking and imagined people rushing over the cobblestones to get out of the rain. He listened to the tinkling jazz piano from Cin Cin. It reminded him of Patrizia, hard at work downstairs, and he chastised himself for not having the courage to ask her what had happened between them. Was she another wasted chance? The revelation from the confrontation with Emily at the restaurant immediately consumed him again. He felt like a failure. He wasted his life waiting for his chance with her. What chance? What was it all for?

He heard a light knocking on his bedroom door. He didn't respond. The door slowly crept open. Alex didn't turn around. He stayed motionless, staring at the window as Emily whispered.

"Alex? Are you awake?" He heard her come closer. He felt the mattress shift under her weight as she sat on the opposite side of the bed. "Alex? Please talk to me. I'm leaving tomorrow. Please don't let me go like this. I don't want this time together to end in angry silence."

A car below had just pulled up. People laughed and shouted with joy. The car doors slammed shut and it pulled away.

Emily finally rose from the bed and opened the bedroom door to leave.

"Wait," he said with his back still to her.

The door stopped.

"Lay down with me?"

The door closed quietly and for a moment Alex wasn't sure if she'd stayed or gone. Then she climbed onto the bed and wrapped her arm around him. Alex shifted to face her and searched the speckles of light reflecting off Emily's green eyes. They stared at each other in the silence.

When he finally leaned in and kissed her, he was surprised at how responsive she was. He shifted onto her, resting on his right arm, as their kiss intensified. Neither spoke. Only the sounds of heavy breathing and the rain, now pouring heavily outside, filled the room as the kisses became almost animalistic. They undressed each other and rolled aggressively on the sheets.

* * *

They lay in bed, warm and sweaty, out of breath and still drunk from the sex. Alex freed his left leg from the tangled sheet and turned his body to once again face the window. Emily lay quietly staring at the ceiling. She eventually shifted on her side and faced Alex's back. Her fingers lightly traced his shoulder blades.

"Alex," Emily whispered.

He didn't respond. He watched the rain falling against the shutters and the light from the streetlamps casting shadows on the walls. The music from the streets below struggled to compete with the sound of the pounding rain.

"Alex, I admire you," Emily continued, still tracing his shoulders and upper back. "You've talked about moving to Europe for a while and you actually did it. Even if you don't know how long you'll stay here, you are here. You are doing exactly what you said you would. And I admire you for that. You know—" She adjusted herself on the bed and continued, "You were right, what you said when I first got here."

"What do you mean?" Alex was relieved that Emily was finally bringing the discussion to him.

"You were right. I did come here to check on you. I didn't like that you'd left. Although we hadn't lived in the same city, I guess I felt comfortable that you were at arm's length. But I didn't realize I felt that way until you left the country.

"When you posted your big announcement about the move to Italy, it hit me. I didn't know what it was that bothered me. I guess I didn't want to believe what it was, what it is, what it could be, maybe?" Emily shifted closer to him, her naked body against his back. She reached over his chest, found his hand, and wrapped her fingers in his.

"Alex, I was selfish. All that time, that you and I kept in contact, wrote each other, sent those mixtapes to each other, I loved it. I loved having that special connection with someone. I didn't want it to ever end.

"Even during these last years that we hadn't spoken, I still thought about you. I followed you online. I knew what you were up to. It just made me feel like we were still, I don't know, connected, I suppose. At least, it made me feel like I still had you in my life. And that made me feel like no matter what might happen, everything would be fine because you would be there, like always."

Alex quietly listened, his eyes fixated on the rain. He didn't know how to respond. In fact, he wasn't even sure he liked what he was hearing.

He wanted Emily to tell him she loved him. That she wanted to leave her boyfriend for him. It didn't sound like that's where the conversation was headed. Nowhere in Emily's speech did she mention romance.

"Alex," she said, "I'm sorry for kissing you when I first got here. And for what just happened. It was wrong of me. I feel so awful about it. When you moved here, I felt like you'd abandoned me. I guess that initial kiss was my childish way of trying to put a claim on you. Stupid, I know. And as for what just happened, I can't even explain." Emily let go of his hand and shifted away. "I don't know. Was this a goodbye?" She lay on her back and didn't say anything more. She was done with her confession.

Alex suddenly felt awake. His eyebrows rose as he shifted onto his back. He took a deep breath. Was this a last goodbye? He had to say something. Even though he had been the one who pushed for this discussion, he wasn't prepared to follow through, to do what must be done. He turned toward her, reluctantly, and propped himself up on his elbow.

"Emily . . . " He wrapped his arm around her waist and held her tight. "I think we both knew how this was going to end. I suppose you're right." The streetlights exposed the glistening tears in her eyes as Alex said the words. "We do have to end this. We both know that we can't be friends. I mean, look at us. Friends don't do this." With his eyes, he gestured to their naked bodies. "This is hurting us."

She pulled away, lifted the sheet around her, and sat up staring at him. "Let's just enjoy this last night. Please?"

She wasn't any better at letting it go than he was.

"Fine." Alex lay on his back again and opened his arms. "Let's not talk about this anymore. Let's just lay here and enjoy each other's company for the last time."

"Shh." Emily tightened the sheet around herself and then settled into his embrace.

Alex couldn't resist. "*This* is really why you came here. Because you knew we had to end this."

"I *told* you why I came here—"

"To pull me back in."

"Stop it."

Alex said nothing more. He lay beside her in the dark and closed his eyes. Soon after, he felt Emily wrap her leg around his torso and rest her head on his shoulder. They fell asleep to the mountainous wails of a jazz soloist and the last of the falling rain.

CHAPTER 38

EARLY THE NEXT morning Alex awoke to find Emily gone from his bed. He was relieved. He didn't want to face what had happened between them in his bedroom, neither the sex nor the conversation.

He heard her coming out of the shower and sliding back into the guest room. He quickly hopped into the shower, dressed, and joined her in the living room, where she was waiting with her packed bags.

They stood at the bar at Cin Cin for a quick coffee. Alex put down his coffee cup, paid the barista, and took hold of Emily's suitcase.

"We should get to the airport," he said. "Morning traffic and all."

Almost unwillingly, he dragged the suitcase behind them to the bus stop. How they would bring themselves to say their final goodbyes, he didn't know. He didn't want to think about it.

On the bus, he kept looking at her sad face as she watched Rome pass her by.

"I'm sorry I didn't say goodbye to Pernille," she said. "I hope the event goes well for her. For you both."

"I'll call her when I get back," Alex replied. "She'll be fine. It's just a tiny live demonstration in front of the press and a book signing. She's used to that."

As he said the words, he knew he was trying to convince himself all was good, but deep down he was nervous as shit. Having Emily there had distracted him from doing his best work for Pernille. He supposed he was limited in what he could do anyway.

"You don't have to come to the airport with me, you know," Emily said to him. "I think I can handle it. I mean, if you could just help me find the train to the airport, once I'm on it, I should be good. Seriously."

"But, I want to see you off."

"Alex . . . " she tilted her chin down and looked at him over her sunglasses. "You have a big day coming up. You need to get back to work. You probably should get back and prepare. You need to be there for Pernille. I don't want you to jeopardize that. You should go."

The bus pulled into the train station. Alex pulled Emily's suitcase to the ticket kiosk and jabbed the buttons. His nerves were getting to him; the ticket machine flashed an error message. Alex slid over to the next machine: same error. He kicked the ticket machine repeatedly until Emily pulled him away.

"Alex!" Emily looked around them, embarrassed. "What is wrong with you?"

"The damn thing's not working!"

"Will you calm down?" She returned to the machine and started the process over in English.

Alex paced in a tiny circle around the suitcase, breathing heavily, as Emily reached into her bag, slid her credit card into the machine, and tapped "Continue" on the touch screen, allowing the ticket to print.

"You need to relax." Emily grabbed the handle of her suitcase. "Now, where's my train?"

"This way," he blurted and led her through the station. It was clear they were both angry, but Alex had no idea why. "Emily, are you upset?"

"No," she said softly as she shook her head. "I guess I just didn't expect to say goodbye like this."

"Like what?"

"With you all angry." She stopped. "I told you, you don't have to come with me."

"Emily, please." He took back her suitcase and started toward the train terminal. "I don't have time to deal with this."

"Alex." She stood her ground. Alex turned around and rolled the suitcase back to her.

"Emily," Alex said as he looked her in the eyes. "Don't start getting all angry with me."

"You kicked the machine—"

"I just wanted to buy a friggin' ticket and move on with my life."

"You mean you just want me gone so you can move on with your life." She wrestled her bag back again and stalked off toward the platform at the far end of the station.

Alex caught up to her standing on the platform, watching the train from the airport pull up. She did not acknowledge his presence.

"I'm sorry, Emily," he said to her. "I don't know what came over me."

She reflexively checked for the ticket in her hand.

"Don't leave like this," he said. "Please don't leave without a proper goodbye. This is the last—"

"Stop *saying* that." In an instant she was crying into his shoulder. "Oh, Alex." Emily wrapped her arms around him. "I'm going to miss you!"

"Shh." Alex stroked the back of her head to calm her. "It's okay. It's all right. Hey, listen. I'm glad you came."

"I don't know when I'll see you." She was calming down, rubbing her eyes. "*If* I'll see you." She pushed away and looked into his eyes. "Do you really want never to see me again?"

Alex knew that the moment to finally close the door on Emily had come. It was like she was standing on the other side of the door, daring him to shut it.

"Emily . . . " He was stalling. "Let's get you on the train."

"Say it!" She was shouting. "Tell me you don't want to see me again. No. Wait. Don't tell me. I don't want to hear it." She lifted her suitcase and turned her back to him.

"Emily . . . "

She put her hand up, still refusing to look at him. "Don't say anything." She breathed deeply, trying to regain some composure. Still avoiding his eyes, she finally said, "Goodbye, Alex. And thank you. For everything." She took a last deep breath and boarded the train.

Alex watched through the window and could see Emily roll her suitcase into a cabin. She sat down and looked back at him, still standing there on the platform where she had left him. The train began its slow roll out of the station. Alex kept his eyes on her until she disappeared into the distance. Never once did she turn away.

CHAPTER 39

ALEX SAT ON the stone bench with the Emperor sprawled at his feet. The cat had crawled through the lower gap of the entrance, circled in the space between Alex and the gate, and then propped himself on the ground.

Alex sat quietly, staring into the ruins and reminiscing about the week with Emily. That even though they had reached it in a round-about way, he felt comfortable that they had finally broached the topic of their relationship. Still, he felt they had not gotten through it all.

Both were to blame for avoiding or deterring each other from following through with the conversation. In the end, Alex was confident that he and Emily understood the inevitable outcome: the idea of them was over. Alex knew his desire for Emily was not about loving her. It was a plea to hold on to his past, his youth, that he felt had gotten further and further away from him. Although, saddened by the idea that his past was never coming back, he did feel a sense of relief, like a heavy weight had been lifted off his shoulders. When Emily's train had pulled away from the platform, it had taken Alex's past, his youth, with it.

Alex knew that it was time to really move on without any reservation or false idea of a possibility with Emily and his past. He hoped that this resolution, this closure, would allow him to move forward both in life and in love. He hoped it meant he would be able to fully commit himself to someone without any thought of Emily or his past.

He hoped too that Emily understood she could not continue reaching out to him for comfort. She had to be fair with whomever she had committed herself to. Alex knew she would probably be married again soon, and he didn't care. He just wanted her, and all of the emotions that came with her, out of his life.

The Emperor meowed, let out a long stretch, and flapped his tail.

"Hey buddy." Alex reached down to pet him, but the cat snuck underneath the bench and rubbed against Alex's ankles. Alex shifted to see him, but the Emperor had made his way back to face Alex and meowed again.

"So, you think I did the right thing? Letting her go? Time to move on, right?"

The Emperor looked back at Alex, got up on all fours again, and let out another long stretch accompanied by a yawn. He circled around one more time and skedaddled back into the ruins.

"Wait!" Alex reached out to him. "Where are you going? What the f—, I'm talking to you! Whatever." It was an abrupt exit, but then again, he couldn't expect more from a cat.

Alex stood up and hailed a taxi.

CHAPTER 40

BUZZ. BUZZ. ALEX sat in the lobby of the St. Regis Hotel ignoring Eleonora's fifth "just checking in" text of the morning. He stared at his reflection in the mirror. He wasn't impressed with what he saw. He wore khakis, a button-down, and a green blazer. If he hadn't made time to talk to that cat like a crazy person, he probably could have taken more care with his appearance.

He was upset with himself over what had happened with Emily the night before. Was that really their last goodbye? He shouldn't have slept with her. What was he thinking? He was angry with himself for letting it happen again. Emily came into his life, took what she wanted, and left him again. He was a fool to think he was the one to let her go. She had left. Again. And she'd do it again. The anger was festering inside him. He wanted to stop thinking about her. He punched his seat, stood up, and paced.

When he looked up, he spotted Teddy at the reception desk closing out his hotel bill. He was dressed in a formal business suit with his briefcase on the floor beside him. After a polite exchange with the hotel staff, he walked over to Alex.

"Good morning, old chap." Teddy shook his hand and sat across from Alex.

"How is she doing?"

"She's doing fine," he replied and reached into his briefcase. "She'll be here in a minute. She just ran to the loo to check her face quickly." He took a moment to reconsider, then leaned closer and continued in a confidential whisper. "Alex, to be honest, she's dreadfully nervous. I think I've calmed her down, but she threatened to cancel today. Worse still, she doesn't even know about *this*."

Teddy handed Alex the morning's paper. Photos of Pernille at the nightclub from the other night showed her dancing with a group of men. The caption read: PERNILLE SPREADS SCANDINAVIAN CULTURE THROUGHOUT ITALIAN NIGHTCLUBS. WHO WILL SHE SLEEP WITH NEXT?

Alex read bits of the article to himself in dismay. "The Scandinavian beauty is looking for an Italian man. Where is Matteo Pozzi? Pernille Bjørn cheats on Matteo Pozzi."

"Like I said," Teddy continued, "she does not know about this. I didn't even turn on the television this morning. I didn't want her to see any coverage of it. I was prepared to tell her that you had worked all night to clear up any misconceptions, but fortunately, I didn't have to. I'm not a very good liar." He sat back in the oversized high back chair.

Teddy wasn't angry, but he was serious.

"I do want to thank you, Alex," Teddy continued, "for being there for her. And understanding. And fixing things when you could. She won't tell you this, but she's been having a tough time of it lately. You can see how jumpy she's been.

"She was extremely happy to hear you were down here waiting for her. She knows that you will protect her today should anything unpleasant arise."

"Of course," Alex finally spoke up. "And I'll be all over this."

"Good." Teddy took the newspaper back and closed it into his briefcase. "I'm sorry I can't be there today."

"You're leaving?"

"I have an unexpected appointment in London this evening. We have an important meeting in the morning and we need to discuss some urgent matters in the office beforehand. I fly out early this afternoon."

Teddy leaned in close again. "You know, Alex, she's been having issues with her former manager in Denmark. Since she fired him, she's been on edge. Yes, that too has been happening. Having you assigned to her in Italy has made her feel so much better. I could see that when I first came here. Even when all that stuff happened with the football match and that guy, she kept telling me she was thankful for you.

"After today's event, she's due back to Copenhagen to discuss her contract. Have you ever considered becoming a manager? It may be something to think about." Teddy stood up and smiled in the direction of the elevators. Pernille had stepped out of one and was walking toward them. Through his smile, he said, "You'll take care of her, won't you, Alex?"

"Of course," Alex replied and stood up to greet Pernille.

She was wearing a long navy-blue skirt that flowed as she walked. Her form-fitting pink-and-white diagonally striped blouse was tucked in. Her waist was wrapped in a thick beige leather belt that hung at an angle on her hips. Her silky blonde hair bounced as she walked up to them.

Although Alex knew Pernille was nervous, she wore her professional smile like a badge of courage. She kissed Alex on both cheeks and thanked him for joining her.

"The hotel is all sorted out, love," Teddy said to her as she kissed him on the cheek.

"You are so kind to me," she replied. "I'm sorry you're leaving so soon. I really am."

Alex felt he needed to give them some privacy.

"I'm going to get a car ready for us, Pernille," he offered. "I'll wait outside. It was nice to see you again, Teddy. I hope that we'll meet again soon."

"I'm sure we will," he replied with a wink. "We'll have to make the effort, of course."

"Indeed," replied Alex, and he walked out of the lobby.

After a few moments, Pernille met Alex in front of the hotel and jumped into the car. Alex could have sworn he saw tears in her eyes, but she immediately covered her face with oversized sunglasses.

"I'm sorry I couldn't go earlier this morning," she finally said. "I hope Eleonora was able to handle the ingredient check without me."

"Yes," Alex replied. He could tell by her tone that she had decided to switch to all business. "Eleonora made sure the kitchen was on time. When we get there, you and I will tour the facilities for a final quality check."

"Great," she replied and waited for Alex to continue.

"There is just one thing," Alex continued gently. "It seems the head chef had an issue with one of the ingredients on the list."

"An issue?"

"Well . . . " Alex could see she was getting a bit short. She was not her typical casual self. "It's the caviar."

"What about the caviar?"

"Well," he continued, trying to deliver the news gently. "It seems they had trouble procuring the specific type you requested. They couldn't get enough for all the sample dishes that are to be handed out."

"And they tell you this now?" she replied, slamming her hand on the seat. "What is wrong with them? Why did they wait until now, the eleventh hour, to tell us something so important like that?"

"Well, they thought they would get some in time." Alex didn't know what else to say.

"Alex," she said, "I'm sorry. I don't mean to be so difficult. The caviar on that dish adds that special quality, especially for this audience. We can't make any mistakes. If the food is off, I'll look bad. You know that."

"I do, but the chef assures me they've come up with a solution that you'll approve of."

"Right," she scoffed. "And how can I trust him? How do I know he's not out there ruining me as we speak?"

"Because this is *our* event, Pernille," Alex replied with assurance. "*We* set this up. Everyone invited—the Italian press, the influential public—is there to celebrate your work and your new Italian book release. They are looking forward to meeting the famous Pernille Bjørn in person. The Scandinavian chef who's taking Italia by storm, remember?"

Pernille looked out the window. Alex followed her gaze as the beautiful baroque villa rose in front of them.

CHAPTER 41

AS THE CAR pulled in, the cameras swarmed, covering the vehicle in bright flashes. The photographers pushed into one another, competing for the best image. The bustling melee forced the driver to stop the car farther from the entrance than anticipated.

"Alex, what is all this?" Pernille instinctively pulled away from the closed window, flinching from the flashes. "I wasn't expecting this."

"I wasn't either." Alex realized he too sounded unsettled. He had to keep her calm. "It's great though," he blurted. "They are eager to see you."

She forced a smile. "How do I look?" She held the smile as she stared at him, waiting for his assurance.

"Great, of course. Just relax." He put his hand on his door handle. "I'll get out first and make them step back. Then I'll open your door and help you out. And don't let go of my hand."

She nodded, still smiling, but exposed her unease with her eyes.

"Don't be nervous."

"Should I stop and pose?"

"Do you want to?"

"Yes. I think I do. It'll make me feel like I'm controlling the situation. I don't want them to think they're ambushing me. I need to look natural. Just please get me inside quickly."

"Okay. I'll allow thirty seconds to pose, then I will sweep you inside."

"Thank you."

Alex opened the door and hurried to the other side of the car.

"*Grazie, signori*," he called out to the photographers. "If you can please step back. We need to make room."

"We want a photo!" shouted a photographer.

"Yes, of course," Alex said as he held up his hands, signaling for the group to step back farther. "But please allow some room for her to pass. You will all get your photograph."

The eager group followed orders and stepped back. When Alex was satisfied with the distance, he grabbed hold of the car door and locked eyes with Pernille through the window. Pernille nodded and smiled back. He opened the door and immediately the cameras flashed.

First to emerge from the car was Pernille's long, white leg, which slipped through the slit of her long skirt. Her open-toe shoe, beige with a strap that wrapped around her ankle, had a heel that accentuated her perfect calf.

Pernille climbed out of the car with a gorgeous, pleasant smile. She waved to the cameras for a moment until Alex put out his arm and guided her toward the entrance of the building.

"This way, Pernille," he called to her over the commands of the photographers. He whispered assurances in her ear. "You did great."

Pernille pulled away from Alex and faced the cameras in full. She put her hands on her hip, let her bare leg out from the slit in her skirt, and posed. The cameras went into a snapping frenzy. The photographers loved it.

"Pernille!"

"Over here, Pernille!"

"*Guarda qui*, Pernille!"

"*Bellissima*."

Pernille continued to look into the cameras as she slowly slid toward Alex. He knew that was his signal to whisk her inside. He reached his arm out again and guided her away.

"*Grazie, ragazzi*," he shouted to the photographers. "We must head inside. We will see you momentarily in the back gardens."

The photographers begged for more and tried following Pernille. When she reached the doorway, she turned toward them again and waved.

"Grazie!" She smiled and blew them a kiss. The photographers climbed over each other to get the amazing shot. She continued to wave as she stepped inside. The doors closed behind her, allowing the silence of the lobby to envelope them.

"Whew," Pernille breathed out, holding Alex's forearm. "That was great. Thank you for being there." She leaned in and kissed him on the cheek.

The kitchens in the back of the building were bustling with cooks. Pots were boiling, plates were clattering, apprentices scurried. The head chef deftly ushered Pernille and Alex through the close quarters while going over the three dishes that Pernille was to discuss with her audience within the hour.

Pernille kept her cool about the caviar. She waited patiently until the head chef brought it up himself. He offered to substitute shaved bits of smoked, salted gelatin for the caviar; he had made a batch early that morning. Pernille tasted the concoction and was satisfied. Although it wasn't caviar, she said it would work.

Alex observed the change in her demeanor. Unrecognizable from the nervous, fidgety woman in the car, in the kitchens Pernille was the cheery personality that the Italians had fallen in love with. In fact, Alex realized, she'd switched it on the second he had opened the car doors. Her professionalism never ceased to impress him.

After the kitchen tour, Alex and Pernille were escorted to an upstairs lounge to await the start of the event. The room was decorated in reds and golds, its satin wallpaper adorned with lavender flowers. Pernille sat in a blue chaise, listening to Alex's rundown of the event.

"We will be escorted down to the side of the stage," Alex read his notes from his tablet. "They will open with a speech from the host, the restaurant manager here. He'll introduce you, and you'll meet him center-stage."

"Will I have an apron on already, or do I put it on when I reach the host?"

"I think we'll have you put it on while you're standing back-stage. This way there's no delay." Alex noted his last-minute decision on his tablet and continued.

"You're making the three dishes we talked about: the grav-lax that impressed everyone when you made it on TV, the wild berries and cream dessert, and the pear cocktail. In that order."

"Correct," she replied. "Well, maybe the cocktail first? So we all can enjoy it as I make the rest of the dishes."

"Ah, great idea." Alex noted the change on the tablet. "I'll inform the staff. And as you make each dish, the waiters will be serving samples to the audience to taste.

"When you're done," he continued, "the host will lead you through some questions, which I have here." Alex handed Pernille the list of questions he'd provided to the host. "It's all about your book and your show."

"These are the questions we reviewed the other day, correct?"

"Yes. And they were approved by your producers in Denmark." Alex looked down at his tablet and continued, "Some questions will be taken from the audience."

"They will?"

"Yes, but they're usually very basic: How did you become a chef? What do you think of Italy? Nothing profound, really." Or at least Alex hoped.

"But this audience, if I recall, is the press. Right?"

"Sort of," Alex replied. "They are book reviewers and TV critics. They've been instructed to focus on the book."

"Okay."

Alex quietly dreaded that part of the event. It could turn out to be a complete disaster. Maybe he could convince the host not to take any questions from the audience. He'd handle that when they got to the stage.

"And after that, we'll take a small break and then you sign books for a bit. And then we're done."

"Good. Because I'm ready to go back home and we haven't even started."

There was a light knock at the door. A server entered with a platter of fresh fruit, set it down on the round glass table, and backed out into the hall, closing the door behind her.

"So, I have instructions to take you back to the hotel after this," Alex said and then popped a strawberry in his mouth.

"Yes," Pernille agreed. "And I cannot wait to soak in a warm tub."

"Sounds nice," Alex replied. "You know, this has been really fun, working with you."

"Let's not say our goodbyes just yet." Pernille stood up and checked herself in the long mirror. "We still have work to do."

Alex smiled at her reflection in the mirror. She winked back.

Pernille returned to the chaise. "Alex, thank you for what you've done for me. You're a good guy. That's what I meant at the club the other night, when I said Emily was not for you. You deserve better."

"I thought we weren't saying our goodbyes yet," he laughed and ate another strawberry.

"I'm not saying goodbye," she replied almost whispering. She put her elbow on the armrest of the chaise and rested her head. "I just wanted to tell you that if you weren't here today, I don't know if I would have come. I'm not feeling like myself, and you keep me sane. I appreciate you, Alex. You're more than a publicist to me. You've become a good friend."

"Thank you, Pernille. And I appreciate you too. But where is this all coming from? Are you okay?"

"Yes." She sat straight and crossed her legs. "Yes, I'm fine. I—" And just like that, tears began to fall.

"Pernille," Alex rushed to her side. "Pernille, it's okay. You'll be great."

"What?" she replied as she pulled a tissue out of the box on the side table. "Oh, the event. No, it's not that."

Alex's mind went frantic with worry. Did Pernille know about the newspaper headlines? Was she freaking out? He had to say something. He kept his hands on her arms and said, "Well, whatever it is, you'll be okay. We will sort it out after."

"I don't know what I'm doing," Pernille continued. She stood up and looked out the window. "What am I doing wrong? How could I keep going like this? Pretending it's all fine, smiling—"

Alex had no idea what the hell she was talking about. He didn't want to ask either. He felt it would only prolong the freak-out she was having. He had to find a way to stop it.

He couldn't allow her to have a nervous breakdown. Not yet. He couldn't handle it. He still was barely holding it together himself.

Pernille's sudden flood of tears brought his own anxiety to a head. He felt a shortness of breath. He needed air. He stood up and paced the room.

"Alex—" She walked over to him. "I'm sorry for doing this to you."

"What?" Alex shook himself from his own anxious spiral and put on his game face. "It's okay. We're both nervous, but I know it's going to be fine. You'll be great. You've done plenty of these before. You know it will be great." The confidence in his words belied his growing uncertainty. He smiled again and held Pernille's upper arms as he repeated the schedule. "It's just thirty minutes of stage time, five minutes of questions, and fifteen minutes of book signing. Done."

Pernille looked at his eyes and breathed deeply.

"You're right." She wiped her eyes. "I can do this. Everything else, we can deal with later."

"Now you're talking."

CHAPTER 42

THE STAGE FOR the cooking demo had been constructed on the villa's back terrace. Pernille was led to a backstage props table where she put on a mustard-yellow apron and received some final touches to her makeup and hair.

Alex walked out to the kitchen counter that had been set in the middle of the stage. He confirmed that all the utensils and partially completed portions of the recipes were in place. He looked out at the crowd just coming into the seating area, which was covered by a yellow-and-white striped tent. To the left of the seating area was a small table displaying copies of Pernille's cookbook. Alex stepped down and grabbed one of the books to display on the kitchen counter.

A few kitchen workers walked onto the stage carrying the cocktail shaker and several salmon, all at different stages of the gravlax process: the whole fish, a de-skinned and deboned fish, and the completed dish. Alex complimented the workers and returned to Pernille's side; she was ready for her intro.

The restaurant manager greeted the guests, acknowledged their applause, and went on to talk about European culture and how his restaurant was proud to celebrate foods from the continent's different regions.

He spoke about Scandinavia and how thrilled he was to host this special event with one of the region's most popular hostesses and award-winning culinary experts. He mentioned her appearance on *Chiacchiere del Cuoco* and her international TV cooking series. He pointed to her new cookbook and announced its recent release in Italian bookstores. Alex stood backstage with Pernille, translating the host's every word.

"And now, please welcome the beautiful Pernille Bjørn!" shouted the host in Italian.

"Good luck," whispered Alex as she walked onto the stage, waving to the crowd.

"Pernille," said the host, "thank you for coming here today." His English was broken, but understandable. "Since you do not speak Italian—"

"Yet," interrupted Pernille, holding her finger up and smiling. The crowd laughed with her and clapped.

"Yes, *yet*," the host repeated and then laughed. "Italy seems to love you, Pernille." The crowd clapped again in agreement as the host led his guest behind the demonstration counter. "What will you be making for us today?"

"Well, I hear Italians love my gravlax," she said. The crowd clapped in response. She grabbed hold of the whole salmon that sat on a platter in front of her and raised it like a prize she shared with the crowd. They cheered and laughed. The photographers clamored again for the perfect chef shot. Pernille set the whole fish down and said, "But first, let's start off with a cocktail. You know, to loosen us all up."

She mixed Aquavit and pear slices in the shaker with dramatic flair and poured two glasses, handing one to the host. Servers in long white aprons began passing out samples to the audience.

"To Italia," she said, holding up the glass.

The host held up his finger and said to the crowd, "Uh-uh. To Denmark." Then turning back to her, he nodded his respect and said, "And to Pernille Bjørn."

Pernille and the host clinked glasses and sipped; the crowd cheered and followed suit. She had them all in the palm of her hand.

The rest of the demonstration went smoothly. The host asked questions throughout, about her experiences and inspirations, just as Alex and Eleonora had instructed him. Finally, as the dessert samples were passed out to the crowd, Pernille waved in gratitude and walked off the stage. The host explained to the audience that they would take a small break and then proceed with a brief Q&A session.

"This is going really well, Alex," Pernille said as she removed the apron and sat at the makeup table. She seemed to be more relaxed and in control than she had been in the waiting room upstairs. Whatever had been bothering her seemed to have been put out of her mind. The makeup artist quickly touched her face with a brush, adjusted her hair, and signaled that she was complete.

After the five-minute break, the host led Pernille back onto the stage. They sat in two high chairs and began the short question-and-answer portion of the event. Alex stood backstage, watching as Pernille answered each question comfortably, just as rehearsed, when Eleonora appeared at his side.

Alex quietly smiled at her and looked at the crowd; they were leaning in intently. "I was wondering where you'd gone."

"She is doing a great job," Eleonora said, ignoring his remark. "You did well today, Alex."

"Thank you."

Alex looked back at Pernille, who suddenly seemed uncomfortable. What had he missed? Then he heard the host.

"Well, there has been some controversy about you lately. Do you have anything you'd like to clarify here while you have an audience?"

"Controversy? Really?" Pernille made a concerted effort to keep the situation light.

"Alex?" Eleonora snapped at him. "Why is he asking her these questions? Didn't you tell him to stick to the script?"

"I think the crowd knows what I'm talking about, right?" He turned to the screen behind them where a large photograph of Pernille had appeared. She was smiling, with a Fendi store bag in her hand, walking arm-in-arm with a man whose face was hidden. It was the same photograph Alex had seen earlier. The host continued, "The papers are wondering. Who is this man?"

Pernille was frowning, confused. She had no idea why that photo was such a big deal.

"That's my fiancé," she finally said. "Teddy."

"And does he know about your Italian lover?" insisted the host.

Pernille gripped the armrest of her seat. Alex was about to rush out there, but Eleonora stopped him.

"You can't go out there," she said. "Not now."

"We can't let her be attacked like this."

Pernille seemed about to contradict the host when a voice rang out from the crowd.

"Here I am!" The audience members turned in their seats, looking for the source of the shout.

Pernille shot a pleading look at Alex offstage, hoping he might have some way out for her. He shook his head in dismay as Matteo climbed onto the stage with a folding chair from the audience in his hand. He set it down next to Pernille and smiled.

"Sorry I'm late." Matteo waived to the crowd.

The crowd cheered with the excitement at the model's appearance. Pernille smiled awkwardly and remained in her seat. The host was thrown, but welcomed the model to the stage.

"Can we stop this?" Alex pleaded with Eleonora.

"No," she replied, her arms folded.

The host fumbled with his words for a moment, then asked Matteo how he knew Pernille. Matteo raised his eyebrows suggestively and replied, in Italian, "We are *very* close friends."

Pernille smiled at him awkwardly and looked at the host.

"In fact," Matteo continued, "her fiancé recently left her. He found out about a passionate night we shared." He looked at the crowd, signaled toward his crotch, and added, "She prefers the Italian."

The crowd cheered Matteo and his Italian pride. Pernille was lost in the flurry of Italian; she had no idea what Matteo had just said. But she knew enough to be shocked by his lewd gesture. She tried to play it off, shaking her head and clucking her tongue as if admonishing a bad schoolboy. The crowd laughed with her. Alex could see she was trying to retake control of the stage. He was, as ever, impressed with her skill.

Meanwhile, the host was enjoying the interaction and knew from the sound of the cameras incessant clicking that his name and restaurant would soon be mentioned in the papers. He turned to his guest.

"It is true then, Pernille? Your fiancé has just left you?"

"What?" Pernille was shocked by the realization of what Matteo had just told their interviewer and the crowd. "How? What? No, it's not true."

"He found out that you and I had sex," Matteo explained. "And it was incredible, wasn't it?"

Pernille's jaw dropped. She looked shocked, confused, and ready to flee. Alex had had enough. Eleonora had let this go too far. He began to think that she had known this was about to happen. Could she have really been involved in some way? Alex walked onto the stage, Eleonora bellowing from behind him to stop. Alex ignored her. He charged at Matteo and punched him across the jaw.

CHAPTER 43

THE AUDIENCE GREW quiet. Alex couldn't believe what he had just done. He'd felt his fist collide with Matteo's jaw. Then, as if in slow motion, he'd watched as the tall model fell over backward onto the stage floor. Pernille screamed; the host sat there in shock.

But Matteo wasn't out for the count. He sat up with fury in his eyes, got to his feet, and charged at Alex. The two men wrestled to the floor, knocking over speakers and chairs. Alex could hear the cameras clicking like crazy around them. He wanted it to stop. He couldn't believe it was happening. It was as if he no longer had control of his own body.

He felt Matteo's punches on the sides of his ribcage. He grabbed Matteo's right arm and tried to hold him down. Unfortunately for Alex, Matteo was leagues stronger than him. The model flipped him over like a rag doll, slamming Alex on his back.

Alex lay flat on the stage while Matteo straddled over him, pinning his hands to the floor. He struggled, trying in vain to free himself. Sensing that resistance might, indeed, be futile, he relaxed for a moment and looked up at the model. Matteo's face was plastered with a snickering grin.

That smug smile would prove to be Matteo's undoing. Alex, in a blind rage, somehow managed to flip Matteo off of him. The model flew into the air and down onto the audience below.

Pernille ran over to Alex and helped him up. The photographers were advancing on the stage. Alex and Pernille backed away, bumping into the kitchen island. The journalists threw out question after question: *Pernille, how many lovers do you have? Did you first meet Matteo at the football match? Are you in love with Matteo? And who is this American?*

Alex's focus was now squarely on getting Pernille out of there. He searched for the clearest exit, but spotted Matteo climbing back onto the stage, making his way toward them.

He didn't know what to do. Matteo was gaining ground, fighting his way through the paparazzi. Alex looked around hastily for something with which to shield himself. He saw the giant salmon glistening on the platter. He grabbed it by the tail and swung it in Matteo's direction.

The cold fish swung from left to right and then toward Matteo's head. But it didn't connect. The fish kept going, swinging farther to the right, slamming into Pernille.

"*Av! Mor F—*" she screamed, holding her cheek.

Alex's jaw dropped. He'd just slapped his client in the face with a salmon. He was definitely fired. Suddenly, Pernille screamed again, pointing at Matteo. Alex swung the fish again, and this time hit him in the chest, sending him flying over the kitchen set.

The photographers were ecstatic. They kept snapping photos, closing in on Pernille and Alex. He had to get her out of there. He quickly handed her the salmon, picked her up, threw her over his shoulder, and ran. He took the stairs from the stage, two at a time, onto the grounds below.

Pernille was on Alex's shoulder, screaming, while swinging the salmon at the photographers that followed. Alex needed the paparazzi circus to end. On his way through the folding chairs, he gave a swift kick to a corner pole, knocking down the giant tent and trapping the crowd and photographers beneath.

Keeping Pernille on his shoulder, Alex ran out of the gate and into the Pincio. He found himself in front of the surrey bike rental area. He put Pernille down but kept hold of her hand, dragging her to the collection of four-wheeled contraptions. He jumped on the nearest bike and Pernille hopped up onto the bench beside him, placing the salmon on her lap. Alex started to pedal, moving the contraption in the direction of the downward slope. It was slow going, pulling both their weight, and so it wasn't until they reached the top of the hill that he realized they had another big problem. His steering wheel was the loose and useless one. It wasn't turning. He realized he had stupidly put himself on the passenger's side. Pernille was sitting in the driver's seat! The quadricycle started to pick up speed as it coasted down the hill toward the puppet theatre.

"Put the fish down and steer," he commanded. "Turn right! Turn right!"

Pernille screamed, fish still in her hands. Alex covered his head to protect himself from the impending crash, when Pernille frantically threw the salmon into the basket in front of her and grabbed the steering wheel. She cleared the puppet theatre, turning them into a head-on course with a rollerblading class.

"Right!" Alex screamed. "Keep going right!"

The surrey bike was practically on two wheels as it took a sharp right toward the busy road that ran through the park. They swung around the rotary and recovered their balance, slowing their pace.

Alex felt they were far enough from the paparazzi. They took a right to the top of the park, where it met via Veneto. From there, Pernille could go directly to her hotel and away from any further issues. They struggled together, pedaling uphill to the far end of the park. They reached a small carousel and a cinema house where they stopped to catch their breath. At the bottom of another hill to the left, Alex could see the museum where he had taken Emily the day before. And now here he was in a surrey bike with Pernille. And a fish that had started to reek.

"Pernille!" The shout came from the park behind them. "*Fermati*, Pernille!"

It was two paparazzi, also in a quad, followed by yet another one driven by Matteo and Eleonora. Pernille gritted her teeth and pedaled down the hill toward the museum.

"Pernille, slow down!" shouted Alex. "There are people all down there!"

She ignored him.

"Let me steer," he pleaded.

"Well, we can't switch places," she shouted. "Tell me where to go!"

"When we reach the museum ahead, take a left!" he shouted back.

Alex looked behind them and saw that the two quadricycles were closing in, with Matteo and Eleonora's gaining on the paparazzi. Eleonora looked angry. Alex knew he was doomed, but there was no turning back. Protecting Pernille was his priority now.

Pernille struggled to steer the quadricycle left. Alex put his hands on the steering wheel to help them keep control. When they'd successfully rounded the corner, she slapped his hands off the wheel and ordered him to keep pedaling. Much to Alex's relief, she skillfully maneuvered the contraption among the tourists just leaving the Bioparco zoo. Alex knew they had to take a left soon, but he couldn't remember where the paved road led. He knew he wanted to get them back toward via Veneto. But how?

"Left! Left," he shouted. The paved road had appeared sooner than he expected.

Pernille took the sharp left. Alex leaned hard to his right to keep the quadricycle from flipping over. They continued through the park and up a slight hill. Alex and Pernille struggled to maintain their speed. The shouts from behind were getting louder.

"*Fermati!* Pernille! Stop the vehicle!"

"Keep going, Alex," Pernille begged. "I don't want to stop!"

Alex didn't know how to end the chase. He couldn't believe a chase was even happening. The road forked ahead of them. He told Pernille to stay to the right, which unfortunately was more of an uphill battle. They were sweating profusely. Alex was breathing heavily; he didn't know if he could keep going. Pernille pushed forward. He marveled at her strength.

At the top of the small hill, the road took them left, onto a wider and flatter path. The quadricycle picked up the pace as they traveled past the Globe Theatre. Alex was finally feeling like they stood a chance when Pernille suddenly turned left into the large flat dirt arena.

"What are you doing?!" he shouted.

"I don't know! I didn't know where to go! They're behind us!"

Pernille and Alex pedaled around the dirt track with the other two quadricycles in pursuit. Alex looked back, then grabbed his new and smelly weapon of choice by the tail and dropped it behind them. The fish carcass flopped in the dirt before rolling to a complete stop. Both the paparazzo and Matteo swerved around the dead fish easily, making the attempted obstacle pointless. Alex flung his hands in the air in disbelief as their bike bumped and skittered over the loose terrain.

Pernille steered them back onto the smooth pavement in the direction toward the main road, but Alex knew their only hope was to lose the two quadricycles on their tail. He ordered Pernille right into a maze of tall shrubs and kept his eyes behind them, while Pernille again steered them away from the paved road. Alex felt almost immediate relief.

"I think we lost them," he said with a smile.

It was then that their quadricycle rattled. Alex turned back to the front and saw that Pernille had steered them out of the maze and onto the grass. Ahead of them, couples rowed around a gated serene pond.

"Stop!" he shouted. "We need to stop!"

Alex pulled up on the emergency break, which snapped off in his hand. Pernille was screaming again. The quadricycle rolled up a wooden ramp and flew into the pond with Alex and Pernille inside.

The cameras snapped profusely. Flashes blinded Pernille and Alex as they splashed their way out of the water.

Alex looked at the crowd that now surrounded the pond. In it, he spotted Eleonora standing, with arms folded, by the police.

CHAPTER 44

HE SAT FACING Eleonora's desk listening to her shout about the embarrassment he had caused her company and her client. His left eyebrow was bandaged, his right nostril stuffed with cotton.

"How could you do this to me, Alex?" she shouted as she paced behind her desk. "What the hell were you thinking?"

He said nothing. He just watched her as she continued to pace. The ride back to the office had been worse. Pernille had cried in his arms in the back seat of the police car that escorted them to the firm's office. Eleonora had met them out front and escorted them upstairs. Somehow, she had convinced the police officers and the park authorities not to press charges.

"Do you realize the damage you've caused?" She slammed her hands on the desk. "Of course you do! Look at you." She leaned on the desk and waved to the hallway as she continued. "I've got a client in the bathroom trying to make herself presentable before getting back to her hotel. A client that you saw fit to hit in the face with . . . with a *fish*? What is wrong with you?!"

He was about to reply, but Eleonora continued before he could muster a sound.

"And not to mention the brawl with Matteo Pozzi. I can get sued for that, you know." She put her hand to her forehead and continued to pace. "A new client, which you could have cost me. And it was all caught on camera. The whole horrid scene!"

"Wait. What?" Alex was confused. "New client? Did you bring Matteo to the event? Why?"

Eleonora looked out the window and remained silent.

"You mean you set that up?" Alex leaned in, trying to get her to look at him. "So, every time Matteo happened to appear, it was because of you? The photo shoot by the fountain? The soccer match? That was you?"

"Alex, this isn't about me."

"But what about Pernille?"

"Pernille is no longer my concern. We gave her what she wanted: a spotlight. And when I saw the opportunity to utilize a new client, I did."

"How can you say that?"

"Do not sit there and question how I do my job. All you have to explain is what the hell you were thinking getting involved like that."

Eleonora's lecture was interrupted by the ring of her office phone. It was her assistant from the front desk. Eleonora picked it up in a huff and then rolled her eyes. Alex sat silently as she tried to tell her assistant that she was in an important meeting. She hung up the phone and pointed to Alex.

"Wait outside my office. I'm not done with you." She picked up the phone again, offering whoever was on the other line her very best sweet greeting.

Alex closed the door softly behind him and took a seat on the gray sofa just outside the office. He sat sullenly, like a child sent to the principal's office, when Pernille appeared from the restroom. Her hair was still damp from the pond. Her makeup was washed off except for a new coat of cover-up she'd used to try and mask the puffy redness left on the side of her face by the salmon. She quietly sat down next to Alex.

"I'm so sorry," he said. "I didn't mean to—"

"It's all right, Alex. I know."

"But your face—"

"I suppose we're in big trouble, huh?"

"Yeah," he scoffed. "Well, I'm the one who's in trouble." Pernille didn't reply.

They sat on the couch not saying another word. Alex replayed the whole scene in his head, over and over. He felt betrayed and used by Eleonora. And what was with all of Matteo's lies and bravado on the stage? Why would Eleonora have planned something so awful?

"I am truly sorry for everything, Pernille. All the stories in the papers. The lies. Punching Matteo. Causing that big scene."

"It's not your fault, Alex."

"Yes, but it was so unprofessional of me."

"Alex, you were brave. You were just trying to do your job. It's me who should apologize to you," she sobbed. "And to Teddy!"

"What?"

"I feel so awful, Alex," she cried. "I really did something awful."

"What are you talking about?"

"Matteo—"

"Yes?"

"It was true!" She whimpered into her handkerchief. "I don't know what I was thinking."

Alex turned to her and held her by the shoulders. "Pernille, what are you talking about?"

"He was telling the truth. Matteo. Teddy did leave me. He left me because he found out about Matteo."

"What about Matteo?"

"That he and I—"

"What?!" Alex stood up, shocked. "When? How? When?"

"It doesn't matter." She sat back, crossed her legs, and put her hand up to her mouth, shaking her head. "I made a mistake and it's over. Italy is over. Teddy is over."

"Pernille—" Alex was now pacing like Eleonora.

Pernille stood up. "Alex, I want to thank you for everything. Really. You are wonderful. And I apologize for all the problems I caused. I must go now. I hope you'll forgive me." She kissed him on the forehead and walked away.

Alex stood in the hallway with his hands at his sides in disbelief, watching his first big European client walk out the door.

CHAPTER 45

AFTER AN HOUR of more reaming from Eleonora, Alex found himself walking across the bridge to Trastevere, head down in defeat. Still in shock over Pernille's confession, he hadn't even processed that Eleonora had fired him. He didn't care.

He found himself stopping in front of the quirky café. It was empty. Inside he noticed Patrizia wiping the counter. She looked up at him and smiled. She soon noticed his bandaged eyebrow, dropped her white rag, and rushed over.

"American Boy!" She grabbed his arm and led him to an empty green chesterfield. "What happened to you?"

"It's a long story," Alex replied. "Never mind that."

"Do you want something to drink?" She didn't wait for his answer. She walked behind the counter and mixed the Campari and soda. She walked back to the couch, handed Alex the drink, and sat down next to him. Alex sipped the cocktail in silence.

"I'm glad you're here," she said. "I've been wanting to talk to you."

"Oh, that's funny," Alex replied. He'd had enough of women. He still hadn't gotten over how his relationship with Emily had ended; nor Pernille's revelation; nor Eleonora's admission of betrayal; nor his being fired. He didn't know if he could handle more bad news.

After her abrupt exit that one morning, Patrizia finally decided she wanted to talk. Alex set his glass down on the coffee table and turned to her.

"What happened to you that morning? Why did you leave? I thought we were getting along well. I mean, we had fun, no?"

Patrizia looked down and stared at her feet. Alex refused to keep quiet. He felt he was owed some sort of explanation.

"Well?" He picked up his drink again, sat back, and crossed his legs. "I'm going to sit here until you speak."

"Alex, I apologize." Patrizia looked up at him. She was twiddling her fingers and spoke quietly. "I did have fun with you. A lot of fun, in fact. It was beautiful. You're beautiful."

"Patrizia—" Alex rolled his eyes. "Enough. I don't want to know. I just thought you should know that I really liked you. And I was surprised when you left like that." He set his empty glass down and shifted in his seat. "I should go."

"No." She put her arm out to stop him. "I want to explain. I do." Alex sat back down.

"I like you too, Alex," Patrizia continued. "I like you a lot. That morning, I was ashamed and embarrassed, but it wasn't about you. I was looking at you lying on the floor and I realized how fast we. . . It's unlike me to go home with someone so quickly. I don't know what had come over me to do that. But, as I was drinking your coffee, I began to feel guilty. I wanted to run away. So I did. Then, when you came into the bar, I saw you and wanted to talk to you, but you had company. I'm sorry for avoiding you."

She reached for her rag, wiped the coffee table, and took the empty glass. Alex said nothing.

"I don't expect you to forgive me, Alex," Patrizia continued. She sat with the empty glass in her hand, about to get up from her seat. "But I felt you deserved an apology and I'm happy you came by." She placed her free hand on his and looked into his eyes. "I know you are probably angry with me right now. But I hope you understand how much I like you."

Alex took what she said in earnest. She was beautiful, he thought. He wanted to stay. He liked her a lot. At the same time, he thought he should probably go home and clear his head. Patrizia took the empty glass behind the bar and busily wiped the counter, waiting for Alex's response.

Alex sat quietly staring at the sculpture of the embracing couple across from him. Behind it was a band setting up for the evening.

CHAPTER 46

ALEX WAS STILL seated on the green velvet chesterfield, every now and again eyeing the sculpture. Patrizia, now seated next to him, wore a smirk, her hands folded, eyeing him with suspicion. They both looked down at the cards laid out on the oval wood coffee table in front of them.

The band in the corner continued a rotating selection of beatnik-inspired music. Alex waited for Patrizia's reading as he sipped another whiskey she had generously poured for him.

"It is in the cards," Patrizia kept repeating as she shook her head, closed her eyes, and sipped her own whiskey.

"Right," Alex replied. He turned toward the sculpture again, glass still in hand. Through the statue's arms, he watched the bass player's head bop to the rhythm.

"It's all here," she tried to convince him. "The cards say so."

Alex turned back, uncrossed his legs, leaned forward, and said, "You are a liar." The last word slurred through his lips. He felt the whiskey relaxing him.

"No, I am not." Patrizia put her glass on the table and pointed to the cards that she had flipped. "The Two of Swords, here, in this position, says that you had a choice to make. And this card, the Three of Cups, tells us that you held on to something from your past." She picked up another card. "And this card—the Page of Swords—tells me that you had a struggle, or maybe have a struggle still." She put the card back in its sixth position and sat back. "You cannot hide from the cards."

"I don't believe you," Alex repeated. "You don't know how to read cards. You are lying." Patrizia scoffed as he continued. "You're just having a laugh at me. After telling you my story, you're having a laugh."

"Alex," she pleaded with a slight chuckle. "No, I'm not. These are *carte tarocchi*. You are American. You don't know how to read these. You are not familiar with them." Alex noticed her smiling behind her tumbler of whiskey.

"I know very well what these cards are. I've played many games with these cards: Scopa, Briscola—"

"Yes, yes." She waved her hands and shook her head. It was obvious the whiskey was getting to her too. "But this deck has more cards. Not for games of old men at the local bar. This here—" She pointed to the intricate layout of the seven cards. "This is the stuff of women. You are a man. You don't know. You can't know."

"Oh, really," Alex laughed. "Then, please, tell me, woman. What does the final card say I have to do?"

"Don't laugh at me." She poured herself another glass of whiskey and took a long sip. "I was only trying to help you."

"Fine, fine." Alex moved closer to her. "Then, please, Patrizia." He leaned in. "Female." He mocked as he gently positioned his arm behind her. "Woman." The aroma of her perfume enhanced the effects of the whiskey, heightening his intoxication. She didn't flinch, despite how close he was now to her face. With his lips close to her ear, he begged in a whisper, "Please, read me the final card."

Patrizia smiled and dramatically reached for the seventh and final card. She flipped it, looked at it, and laughed out loud

as she placed it face up in the seventh position. Alex looked at
the card and then sat back in disbelief at his luck. Staring at
him from the coffee table, defiantly, was The Fool.

"Well," Patrizia said, still laughing, "I can't say I'm surprised
that this card appeared." She took another sip of her whiskey.
"Come on, Alex. It's not as bad as it looks."

"Oh, really?" Alex sat up. "It's obvious." He reached for
his whiskey. "The cards are telling me I'm an idiot. Which I
already knew, by the way."

"Ha, ha." Patrizia put down her glass and pointed to The
Fool. "This card is in the position of outcome and guidance."

"Oh, so it's telling me I will *always* be a fool."

"No. No. Not at all." She leaned against his shoulder. "The
card is telling you how to move forward."

"Forward?" Alex leaned in closer to Patrizia. "Be stupid?
And all the problems will resolve on their own? Ignorance is
bliss?"

"Maybe," Patrizia replied softly. Her perfume trickled back
into his brain. "This card is the Fool of Love. Maybe it's telling
you to move forward, ever the fool."

"Forward?" he repeated, this time a little softer, with less of
a slur. "Like this?" He moved in, his lips brushing her cheek.
Patrizia exposed her slender neck. The warmth from it was
reaching out to him. "Am I closer now?" His breath ricocheted
off her neck. He lightly kissed it, feeling her pulse quicken with
every kiss. Slowly, she turned toward him, wrapped her long,
slender arm around his neck, and kissed him on the lips. Alex
helped guide their bodies down onto the chesterfield. They
continued to kiss.

"Alex," Patrizia managed to say, breathlessly.

"Shh." Alex didn't want to spoil the moment.

"Alex," Patrizia snuck out another word. "I have to confess
something."

He didn't want to stop the kissing. He continued, caressing the side of her hip.

"Alex—" Patrizia stopped the kiss. They lay on the couch, faces still close. Alex tried to kiss her again. "I have to tell you something." She was insistent.

"What's that?" He kissed her again. She reciprocated for another second, then stopped.

"Alex," she whispered, as he nipped at her earlobe. "I made it all up. I don't know how to read cards." Alex stopped. He looked at her as she lay there, underneath him, smiling. He laughed and buried his face in her neck.

They would continue to kiss for hours, on that green chesterfield, by the embracing sculpture in the dark corner of the bar, both of them thanking the tarot cards and that ridiculous Fool.

THE END

AUTHOR'S NOTE

I started writing this book when I temporarily moved to Rome in the autumn of 2011. I had always thought about writing a book, but I had never attempted to put down on paper what many exceptional actual writers do so easily. But, living in Rome, I guess inspired me. So, I started to write.

I never thought I'd actually have something until the story just poured out of me like a never-ending flowing river of gold. After four months, I returned from Rome with a large chunk of the first draft, then completed it in my spare time (after my full time job). After several cycles of reviews and feedback from several clever beta-readers (you know who you are), and being slapped and pleasantly butchered by awesome editors . . . six versions later, I had the beautiful final manuscript for *The Love Fool.*

This book had taken up my spare time for over five years. Was it a lot of work? Heck, yeah! But, through this whole process, I've learned so much and am still learning at every step.

I've written this note to encourage anyone out there that has thought about writing a novel, to just do it. I mean, if I did it, anyone can. I'm serious. I'm not a fancy writer. I'm no Fitzgerald. No Hemingway. I'm just a guy with some stories.

So, don't be discouraged. Sit down and write. Worry about organizing it all later. Get out there and write, people. But, before you do, read my story because it's awesome. And thank you for picking up my first book.

ACKNOWLEDGMENTS

I would like to express my gratitude to the many people who saw me through this book: to all those who provided support, talked things over, read, offered comments, and assisted in the editing, proofreading, and design.

I would first like to thank my beta-readers Kath, Morgen, Connie, Kerry, and Peter. Without your feedback, my story would have been one hot mess with missing elements and confusing timelines. I would also like to thank my content editor Shanna for slapping me around and getting my story straight. And to my proofreader Lauren for constantly hitting me with her ruler only to improve my grammar, spelling, and sentence structure.

I also would like to express gratitude to local authors L. S. Kilroy, Kate, and others that allowed me to pick their brains on the book business, writing, and tips for coping with time and organizing my thoughts.

To my family, friends, and extended family—near and far. Thank you for all of your generous support.

And finally, I beg forgiveness from all of you who have been pleading to read my darn book. I appreciate your patience and am happy to have finally been able to share this story with you. I hope it was worth the wait.

GRAND PATRONS

Exhibit Express, Inc. – Wilmington, MA
Northern Lights Development – Dedham, MA
Power House Systems – Walpole, MA
San Marino Landscaping – Dedham, MA
Supreme Companies – Dedham, MA
Vincenzo's Italian Deli – Dedham, MA

Mark & Olimpia Berg
Anthony & Sabrina DiMascio
Domenico Vito Fabiano
Sylvia Fabiano Lanzillo
Tracy Noga
Clementina & Armando Petruzziello
Susan Read
Peter Reynolds
Terisa Rupp

INKSHARES